Pride Publishing books by E Rose. Lynn

Heated
Heatless

I0527724

Heated

HEATLESS

E. ROSE LYNN

Heatless
ISBN # 978-1-80250-729-4
©Copyright E. Rose Lynn 2024
Cover Art by Erin Dameron-Hill ©Copyright April 2024
Interior text design by Claire Siemaszkiewicz
Pride Publishing

This is a work of fiction. All characters, places and events are from the author's imagination and should not be confused with fact. Any resemblance to persons, living or dead, events or places is purely coincidental.

Published in 2024 by Pride Publishing, United Kingdom.

Pride Publishing is an imprint of Totally Entwined Group Limited.

HEATLESS

Dedication

To Ana Maria and Juliet.
This wouldn't exist without you.

Chapter One

The note is taunting her.

Kara has it creased from being crumpled then hastily uncrumpled and refolded in the pocket of the mid-weight jacket she's wearing as a concession to the chill in the brisk March air. The attempt at warmth is undercut by her dress, which shows so much skin she might as well not be wearing anything below her waist.

It came on nice paper, the note, tucked in an envelope that was also made from nice paper, the sort that looked like it should be saved in some box of treasures instead of shredded into uneven pieces before a non-existent person could come into Kara's shitty apartment and see who was writing her. Not that anyone has been in her apartment since she walked through the initial inspection with her Beta landlord almost a year and a half ago.

The shredded envelope went into the trash, but she kept the note, which she's sort of regretting now as she walks into *htls*, the hottest A/O nightclub this side of the Mississippi. It's the sort of place she never would have gotten into if her name hadn't been on The List, which is the main reason she knows this whole thing isn't a joke. It's warm inside the club, the sort of humid heat that comes from bodies and hormones rather than central air. Two steps in, a wave of scent hits her, smoky Alphas and bright citrus Omegas all mixed into something heady, intoxicating.

Kara sways where she stands — then a woman appears at her elbow, saying over the noise, "If you'll follow me."

Kara does, because she's not sure what else to do, is barely sure which direction is up, only knows where the floor is because it's what her feet hit every time she steps. She hasn't been around this many Alphas and Omegas in one place in...years, it must be, and she'd forgotten how hard the scent hits her, need and hope and arousal and that very specific smell of *looking for a mate so look at me.*

All around her are tables with cushioned booths, the sort that feel like they should have a drug dealer Alpha with his barely legal Omega girlfriend chatting with a business partner, like in the syndicated cop shows that are on all day when she's home. But instead it's all well-dressed men and women, too far away and drenched too heavily in the mix of scents in the air for her to tell who is who. Maybe fifty years ago, when it was taboo for Omegas to wear black or Alphas to bare their collarbones, but society has come a long way since then.

Kara and the as-yet-unnamed woman skirt around the edge of the half-filled dancefloor, then head up stairs just steep enough to make Kara's calves ache as she walks in her single pair of four-inch heels. The woman says something in the ear of the guard at the top of the stairs, and he nods and steps away to let them pass. From this close, Kara can tell that he's a Beta. She wonders if all of their staff is.

"Mr. Silva is at the last table," the woman says before disappearing back down the stairs, leaving Kara alone on the mezzanine. Panic hits her, high and acrid, and she swallows it down, touching the note in her pocket to remind her that she's supposed to be here, no matter how fake that feels right now.

But leaving Damon Silva waiting seems like a bad idea, so she takes a deep breath that isn't as steadying as she would like, steels herself and starts walking toward the table at the end of the mezzanine.

As Kara gets closer, she can tell that it's him—not because she knows his face that well, but because he's the only person in the entire place that's sitting alone. And he's watching her, too, eyes behind dark-rimmed glasses fixed on her as she walks toward him and tries her damnedest not to fall flat on her face.

She's going to regret the hell out of wearing these shoes tomorrow.

Frankly, she's already regretting the hell out of wearing them. They might make her legs look worth enough for an Alpha like Damon Silva, but she can feel every single place where they're rubbing blisters on her feet.

When she's almost at his table, he stands—and he's still taller than her by a good few inches, even in her ridiculous heels, tall in a way that should be gangly but instead feels all-encompassing, like he could close his arms all the way around her, like she could press her nose to his throat and smell only him.

Which she is not going to do, because she still has some goddamn self-respect.

"Kara," he says, his voice a low rumble. When he offers his hand, she extends her own—and almost jumps out of her skin when he turns it over and bends to skim his lips across the delicate skin of her wrist. It's the sort of courtly greeting that no Alpha has offered her in years, not since before everything went to hell.

Her breath catches, and for a second all she can feel is the touch of his lips against her skin, his inhale as he takes in her scent, the warmth of his hand on hers.

Then he straightens, releasing her hand, to say, "I've been looking forward to meeting you."

"Hi," Kara says inanely, because all of her brain has shut down except for the part that wants him to take her hand again.

His lips curl up at one corner. "Hi." He steps back, saying, "Please, sit."

Kara sits, keeping one hand on the bottom of her dress to stop it from riding up as she scoots over a little in the booth. He sits across from her. At this angle, he can watch both her and the room, but all she can see is him.

A man appears at their table almost as soon as they're both seated, like he was waiting for just the right time, to ask, "What can I get you?"

His eyes are on Silva, but Silva just gestures toward her, so she says, "A ginger ale, please." Not her usual drink by a long shot, but getting even tipsy here seems like a terrible idea, and ginger is one of the best ways of mitigating the effects of scent overload.

"I'll have an Old Fashioned," Silva says.

The man leaves as silently as he appeared.

"So," Kara says, fifteen seconds into a silence that's at least fourteen seconds too long. She pulls out the note, smoothing it out on the table and wishing, not for the first time, that it wasn't so obvious she had crumpled it up into the smallest ball she can manage. She doesn't look at it. She already knows what it says. "You want me to pretend to be your Omega."

He blinks once, twice behind his glasses. "I never said that."

"No," Kara concedes. "You just wrote a courting letter to an Omega who is known publicly to be heatless. No heat, no bonding. No bonding, no kids. No kids, not a real Omega. So." She spreads her hands in front of her. "A pretend Omega. Here I am."

"I wouldn't have thought you would subscribe to the idea that the ability to bear children is what makes someone an Omega."

"Because I can't have them, you mean?" But she's not doing him justice, or herself, and she drops her hands, admitting, "I don't think that. I wouldn't have to deal with all these fucking hormones if I weren't a real Omega, and I wouldn't *feel* like an Omega. But an Alpha in your position—"

"Has the ability to decide what I want with my life, the same as anyone else." Someone comes bearing drinks, and Silva stays silent until they are gone. Kara doesn't know if he doesn't want anyone to know what she's doing here or if he just doesn't like talking in front of the waitstaff. "To be very candid with you, I am not looking to spend a heat with an Omega—not now, not ever. Neither is anyone in my set. But time is coming up where, if we don't find ourselves an Omega, one will be found for us—and at some point, we won't be able to say no."

This sounds too good to be true, which means that it almost certainly is. Men like Damon Silva don't up and decide one day that what they really want is a heatless Omega when they could have, almost literally, any

Omega in the world. Or Beta or Alpha—and maybe that's what this is, them getting an Omega beard so they can have whoever it is they want to have.

"What would you want from me, then?"

Silva surveys her over his sip of his drink, then sets it down on the table to say, "We need someone who will live in the same house as us, who will stand by us at events, who won't take other lovers without them being agreed-upon by us first. Most importantly, we need someone who can commit to being with us even without a bond. In exchange, we can provide you with whatever you need from a material or networking standpoint. You would gain the protection of being part of the set, and all the benefits of it. You could cook and clean and nest as you would like, or not—we don't need a housekeeper."

"And when you decide you want a bonded Omega?" Kara asks, even though she shouldn't even be entertaining this idea. This isn't the sort of thing that happens, especially not to people like her.

But Silva just says, "We won't."

"That's great reassurance," Kara tells him, "until the day that you do, and I'm left right back where I started, but older and untouchable because nobody wants to piss you off by having me."

"We can write in legal protections for you," he says, like it's no big deal. "Assets that would be yours, in case of a dissolution of the agreement, and an allowance. We have no interest in entering into an agreement with somebody who feels trapped or obligated."

"I—" Kara swallows, taking a big sip of the ginger ale. It clears her head a little, the sharpness making it easier to think. "I can't agree to anything right now. I need to—I need to think."

"Of course," he says. He pulls out two things from his inside jacket pocket—a business card, which she sticks in her own pocket, and a black silk square. "From the set," he tells her. "So you can know us."

* * * *

Damon Silva is in the top one-hundred richest people in the world.

He's not as well-known as most of the ninety-nine above him, and certainly not as public, but what the internet can tell Kara is that he's part of a four-Alpha set, he lives in northern Virginia and he's been seen with every female Beta and Omega under the sun but hasn't bonded with any of them.

Kara read all of these articles about him when the courting letter first arrived, when she was trying to figure out how likely it was that someone was fucking with her, but reading them again feels different now that she knows that this is real.

Or real enough, at least—enough for Silva himself to show up in person to tell her that he wants her—Kara Igan, academic researcher, heatless Omega, second child of an upper middle-class family of mostly Betas—to be his set's Omega.

And to give her a scent square that smells of four Alphas, heat and smoke and sugar. Each of them must have carried it for some time, for it to be this saturated with their scents—or they all jerked off with it, she thinks, then sets that thought aside before she can get too deep into it.

And scent compatibility has been debunked, but there's something about their scents, about the way they fit together, the four of them distinct yet complementary. Silva's strong smoke mixes with a scent as sweet as a bakery, and on top of that is one as sharp with heat as a fire—and a fourth, like water running underneath, so smooth it's barely there.

All that's missing, she can't help but think, is some Omega citrus.

So before she can talk herself out of what is undoubtedly a terrible idea, Kara opens her phone and calls the number on Silva's business card.

It rings once, twice, just long enough for her to begin to regret it—then it clicks over, and an unfamiliar man's voice says, "Hello?"

"I'm so sorry," Kara says, pulling her phone from her ear to check the number that she dialed. Irrational disappointment hits her. "I must have dialed the wrong number. I didn't—" It's definitely the number on the card, which means that Silva must have given her a fake number, which means that this was all actually the world's most elaborate way to fuck with her.

"No, wait," the man says, tinny from the way her phone is away from her ear. "Are you Kara?"

Kara puts the phone back up to her ear. "Who are you?" she asks, suspicious.

"Eric," he tells her, like that gives her any useful information. "Damon—he said to pick up his phone if it rang. He's on a video call with a couple of his people in Spain right now. You are Kara, right?"

"Yeah."

"It's great to meet you," Eric says. "We've—well, *I've* read your work, and your analysis of how the American public understands the concept of war was fascinating."

Kara blinks down at her desk, and at the scent square sitting on it, smoothed flat by worried fingers.

"You read my work?" Her voice sounds like there's something stuck in her throat.

"Yeah, of course," Eric says. "Everyone else will tell you that they read it too, but Jason's idea of good reading is a physical car magazine and Damon gets off to earnings reports, so I wouldn't believe them."

"Why did *any* of you read it?"

"I mean," he says, a little slower, "if you do end up with us, I have to assume you'll want to talk about your work at some point, and it's better that we know what you're talking about." There's a sound like he's clapping his hands together. "Anyway. I know you were calling for Damon, but is there anything I can do for you? I'm great at phone sex, in case you were wondering."

Kara's entire body goes so hot it's a wonder her phone doesn't overheat, but she manages to choke out, "No, I'm good."

"Shame."

"About the phone sex, I mean," she clarifies before she can lose her nerve. "I was wondering—I was hoping to meet you, if that's okay. All of you. Before I make my decision, I mean."

"Of course." Eric laughs, but he sounds more incredulous than mocking. "Yeah, of course, we'd love to meet you. And if Damon didn't say it, you don't need to make a decision right this second. All we're looking for right now is an answer to the courting letter. Obviously there are commitments that go along with that, but we're not asking you to move in tomorrow."

Kara says, a little faintly, "Oh."

"But yes, we would love to meet. Does tomorrow evening work? We can have someone pick you up and bring you here, have dinner. How does that sound?"

"Good," Kara says, even though it sounds better than good — and more absurd, too. She has no business having dinner with Damon Silva and his set.

But she's a twenty-seven-year-old Omega academic who works mostly from home and never meets anyone or goes anywhere, who hasn't since a doctor with a pitying look and cold hands told her three years ago that there was a defect in her scent gland and she was never going to have a heat, that after four agonizing days they couldn't manage to trigger one, no matter how many hormones they flooded her body with.

Her life isn't going anywhere and it never will be, and she doesn't think that Silva's set would ever decide that they wanted her permanently. But even if all she gets out of it is a dinner, well...

It'll probably be one hell of a dinner.

Chapter Two

The next night sees Kara running late, still scrolling through an article about Ethiopia on JSTOR even as she finishes doing up the zippers on her booties and shoves earrings of some sort into her ears. She knows better than to start reading so soon before she needs to leave, but then she saw it referenced in her department chair's tweets, and, well—

Here she is, hair still twisted up in a messy bun, fingers stained with ink, as there's a knock on her apartment door.

Kara takes a deep breath, decides discretion is not the better part of valor in this case and opens the door.

The man standing in front of her apartment is the tallest Alpha she has ever seen, six-five or six-six and so broad-shouldered he fills up her entire doorway. His dark hair is cut short on the sides and longer at the top, a riot of curls. He's gorgeous.

Kara wants to shut the door in his face.

Instead, she musters up all of her bravery and offers him a hand, saying, "Hi, I'm Kara."

"Jason," he says, before dipping down and skimming his lips over the inside of her wrist, just as Damon did a couple days ago.

Her knees go weak, and she blurts out, "The one who reads car magazines," to distract from what a mess she is.

Jason laughs, keeping hold of her hand so he can tug her forward. She pulls the door closed behind her, locking it one handed because she doesn't want to pull her hand out of his warm grasp. This close, Kara can smell him, that sharp heat that makes her mouth water. She wants to taste him, wants to lick his skin until that scent is heavy on her tongue.

He sucks in a deep breath, and Kara realizes that he can smell *her*—her want, her need—as her own scent sweetens from lemons to lemonade.

"We should go," he says, letting go of her hand so he can put his hand on the small of her back. She lets him. "Otherwise, I might do something unwise."

"Like what?"

"Like trying to convince you to let me into that apartment of yours and let me strip off your clothes one by one until you're wearing nothing but that beautiful smile." Kara sucks in a breath, and Jason grins at her with very white teeth. "But we won't get to that just yet."

He heads toward the elevator bank, but she redirects him toward the stairs, leading him down the two flights to the entryway. He darts forward to try to get the door before her, but she pushes it open, holding it pointedly until he gets the picture and exits.

"You don't like Alphas holding the door for you?" he asks, settling his hand back on the small of her back as he heads toward a sleek black car.

"I don't like Alphas who don't like Omegas holding the door for them."

"Noted," Jason says with a smile. "Well, I am pleased to inform you that I, at least, am happy for you to hold the door for me." He unlocks the car, sweeping his hand out to indicate that he's leaving her to open her own door before heading around to the driver's side.

Kara smothers a grin behind her hand, climbing in. It's nice he has a sense of humor, at least.

Once they're on the road, Jason asks, apropos of nothing, "If you had five million dollars, right now, what would you do with it?"

Kara blinks at him. "Is this some sort of test? If I give the secret answer, do you throw me out of the car?"

"If you told me you wanted to go commit mass murder, I might reconsider this whole thing." He shakes his head, laughing a little. "Answer the question, sweetheart. What would you do with five million?"

The word 'sweetheart' sounds good on his tongue — but it was clearly reflexive, the kind of thing he probably calls every Omega he meets. She can't look too deep into it or she'll never dig herself out of this hole when they inevitably decide she's not what they want.

She's already letting herself hope, and that is a dangerous thing.

So Kara just clears her throat and says, "If I had five million, I think I'd buy myself a house. So that's eight, maybe nine hundred down. I have some college debt left, so I'd cover that next — or first, but let's assume I'm doing this all at the same time. I'd save some of the rest, and probably go out and spend some ridiculous amount of money on clothes, and then I guess everything else I'd donate."

"No car?" he asks.

"I prefer riding in other people's."

Jason glances at her, and she realizes how that sounds, given the circumstances. But she doesn't take it back, and his smile just keeps growing. It lights up his face, makes his eyes look like they're shining from the inside out, and it would take her breath away if she weren't trying so hard to take slow even breaths and not look too hard at him.

The car is already flooded with his scent, so entrenched she's sure it's in the stitching of the leather seats, and her own scent layers on top of it like a gauzy piece of fabric, just there enough for her to smell an embarrassing amount of *want* in it — want for him, for this, for something to make her life something different from what it is right now, alone and lonely and so aggressively isolated that she feels some days like she might never dig herself out of it.

"You smell sad," Jason says, his smile fading.

Kara's face burns hot at that, and she cracks open the window just enough to air out the car a little. "Shit, sorry." Whatever they're looking for, it's not a mess of a woman whose idea of flirting is to immediately start having an existential crisis.

But he just shakes his head, saying, "You don't need to apologize for it."

"I know it's not..." She waves her hand to encompass whatever the hell this is. "Anyway. The internet told me what Damon does — more or less — and obviously you all have looked me up, so...what do you do?"

"You mean other than drive beautiful women around?"

"Unless that's what you do with your life. I won't judge."

Jason laughs. "If only that were my lot in life. But alas, I have the far less glamorous job of being a consultant."

"The true DMV lot in life."

"Excuse me," he says loftily, "but we call it the National Capital Region."

"Oh," Kara says, mock-despairingly, "a *government* consultant."

"You caught me."

He makes a turn, and suddenly they're on an empty road, nothing but an unrelenting set of trees on either side of a one-lane road.

Kara glances around, then asks, a little less casually than she intended, "Is this where you're taking me to murder me?"

"Is this where I'm —" Jason looks around too, then snorts out a laugh. "Oh, okay, that is the vibe here, isn't it? No, this is the road to our place. We own all this land."

"Which would be a great place to murder me," she points out, but that little bit of instinctive tension eases. Not that he couldn't still be planning on murdering her, but she already came this far with him without him being the least bit creepy, so it's not like she's going to ask him to turn back now.

And even now, a gate comes into view, and far beyond it a house, pale in the distance. Jason slows when they get near the gate, stopping next to a discreet box so he can roll down his window and press his thumb to it. The gate slides open, and he drives them in.

It's a long driveway, but not absurd, ending in a circle in front of the door, though there are paved offshoots that she assumes lead to garages or wherever else rich people store cars. Maybe they have one of those car elevators where the cars stack and can be called up like dry cleaning.

He parks them at the top of the circle, closest to the door, then says, "I'll let you get your own door."

"Thanks ever so much."

That gets her a grin and a blown kiss, and both of them climb out. Kara's closer to the house, and she is *definitely* not opening that door on her own, not when it's someone else's house, so she just waits by the car as Jason walks around it.

She expects him to head straight to the house, but instead he comes over to her, settling a hand on the small of her back just like he did in her apartment and walking with her toward the house.

It would be presumptuous, but she doesn't mind, not when his hand is so warm and he smells so good.

The door pops open before they even reach it, and a man with a familiar voice says, "Okay, okay, you've gotten enough time alone with her, you don't need to slow-walk her to the house."

Jason flips Eric off, and he's clearly attempting to be discreet, but it's very obvious, and Kara smothers a smile.

Eric is a lot shorter than Jason, which still puts him at quite a bit taller than her — and she's not used to feeling this short, at five-foot-six — with auburn hair and eyes that are startlingly blue even from a distance. When he pulls her away from Jason to tug her into the house, she can feel the calluses on his fingers, the muscles in his arms.

"Welcome!" he exclaims, tangling his fingers with hers so he can pull her deeper into the house.

Kara forgot how tactile Alphas are with Omegas—
to the point of being presumptuous at times—but
everyone knows the stories about how courting Alphas
are with the Omegas they're pursuing, practically
rubbing themselves all over the Omegas to get their
scents to mix, to get even a little bit of the far less
transferable Omega scent onto their own skin and
clothes.

Good Alphas stop when asked, but it's the
culturally-accepted default, for Alphas to touch and
touch and touch until the bond is set and the scents mix
on their own.

And damn if she hasn't missed that.

Nobody touches her these days, except for hugs
when she goes back to see her parents up north of
Baltimore, and the occasional kiss on the cheek from
her Beta aunt's Alpha wife.

"You have a beautiful house," she tells them, and
means it—it's open and airy, but there's
personalization that keeps it from feeling like a
magazine photo, including a gorgeous geometric
feature wall.

"Thank you," Eric says brightly. "I can take no credit
for it."

That makes her laugh, and from the pleased look on
his face, that's what he was aiming for.

"But really," he continues, directing her through a
doorway into a dining room with five places set, "I'm
glad that you like it. If you do end up with us, this
would be your home too."

That's a jarring thought—not of moving out of her
apartment, to which she has very little emotional
attachment, but of living *here*, in someone else's house.
In a set's house.

But that's what this is all about, ultimately. Joining a set, becoming their Omega, keeping house and home and set. Something that she gave up on years ago, when it became clear that she was the one of the few Omegas who will never go into heat.

There are infertile Omegas, of course, but even they go into heats, because heats are not just about pregnancy but about bonding. And gland implants have let transdynamic Omegas go into heats for almost a decade now.

So it's just her and maybe a dozen other Omegas in the country, the literal one-in-a-million whose glands are so wildly fucked that they just can't do any of it.

The fact that they're giving her this opportunity, without prompting, without her seeking them out first to beg and plead for *someone* to take her — she doesn't know how to trust it.

"Well," Eric says, after she's been silent for too long, lost in her own head, "there are two options — we can hang in the kitchen where Damon and Ry are finishing cooking, or Jason and I can ply you with alcohol and good company in the living room."

"The kitchen and the alcohol aren't mutually exclusive," Jason specifies from the other side of her. "Though the kitchen and the good company might be."

Meeting everyone seems a bit overwhelming — but sitting in a living room while two people she doesn't know are cooking for her seems worse, and she does want to meet the fourth member of their set, so she says, "The kitchen sounds good to me."

"The kitchen it is." Eric sweeps his arm out in a mock bow, then heads over to a pair of sliding frosted glass doors.

"She doesn't like Alphas to open the door for her," Jason calls after him.

"I'll take my chances," Eric says, and slides open both sets of doors to reveal a massive kitchen, all white marble with a huge range and multiple ovens and a fridge that looks big enough for her to live in.

Damon is at the central island, chopping some sort of herb on a wooden cutting board, and beyond him there's a man with his back to them stirring something at the stove.

The smell of food hits her, rich and savory.

"Come in," Damon says, putting his knife down and wiping his hands on his apron—because he's wearing an honest-to-god apron over what looks like slacks and a white button-down shirt—before he strides over to take her hand.

Just like last time, he touches his lips to her wrist, no more perfunctory for having done it before. And just like last time, it sends a shiver down her spine, makes her want to curl her fingers and grab onto him, to cup his face and bury her face in him, in all that smoke.

And then Eric exclaims, "Oh, I know what I forgot to do," and takes her other hand and does the same, so she has two Alphas bent over her, both of her arms outstretched. A strand of Eric's hair brushes her wrist, and she feels it all the way up her arm.

When he straightens, Damon is smiling. "Welcome," he says. He lets go of her hand so he can take a step back, but not far. She feels very small surrounded by these three men, three Alphas. "We're glad that you came."

"Thank you for inviting me." Eric lets go of her hand too, and she tucks both of her hands behind her back, clasping them together so nobody can see them trembling a little. She isn't *used* to this, to the attention, to even the lead-up to courting. "I wanted to meet you all before I—before I decided."

"Of course." He heads back to his cutting board, pulling her gaze toward him—and toward the fourth member of their set, who still hasn't turned to look at her.

She's not sure if he doesn't want her here, if he doesn't want her at all. She wouldn't blame him if that were the case.

"We weren't sure what you eat," Damon continues, "and *someone* didn't ask—"

"It's not my fault I was distracted by how hot she sounds," Eric exclaims.

"—so we made a mix of everything. And if there's nothing here that you eat, we can find something else."

That seems like a lot of work just for her, but Kara does appreciate the thoughtfulness. "I eat basically everything, unless everything you made has eel or chestnuts in it. And it smells great."

"That is...very specific," Jason says. "Did you have some traumatizing childhood experience with eels on a chestnut farm or something?"

"I am part of the small set of people with a chestnut allergy," Kara says. "And I just find the concept of eating eels disconcerting."

"I can guarantee you that we have no eels *or* chestnuts in anything we made," Damon assures her. "Would you like something to drink? I noticed you didn't drink at the club, but I didn't want to assume one way or another."

"I would love some wine." Feeling bold, she heads over to the island, which is big enough that she can sit on one of the tall stools across from Damon without getting in his way. "White, if you have it."

"We have," Eric says, "and I am not kidding with this, hundreds of bottles of white wine in this house. We have a white wine fridge downstairs. We are overflowing in white wine. We have an *embarrassment* of white wine."

"Just because you're a philistine," the fourth member of the set says, a little sharply, "doesn't mean the rest of us need to be."

No matter the tone, Eric doesn't seem to take offense, saying cheerfully, "I like to think of myself less as a philistine and more of a connoisseur of fine beers." He heads toward the fridge, asking, "Any specifications on the type of white wine?"

"Sauvignon blanc."

"One sauvignon blanc, coming up," Eric says. In short order he's offering an expertly-poured glass of wine to her. Whatever his preferences for alcohol are, he's better at pouring wine without spilling than she is on her best day.

Fortunately, the stain on her apartment ceiling is less obvious because it was made by white wine.

Jason sits in the chair on one side of her, and Eric takes the chair on the other side. He hands a beer to Jason, something that looks fancy and artisanal, like the sort her cousins would drink while watching soccer.

"So," Kara says, to jump all the way through the ice, "why me?"

The fourth member of the set goes very still.

But it's Damon, confidently chopping a new herb — one that's either parsley or cilantro, or maybe some secret third herb that only rich people know about — who says, "As I said, none of us are looking to go through a heat with an Omega. It made you an... obvious candidate."

"Maybe you could sound more mercenary," Jason drawls next to her. He takes a long drink of beer, and she watches his throat work as he swallows. "Yes, that was how we found you originally, from the *WaPo* article—"

That fucking article. "It didn't list my name." *First Instance of Heatless Omega Identified in D.C. Metropolitan Area.* Because that's what the whole world needed, to know that somewhere in the broader metro area, there is a fucked-up Omega.

"When you have as much money as we do," Damon says, almost apologetically, "you can find the information you're looking for."

"Great." Kara takes a too-big sip of the wine, swallowing too fast to savor it. She's starting to regret bringing this up.

But Jason continues, "As I was saying, that was how we found you. But when we looked into you, we found someone who's clever, who seems kind—and that seemed like a pretty good potential for a courting. And if you decide that the courting isn't for you, or we start it and you don't want to go all the way, there won't be any hard feelings."

From the set of the spine of their fourth member who still won't look at her, that isn't universally true.

"And what does 'going all the way' mean to you, without a bonding?"

She's asking Jason, but it's Damon who says, "We can get married, for one thing. Almost sixty percent of A/O pairings or sets are married at this point, so nobody would question it. And there are ways to mimic a bonding, scent-wise."

"So you want to pretend that we're bonded?"

Damon shrugs one elegant shoulder. "I want to let people assume. It's none of anyone's business whether or not we ever bond or what the formation of our set is. I see no reason why it should be a concern."

"Stop it."

Kara opens her mouth to respond — then realizes it was the fourth member who spoke, his voice so sharp it's almost a whisper.

He turns off the heat and shoves a pan off of the burner, then turns and says again, louder, "Stop it."

He's...not what Kara expected, seeing the rest of them. He's attractive, sure, but in the way a blade is attractive, or glass — sharp, too-thin, more edges than curves. But most of all, he looks *tired*.

"I appreciate this," he says, even though he looks very much like he doesn't appreciate it, whatever *it* is, "but we all know that this is not the solution to this problem. *She* is not the solution to this problem."

That hurts, even though it's very much not a surprise, and Kara is proud of how calm her voice is when she sets her glass down on the island and says, "I understand."

But they're ignoring her now — which feels better, honestly, because she's pretty sure she's about to cry, and she doesn't want to do that here, surrounded by these Alphas, stuck in a house she can't leave without one of them.

She never should have agreed to this.

It's Jason who asks, "And what do you think the solution is, if not finding an Omega we can all be with?"

"Finding an Omega you *want* to be with," he snaps, and that hurts even more, more than Kara thought it would. She really doesn't want to cry here. She really doesn't. She shouldn't be here. This was a mistake.

"Find someone you can bond with. Don't make your life decisions based on me."

"And who should we be making our life decisions based on?" Damon demands.

"Based on what *you* want. Not this mess."

The first tears slip out, and Kara stands and hurries out, trying to find a bathroom or a closet or *anywhere* where she can cry without them seeing.

All of this was such a fucking mistake.

She's made peace with what she is—she's had to, or she would have just given up and laid down and died—but it still hurts to hear someone talk about her that way. She knows she's broken, she knows she's fucked up, she knows she's a mess, but she doesn't need some asshole to invite her to his house to say it to her face.

She's so goddamn mad.

But mostly she's mad at herself for having this hope, when a child could have told her that this was doomed to fail from the start.

And she has no fucking clue where the bathroom is, so she stumbles outside and sits down right on the steps leading down to the driveway so she can put her head in her ink-stained hands and cry in peace.

Chapter Three

It doesn't take long for Kara to be cried out—she did most of her crying about this years ago, and she's not all that interested in going back—but heading back in is wildly unappealing. She'll have to at some point so she can get a ride home, but at this point, avoidance seems like the best possible option.

At least it's a nice day out, not too hot with the sun starting to get low on the horizon, and there's a good breeze. They're tipping into the warm side of March, where days still shift unpredictably between cold and lovely, but sit more on the latter half than on the former.

And it's not raining, so she has that going for her.

Not that that makes her any less braced for an uncomfortable conversation when the door opens behind her and Damon says, "I'm incredibly sorry about that."

"It's fine," Kara says, even though it's not.

"No," Damon says, "it's not." He walks past her to stand in front of her, offering a hand, and she takes it because she doesn't want to be rude. He helps her to her feet. "But I need you to know that that wasn't about you."

Kara looks away. She doesn't need him to lie to her. "It sure felt like it was about me."

"It wasn't. I promise." He hasn't let go of her hand yet. "We'll explain everything if you come back in with me."

"I think I should just go home."

Damon looks, for one brief moment, gutted. Then he visibly packs it all back up and puts it away, his expression smoothing out into something neutral. "We'll take you home if you want to go," he says. "I promise. But just give us five minutes to explain, and then you can decide. Please."

She doesn't want to, because this whole thing has been like a fever dream, and now the fever has broken and she's back in the reality where no matter how much she likes herself, no Alpha is ever going to want her, not really.

But she also wants an explanation—she deserves an explanation—so she can get one then leave and never think about these few days of insanity again.

So she sucks up her hurt feelings enough to say, "Yeah, okay."

Damon closes his eyes, just for a second, like he's trying to hide whatever is on his face. "Thank you."

Kara pulls her hand away and follows him back into the house.

They're all still in the kitchen, in more or less the same positions as when she left, except Jason is back all the way against a far wall near a floor-to-ceiling set of windows, watching them with his arms crossed, a bottle of beer in one hand.

It makes an odd tableau, the three of them so far apart in that big white kitchen that still smells like the best home cooking she's ever had in her life.

"I'm sorry," the fourth member of the set says as soon as they walk in. "I didn't mean — can I come over, greet you properly?"

She doesn't want him touching her, not like that. "I'd rather you not."

He nods once, a sharp jerk of his head. "I understand."

"So," Kara says, when nobody else fills the next half-second of silence, "that's the apology out of the way. Now that we've established that this isn't going to happen, does someone want to give me a ride home?"

Damon's lips tighten. "I understand if you've changed your mind."

Kara laughs, because the alternative is starting to cry again. "If *I've* changed *my* mind? It's pretty clear that this was never going to happen, so let's all stop pretending that I'm the deciding factor here. When one of the members of your set doesn't want me, we haven't even gotten close to the point where it's my call."

"I didn't —" The fourth shoves his hand through his hair, his too-thin face twisting into a grimace. "Fuck. Sorry. Okay." He pushes away from the stove. "Let's start over. I'm Ry, and I'm the reason you're here in the first place."

"You have a funny way of showing it."

Ry shakes his head. "What I meant is, I'm the reason that they're looking for an Omega who doesn't have heats to begin with. Damon, Jason, Eric, they would all be perfectly happy to find an Omega to bond."

"Ry —"

"Don't pretend you wouldn't be," Ry interrupts Eric. "The only thing stopping them from doing that is me."

"Because you don't want to bond?" Kara asks.

"Because I can't bond."

"You don't need to tell her this," Damon interrupts.

Ry just shakes his head again. "I do if we want her to stay, and you know it." His eyes settle on Kara again, and even across the room she can feel them like a weight. "I have what's known as Bond Rejection Disorder, which means that the hormones that come from bonding will more than likely kill me. I'm not telling you this to feel sorry for me—I'm telling you this so you understand why this set is looking for an Omega like you."

"But you can go through heats without bonding."

"You can," Ry concedes. "But I have...other health issues that make the likelihood of me getting an Omega through a heat low at best."

"So you're looking for someone where that just won't be an issue," she realizes.

He inclines his head. "That's why none of that was about you, not really. But I'm sorry anyway. It's not your fault that your presence here reflects, well..."

"The opportunities your set won't have."

"That's not true, though," Jason says, pushing off from the wall he's been holding up. "If we end up with you, Kara, it's not some missed opportunity—it's just a different opportunity, to have our whole set be with someone equally, to be with someone who is smart and funny and forgiving enough not to walk over and kick each of us in the balls for making you sit through that."

But Kara knows what Ry is saying. When your own body ends up as the vessel for everything you thought you would be able to do but can't, everything that reminds you of it hurts.

Which is why she lives her life holed up in her apartment, keeping life close but everything else far.

Damon says, "So one of us can drive you home now, if you'd like, and you can think about it — or you can tell us you never want to hear from us again, and we'll leave you alone. But we'd like you to stay for dinner, if you're willing, and give us another chance to try to convince you that we're not as terrible a bet as we've just made ourselves seem."

She should just go home, say to hell with all of this and walk away. But she doesn't want to keep everything far anymore. And she has no illusions that they'll fall in love with her, no expectations that this will be a great love from the movies, but maybe it doesn't have to be. Maybe it can just be people helping each other out, giving each other what they want and what they need and having some half-decent sex in between.

So she says, "I'll stay."

Eric beams at her. "You're not going to regret this."

* * * *

To Kara's surprise, they eat family-style, food in serving bowls and plates on trivets on the table, and with her permission Damon spoons out a little of everything onto her plate, bœuf bourguignon topped with parsley and roasted carrots and herbed mashed potatoes and a peppery salad with mustard vinaigrette.

It is, she tells them, "Amazing. I can cook, but not like this."

To her astonishment, Damon's face turns a full red, though it's Eric who says, "Thank you, though I can't take any credit for this either. Ry and Damon do ninety percent of our cooking."

"We get a lot of practice, cooking for four every day," Ry says. He doesn't seem sure how to talk to her now that trauma-sharing time is over, his voice careful. "Though Damon keeps abandoning me to the hordes to take business calls."

"I wouldn't call it abandoning," Damon protests around a mouthful of potato. "More like strategic retreat."

"Sure, sure."

"So I know Jason is a federal contractor and Damon does...business, but what do the rest of you do?" Kara asks.

Business, Eric mouths at Damon, then says, "I'm an ER charge nurse."

That's not a stereotypical Alpha job, or a standard male one — most nurses are still Beta or Omega women. But academia hasn't been friendly to Omegas until recently either — or women — and Omega women least of all, so it's not like she has any ground to stand on when it comes to traditional dynamic or gender roles.

"What about you?" she asks Ry.

"I'm what you might call a house-Alpha," Ry says, mouth quirked up into a half smile.

"You'll have to negotiate with him for nesting rights," Jason says with a laugh, and Ry's eye roll makes it clear this isn't a new joke.

"My apartment is an absolute disaster area," she tells them. "I am solidly mediocre at and wholly uninterested in the vast majority of nesting ninety-five percent of the time. I would steal all of your pillows, though."

"We have more than enough pillows," Damon assures her.

Kara thinks of the literal wall of pillows on her queen bed and says, "We'll see." She looks around the four of them, these four very different people, then asks, "So, how did you become a set?"

"Ry and I have known each other since we were born," Damon says, "and I met Jason in college."

"And Eric and I met in the Army when he saved my life," Jason adds. "And when we got out, I reconnected to Damon, who had just made his first billion, and I decided a rich set was the way to go."

"Romantic," Kara jokes, even though most single-dynamic sets aren't.

But Ry just smiles and says, "We do love each other. Maybe not the same way we would love an Omega, but we do." He smirks at her. "And we do share well."

"Oh," Kara says, throat dry. She feels very brave and very scared all at once. "Any chance you'd be willing to show me? Just for evidence gathering, you know."

"Of course," Damon says. His gaze is hot behind his glasses. "After we get you well fed. We wouldn't want our potential Omega going hungry, you know."

Next to her, Ry's throat works like he's swallowing and swallowing again, then he says in a rough voice, "She doesn't smell like she wants to wait that long."

Kara squeezes her thighs together, like that will mask the rush of sweet arousal coming from her—or how wet she is, just from their scents and the thought of her between them, below them—

"That's not helping," Jason says. He takes a long drink of his beer. "You smell so fucking good, I just want to bury myself in you, lick you until you're all over my face—"

"Okay," Eric cuts in. Kara's gratified to hear that he sounds as hungry as the rest of them. "Okay, let's just— put a pause on this, until we've eaten, because otherwise we'll never finish."

"I certainly plan to finish," Jason says.

Kara bites the inside of her cheek, because the alternative is saying something stupid and horny and needy —

Then Jason is on his feet and heading toward her, and he pulls her up out of her chair to get her leaning on the table, off-balance and so desperately horny, so he can bend down and kiss her.

He kisses like someone who's kissed a lot of people, mouth hot and wet and tasting just a little of beer as he licks his way into her mouth, and his hand at her back is the one thing that's keeping her upright as her head spins and she *burns* with need. His smell is all that's in her nose now, so strong she thinks it'll be imprinted on her skin, and it's intoxicating in the way only an Alpha's scent can be, burying its way deep into her brain.

His other hand skims up the inside of her thigh, burning hot even through her pants, then he presses between her legs and she gasps into his mouth.

"You like that?" he asks, sliding his thumb up and down the seam of her pants, just hard enough for her to get a little bit of friction, a little bit of pressure. "You like my hands on you?"

Kara nods, reaching up to tangle her hand in the short hairs at the back of his neck, and he groans.

"Just like that, sweetheart," he breathes. "You pull as hard as you want."

His lips travel down her throat to worry at her collarbone, a couple inches from her scent gland, and she tips her head back to give him more space — then she feels another hand touch her lips, and Eric says, "You're not showing her what a good job we can do of sharing."

"Fuck," Kara gasps out, opening her eyes just a slit to see Eric there too, almost as close, the caramel sweetness of his scent a heady mix with the heat of Jason's. Her lips move against his thumb as she talks, and he slips his thumb inside, and she closes her lips around it, scraping the pad of his thumb with her teeth.

Eric groans, and Jason sucks so hard on her skin that she knows it'll be bruised, and she has to close her eyes against the sensations, the taste and smell and feeling of these hands on her, these bodies crowding hers.

"Do you want to come now, baby?" Eric asks in her ear, his lips so close they're brushing against the sensitive skin there. "Or do you want to come later, when we're all in bed together?"

"Or both?" Jason asks against her throat. His hand strokes up and down between her legs, just on the edge of giving her enough pressure. "It's not an either-or, sweetheart, if you don't want it to be."

Kara can barely think—but she can think enough to know what her body usually wants, so she gasps out, "If I come now, I won't want to come later—and I want to come later."

"Thank you, sweetheart," Jason says, and his hand slows. "You smell so good. We're going to make you feel so good."

Adrenaline is still pumping through her, but as Jason drags his hand back down her thigh and around her hip so both of his hands are bracing her, she forces herself to take deep breaths to try to calm herself. The waves of scent she's getting from both of them—and from Damon and Ry underneath—are not helping her ratchet that arousal down.

But Eric pulls his thumb from her mouth to stroke her hair back, Jason pulls his mouth from her throat and everything steadies into something a little less shivering hot.

When they step back entirely, the embarrassment hits her.

She just almost let two Alphas get her off in the middle of their dining room, in the middle of dinner, while two other Alphas watched—and she doesn't even know if Ry and Damon wanted to see that.

So now she's wet and reeking of arousal, and they're going to go through the rest of dinner having to smell that.

"I am," she says when Jason and Eric step back enough for her to turn and look at the rest of them, "so sorry."

"You have nothing to be sorry for," Damon tells her. His eyes are bright, his lips red. "That was the hottest thing I've seen in a long time."

"I could watch them take you apart for hours," Ry adds.

"I—" Kara sits back down, pressing her thighs together to keep from getting distracted by how *wet-hot-sensitive* she is. Jason drags a thumb across the nape of her neck before heading back to his seat. "I didn't come here to sleep with you. I really did just come here to get to know you."

"And we didn't bring you here to sleep with you," Damon says. He shifts in his seat, and she has the sudden thought that he might be as aroused as she is. "But we want to court you, Kara—and the fact that we want each other, that can only be good. And you are...very, *very* sexy." He gestures toward her half-full plate. "Now eat. You look hungry."

She is—more for them than for the food on her plate, as delicious as it is—but she picks up her fork anyway and makes herself take a bite of bœuf bourguignon. It's cooled a bit, but it's still tasty, and she realizes just how hungry she is for actual food, too.

"This is really good," she says around a mouthful of beef, scooping up some mashed potatoes with her fork. "You are a very impressive house-Alpha."

Ry's face goes pink with pleasure, and Damon says, offended, "Hey, I helped too."

"People probably tell you you're impressive all the time," Kara says.

"She has you there," Eric says, laughing. "Nobody needs to inflate your ego."

Damon glares at him, but it's a hard sell when she can smell his arousal, can almost taste it in the air. "And how many people have you picked up with 'I save people for a living'?"

"A *lot*," Eric says unselfconsciously. "But in fairness, I *do* save people for a living."

"And I'm impressive," Damon counters.

"Making money is nowhere in the same ballpark as nursing," Eric says.

Loftily, Damon says, "I do support our hedonistic lifestyle."

Ry snorts. "Our hedonistic lifestyle of spending ninety percent of our time holed up in your secluded mansion?"

"It's *our* secluded mansion." Damon shakes his head. "We're really giving Kara the wrong idea of how fun we are."

"You're talking to someone who spends *her* life holed up in her mediocre apartment. If you were going to expect me to go to parties every night, this definitely wouldn't work."

Something shifts in Damon's expression, and he says, "If you agree to the courting, we'll figure all of this out, but I need you to know — we wouldn't expect that from you, if you didn't want to do it. We wouldn't expect you to entertain if you didn't want to, or to cook or clean or do whatever it is Omegas are 'supposed' to do."

Kara swallows, her throat dry. "You said that when we first met."

"And I meant it," he says. He glances at Ry and Eric and Jason, then looks at her again to say, "We are, ultimately, asking you to give us your life, with everything that comes with that—with the scrutiny, with the judgment, with the commitment to be with us for the foreseeable future. So, frankly, it's important that you like us, because nothing will make all of us more miserable than being with an Omega who hates being with us. We'd know if you were unhappy."

"We wouldn't be bonded," she protests, even though she's not quite sure why she's protesting. Maybe because this keeps creeping closer to actually being real. Having sex with them is one thing, but what they want is forever—and that's almost too long to contemplate, when up until a few days ago she assumed she would never have an Alpha, much less a set.

"Do you think," Ry asks, "that just because we won't be bonding, that we won't have all of the same instincts Alphas have about their Omegas?"

She did think that, a little bit, actually.

"I want to mark you up," he continues. "I want to worry the darkest bruise right over your scent gland, even if it wouldn't do anything, because it would be so pretty there, and everyone would know that you're ours. We would keep you marked up there, if you'd let us, so nobody else would ever think that they could have you."

"We'd give you shelter," Damon adds, "and food, and cover you in gold or jewels or whatever it is that you want on your body to show off the fact that you have a set, and it's yours."

"We'd keep your scent sweet and bright," Jason picks up. "We'd open you up and knot you all night, we'd make you feel so good and then we'd take you out and show you off so everyone could smell that we belonged to you."

"And we'd keep you safe," Eric finishes. Kara can hardly breathe. "We'd stand between you and anyone or anything that tried to do you harm."

"All we're asking from you," Damon says, "is for you to give us a chance to prove it to you."

"Yes," Kara says, because she wants all of that. "Yes, I'll give you that chance. I accept your set's offer of courting."

* * * *

They touch each other carefully that night, five bodies in a bed that can fit more, hands and mouths and slick against skin. Damon's the one who undresses her, reverent when she would just go for expedient, pressing kisses to her stomach until Jason says, "You don't get to be the only one who touches her tonight."

"It's not my fault you weren't faster," Damon says, but he's laughing, moving out of the way on their massive bed to give Jason access to her mouth. Kara pulls him down, tangling her fingers in his hair until he moans and kisses her. A third set of hands slides up her thighs, all the way to the edge of her lacy panties, her special pair that she wears for dates.

Then the hands pause, resting there almost hesitantly until she opens her eyes and leans up to look past Jason and see Eric between her legs. There's a question visible on his face.

"I thought you were going to show me how good you are at sharing," she says, because *please do whatever you want to me* feels a little much for a first date.

Eric grins, then tugs her panties down her legs and slides two fingers against her clit.

Her gasp is caught in Jason's mouth. She can feel his grin against her lips.

"Beautiful," Damon says, thumbing her nipple until it hardens under his fingers.

She can smell their scents in the air, thick with arousal, her citrus a bright note over their smoke and heat, and she's losing herself in it, in the wash of pheromones all around her.

Eric's fingers play between her legs, and she groans into Jason's mouth, tugging him even closer.

"What do you want?" Jason asks against her lips. "What do you want, Omega?"

"What I want," she says, "is to get one of you inside of me, right now."

"We can do that," Eric says.

She ends up riding Damon, one hand braced on his chest as they find a rhythm. She gets one hand between them, around his knot, so it doesn't end up slipping inside of her by accident. He's hot inside of her, and thick. It's been a while since she's slept with anyone and even longer since she's slept with an Alpha, but it's even better than she remembered.

Jason is a line of heat against her back, callused hands on her hips, and Eric and Ry are both watching. From her angle, she can see Eric jacking himself off, and it makes her want to get him in her mouth.

"Omega," Damon groans, fucking up into her. "You're going to kill me."

"But what a way to go," Jason says. "Fuck, Kara, you smell like heaven."

"I bet you say that to all the Omega girls," she jokes, then drags one of Jason's hands up so she can suck it two fingers into her mouth. He makes a guttural noise behind her, his other hand tightening on her hips so hard she thinks she might bruise from it.

Between their joined bodies, Kara squeezes Damon's knot, and he's coming, and she follows behind him, her rhythm faltering as she tips over into the edge into heady pleasure.

Chapter Four

Kara wakes to an empty bed.

It's a set king, which means it's made to fit six comfortably. It also means that, when she wakes alone in the dead center of it, tangled in a veritable bolt of fabric, she's faced with no graceful options for getting out.

Not that she wants to get up, not yet—there's a throb between her legs that's just on the edge between *a reminder of a great night* and *will be uncomfortable to sit for a while*, and she's naked but for a tank top that didn't belong to her at the start of the night. And, most important, getting up means facing the cold light of day and everything that comes with it, like the fact that she agreed to a courtship with a four-Alpha set, promptly had mind-blowing sex with them then woke up in an empty bed in an empty room somewhere in a house she doesn't know.

There's something very awkward about being the last person to wake, about knowing that everyone else saw her sleeping sprawled out on their bed, undignified, then left to go about their day knowing that some Omega they barely know is still sleeping, oblivious, in their bed.

It's so rare that she sleeps anywhere that isn't her sham of a nest in her apartment or the remnants of her childhood nest that her parents never dismantled, and she can see the signs of where she started to try to build one in their bed while she was half-asleep, pillows layered just so, and one put at the end of the bed to symbolically close it off.

Face burning, she snatches that last pillow up and puts it haphazardly back with the dozen other pillows at the head of the bed, ignoring how good the weight is and how nice the texture. They do not need her turning their bed into her goddamn nest.

But she hates how that looks, all the pillows in such disarray, and so in short order and without any prior experience, she ends up standing in front of a basically-made set king bed, which has the largest goddamn sheets she has ever seen in her life.

And if she's a little out of breath, well, nobody is around to see it.

And if she's wet between her legs from the way the entire room smells like four aroused Alphas and the scent of the five of them having sex, nobody is around to tell that either.

She can't find her panties—not that she looks all that hard for them—but she puts on her bra under whoever's tank top that she's wearing then pulls on her pants. They're not the most comfortable to wear when she's panty-less and wet, but they're a better option than going naked from the waist down.

When the stalling gets to be a bit too much even for her, she smooths down her shirt—someone else's shirt—one more time and heads downstairs.

The one place she knows how to get to in the entire house is the kitchen, which is where they seem to be congregated. Kara can smell food as she gets close, mostly bacon, and she can hear the sound of multiple male voices.

When she gets close, she hears one of them — Jason, she thinks — ask, "What time's your call?"

Damon says, "I have half an hour or so. Ask her to give me a chance to say goodbye, if she wants to head out before I'm off it?"

The fact that he wants to be able to say goodbye to her — even something so small as that — makes something warm deep in Kara's chest, and it gives her the courage to push into the room and say, "You can ask me yourself, if you want."

"Good morning, sweetheart," Jason says, heading over to take her hands and spin her in a circle like they're in a waltz or a ballroom dance. She ends up in the circle of his arms, her back to his chest, and he tips his head down to press a kiss to the top of her head. "You look ravishing this morning."

This close, his smell is intoxicating, arousal and sweat and *Alpha*, all heat and need. It smells like one of the scents on her skin, and there's something particularly heady about that, knowing that last night, he was *hers*.

"Did you sleep well?" Damon asks. He sounds nonjudgmental, and Kara manages to shove down the instinctive defensiveness. They let her sleep in their bed. They aren't going to be upset that she was, well, sleeping in their bed.

So she smiles at him, at where he's sitting at the kitchen island in a Henley shirt and jeans looking very put together, and says, "I did, thank you."

"I'm glad." He walks over to stop in front of her, so close she can feel the heat of his body, tucks a finger under her chin, and tilts her head up to look at him. It's a soft enough touch that she could resist if she wanted to, or pull away, but she can feel the unexpected calluses on his fingers and the warmth of his skin, and she doesn't want to pull away.

So instead she lets him tilt her head up and press a kiss to her lips. It's chaste for one brief moment — then his lips part, and so do hers, and he licks into her mouth, biting down on the meat of her lower lip in just the right way to send a hot spark of pain down to the base of her spine, and she's wet between her legs again just like that.

"Fuck," Damon mutters against her mouth, and she thinks, *yes please*.

One of Jason's hands slips up under her shirt, pressing against her stomach, and he says in her ear, "You smell so good, sweetheart."

Damon's lips lift off of hers, just a little, and she goes up on her toes to chase his kiss. Her blood is burning, and she feels almost drunk with need, with the ache between her legs for something, anything, for touch, for friction. It's the pheromones — she knows it's the pheromones — but the air is so thick with them that she can't think.

"So beautiful," Damon whispers, dragging his tongue across her lower lip once, twice, before nosing down to her throat. He presses a wet, open-mouthed kiss to the sensitive skin there, just on the edge of her gland —

And the sensation is so startling that she jerks away from him, a rush of cold shaky adrenaline running through her body.

"Don't," she says through swollen lips, "touch me there."

"My apologies," Damon says, taking a few steps back. He looks as taken apart as she feels, lips bright red and face flushed and hair all a mess. "I didn't—my apologies."

Kara pulls away from Jason, too, because she suddenly can't stand to have his arms around her. She's shaking, stupid pointless adrenaline for something that she knows isn't an attack no matter how much her body wants to convince her it is.

"Are you okay?" Ry asks, and she realizes for the first time that he's been standing over by the stove the whole time.

He was the only person who didn't fuck her last night, and she wonders at that.

"I'm fine," she says, clapping a trembling hand over her scent gland. "Sorry. I'm fine. Just don't—please."

"Does it hurt?" Ry asks.

Kara shakes her head. It doesn't hurt. It doesn't feel like anything.

"What would you like to eat?" Ry asks. Jason and Damon step away like they're trying to reset back to an earlier moment. "I have bacon, maple bacon, scrambled eggs, fruit, the ability to make other eggs. Also toast."

As awkward as it is, she appreciates them not pushing. "What's the difference between bacon and maple bacon?" she asks, heading over toward him. He gives her a look that's half-hopeful, half wistful, but he doesn't reach out to touch her the way the others do.

What he does is clear his throat and say, "Maple bacon was cooked with maple syrup on it."

"That sounds amazing," she tells him. "And I'll take everything." She grins at him, the shaking ebbing a little bit. "I could learn to live with this."

The look on his face shifts, turning into something thin and delicate and yearning, and it hurts to look at, because she's seen that same look in the mirror at the thought of being somewhere like here, doing something like this.

But all he does is pile a bunch of food onto a plate and carry it over to the island, where he sets it in front of a chair. "For you," he says with a little flourish.

"Thank you, Alpha," she says, and is gratified with a bright smile on his face. "Did you all eat already?"

"We did," Damon says apologetically. "And I need to go prep for my meeting. Stay until I'm done?"

"Sure," Kara says, because she doesn't have anywhere else to go right now.

He gives her a smile, then brushes a hand against her back and heads out of the room.

"I, unlike our illustrious billionaire and intrepid nurse," Jason says, sitting down next to her, "am living a life of leisure on this fine weekend, so I can keep you company." He reaches over to steal a berry from her plate, an old Alpha tease, and she hits his hand away. They're not together yet, barely even courting. He doesn't get to steal her food. "Ouch."

"Keep your hands off the food I made her," Ry says, without looking back at them.

Jason pouts at her. "Please, Omega."

"It's mine," she tells him, and eats that berry in particular. Then she realizes what he said and asks, "Where is Eric?"

"He's on shift," Jason says. "Saving the world and all that. He would have been here too, if he could have."

Kara takes a bite of maple bacon — sweet and salty and delicious — then says around a mouthful of it, "I think saving lives gives him a pass on not waiting around for me to wake up."

"It gives him a pass on a lot," Jason says with a laugh. He nudges her thigh with hers and says, "C'mon, eat."

She eats.

* * * *

The grounds around the mansion are beautiful.

The entire back of the mansion, when Ry and Jason lead her through there, is lined with flowering dogwood, beautiful white petals blooming in the spring air. Farther out, lining a path, are what might be plum or cherry blossom trees, as far as she can see. To one side is a vegetable garden, and to the other side is an enclosed patio and pool.

It looks like a dream.

The sort of dream that you wake up from half-remembering, feeling like you lost something, because nothing this perfect can exist in real life. Not in her world, at least.

They have this entire world — they have *the* entire world — and there will be absolutely nothing to hold them to her but some courting promises.

If she gets attached, if she convinces herself that their affection means something that will tie them to her, all it's going to do is break her heart.

"I grow some of what we eat here," Ry tells her. "Last year I ended up with about a hundred times as much zucchini as four people can physically eat, and somehow everything else ends up a tomato, but I like to think that I'm proficient at it."

"You're more than proficient," Jason says. He's standing a little too close to Kara in that Alpha way, crowding her, but she doesn't step away just yet. "The greenest thumb of the set."

"That is not a high bar." Ry tilts his head up toward the sky, and he looks better out here, less pale.

But then he turns a bright smile on her, warm and a little bit wicked, and all of her thoughts about his health go out the window. "Can I help you with something?" she asks.

"Just looking," he says. "You're beautiful."

"You're just saying that to get in my pants."

"I assure you, I'm not." He reaches out to brush a hand against her cheek, petal soft. "I didn't think I would ever get to have someone like you."

Something strikes Kara, and she starts to ask, "How long have you…"

"How long have I…?" Ry prompts, when she realizes how inappropriate her question is and cuts herself off.

She shakes her head. "Never mind. Ignore me."

"No, what were you going to ask?"

Kara scrubs a hand against her mouth, then steels herself and asks, "How long have you known about your Bond Rejection Disorder?"

Jason flinches, but Ry just gives her a long, steady look. "Since I was a teenager," he says. "It shows up on some standard blood tests."

"I'm sorry," she says, because she knows what it feels like to get results like that. "That must have been hard."

He shrugs. "I've had time to get used to it."

"I mean, I've had time to get used to being heatless, and it was still hard."

Ry tilts his head to the side, more like he's acknowledging her point than like he's conceding his own. Alpha bullshit all around, but Kara's used to it, and it's certainly not Alphas' greatest sins or their greatest problems.

The fact that they can order Omegas to do their bidding and Omegas will have to do it... that's probably both. It's something that Kara's never had happen to her, because it's illegal in all but a few cases—like courting or bonding—but, well. If she had to pick an Alpha, she'd pick one who's a little too stoic over one who does that.

"Also," Ry says, changing the subject with all the subtlety of—well, an Alpha, "we wanted to talk through some of the logistics we didn't get through last night. Would you be able to stick around until Eric is back from his shift this afternoon?"

It's a Sunday and Kara's caught up on everything she needs for her classes on Monday, so she says, "Sure, I can stay."

* * * *

"What we'd like to do," Damon says, "if you're amenable to it—"

Jason mouths *amenable* at Kara, grinning.

"—is take you out for dates. Each of us, individually, so you can get to know us as people and not just as one amorphous mass."

"I don't think four people can count as an amorphous mass," Eric puts in, and Damon reaches over without looking and hits him in the chest. Eric blows him a sardonic kiss in response.

"I'm good with going on dates," Kara says, trying to play it more casual than the giddy terror that she's feeling. "But don't you want me to get to know you as a collective, too?"

"Our hope for that," Damon says, "is that you'll be willing to come here sometimes, too. We want this to be your home, one day, for you to live here, to build a nest here. And so you should feel welcome here any time."

Kara can't imagine that, but she supposes it is the goal of this whole thing. To move in eventually, probably a few months into the courting if they get that far, to build a nest and prove to them that she can provide the sort of home Alphas need. Then by the end of the courting in a year, they'll decide to get bonded — married, she supposes — or go on their merry ways.

It's simpler for Alphas. If they decide she's not right for them, they can just end the courtship, and nobody will blame them. Especially not rich Alphas like them with an Omega who can't bond or give them children.

And there are ways for her to end the courtship without torpedoing any of the infinitesimal social clout she currently has, but they're neither simple nor guaranteed to work.

For so many reasons, seeing this courtship through is best for her — even if she's terrified of the concept of it, deep in that part of her that has spent the past few years internalizing all the reasons it's just as well that she could never end with an Alpha anyway.

"It's a beautiful house," she says, for lack of anything else to say.

"Thank you," Ry says. "I've done my best to keep it from turning into an Alpha mancave."

That's not the first—or second or third—thought Kara would have to describe the home. It's modern but comfortable, with art all over. Some of the art looks wildly expensive, but a lot of it doesn't, necessarily. None of it's bad, but it's a huge, unpretentious range.

"Where do you get the art from?" Kara asks, curious. "I know there's a rich person art world, but somehow most of your art doesn't seem to fit that."

"We have some of that," Ry says, "but most of what's here is just art that we enjoy looking at. Maybe a quarter of it is local artists, but there's definitely a mix."

"I refuse to live in a museum," Jason says, like it's an old argument.

Damon sighs. "I was never trying to get you to live in a museum."

"I've seen your parents' house." Jason grins at Kara. "It's *a lot*."

"And there's a reason why I don't live there." Damon waves his hand like he's pushing that conversation away. "So you'll let us take you on dates?"

He sounds oddly hopeful, not like a billionaire who's dated up and down the eastern seaboard.

"I'd really like that," Kara says, and means it. "I—thank you for doing all of this."

"It's not something you need to thank us for," Damon says, voice low and serious. His gaze darts to Ry. "What you are giving us is more than we could have hoped for."

* * * *

The first thing Kara does when she gets home is turn in her Muse-In to her *what is my life* playlist, crank up the volume and scream into a pillow.

There's nothing that feels real about this. A billionaire Alpha set courting the nerdy Omega academic—that's the sort of thing that happens in Hallmark movies, not real life. Alphas like that don't want Omegas like her, heat issues notwithstanding.

She pulls out her phone to call someone—her mom, maybe—then stops. Her mom would hate the idea of this, no question about it, and there's no point in telling her when she has no idea if it'll go anywhere. No point in opening that can of worms just yet.

She could call Sue Ann, but her entire family has been down with a stomach bug for days.

And beyond that, there's nobody else to tell. All her friends from college have moved away or started their own lives, and Kara didn't include herself in them. For so long after her diagnosis, she couldn't stand to see that happiness when all it did was remind her of those things she couldn't have.

And now, years later, she's looking up and finding her own life empty, and it's her own doing.

All at once, her apartment looks sad—and it's not that she hasn't had this thought before, that this isn't a true Omega's apartment, but there's a loveseat and one chair and one small table and barely a kitchen and barely a nest. It all feels so isolating. She's never had people over, never hosted anyone or even thought to invite people for drinks or dinner. The limited sex she's had over the past few years has been just a step above anonymous and always at their place, not hers.

It's a place made for being alone, and she's certainly done that well.

So she puts her phone away and curls up with a pillow on her too-small loveseat and listens to the music blaring around her.

Twenty minutes or so in, the wallowing gets old, and she forces herself up to do a good, overdue deep-clean of her apartment. There's something very cathartic about scrubbing every bit of grime from her shower and leaving it as close to shining as textured plastic ever gets.

The perfect maintenance of a clean home is one part of Omega education that never really stuck, but sometimes she just needs to take some farm-fresh, organic caustic chemicals and clean the hell out of something.

And in the end, she's pleasantly exhausted and has largely quieted the noise in her head, with a nice, clear apartment.

At the end of the cleaning, she sprays some aggressive descenter all over herself to get rid of the chemical smell, then strips all of her nest pillow cases and her sheets to wash them. She has special laundry detergent that she uses just for her nest, with a pleasant neutral smell that helps them take her own scent well. It's probably the single most expensive recurring purchase she makes, but it's absolutely worth it to have a nest that smells just right.

Once that's all done, she reassembles her nest, such as it is, then climbs into it.

There, she can relax.

* * * *

A few days later, Jason invites Kara on their first date to a nearby ice rink.

She gets there early. He's not there yet so she texts him to let him know she's heading in, then buys a public skate pass and gets her skates on.

Once she's all set, Kara takes a couple turns around the rink, just getting her feet under her, then heads to the middle of the rink to do a couple jumps while she has the chance. She's not warmed up enough to attempt an actual single jump — and frankly, she hasn't been on the ice recently enough to have much confidence she can do one without breaking something — but after a wobbly first attempt, she gets through a couple solid waltz jumps, left foot to right toe pick, then step and go again.

After the third, she turns to see Jason halfway across the ice, watching her, so she breaks off from her circle to skate over to him.

He looks steady on his feet, and between his confidence standing a few feet from the wall and the fact that his hockey skates look owned rather than rented, she has the feeling he's done this before.

"Wow," he says when she reaches him, holding out a hand to pull her close. "I was planning on showing off and catching you when you fell, but I think *you* can catch me when *I* fall instead."

"You might be a little too big for that," Kara says with a laugh, tugging him forward so they don't become those people she hates who stand in the way of everyone else. Not that there are many people on the ice right now, but most of the people who are here look like people who actually know how to skate, which means that they're the people most likely to get irritated at them.

"No swooning in your arms?"

"You're welcome to try," she says with a grin.

"Damn." He tangles his fingers with hers, keeping easy pace with her as they make their way around the rink. "This is probably a bit of a stupid question, but…did you grow up skating?"

"Yep," she says, popping the 'p'. "They get weird about Omegas playing in team sports once we present, which limited my athletic options. I wasn't good enough to compete in the all-Omega competitions, but I've stuck with it since I was a kid, so I'm decent. How about you?"

"Hockey through high school," Jason says, letting go to do a noisy hockey stop, sending ice shooting up against her ankles. She makes a face at him, and he laughs. "I grew up outside of Capron, which is near the Illinois-Wisconsin border, and it's the sort of place where most of what's around is churches and more churches. Hockey was my parents' way of getting me out of the house. There weren't enough people around to have separate Alpha leagues, so everything was mixed teams for the most part."

"Probably not a lot of Omegas on those mixed teams," Kara says.

"Not many," Jason concedes. He takes her hand again as they skate around a couple kids clinging onto the wall. "We did have a couple — there was an Omega guy on my team in high school, and one of our main rivals had an Omega as their goaltender."

That's better than Kara expected — most mixed teams in the DC area are all Alphas and Betas, especially for men's teams. "Do you still play?"

"In all my copious spare time?" Jason laughs, but it's not mean. "Nah. I thought about it, but I wasn't interested in trying to keep up the practice schedule. I try to skate when I can, though."

"We'll have to skate together again," Kara says before she can think about it, and she's rewarded with his beaming smile. Heat flares in her chest, and she can smell her own citrus scent in the air.

Jason's nostrils flare like he's trying to catch her scent, and he makes a face when he doesn't seem to be able to catch as much of it as he wants. The cold air deadens smells, which always seems to drive Alphas a little nuts.

So she says, "If you're good, I'll let you scent me once we're off the ice."

"I'm always good," he says with a grin, even as he lets go of her hand to press one hand low to her back, almost on her ass. She considers pushing his hand off, because they're in public and anyone could see, but she doesn't mind as much as she probably should.

There's something nice about the feeling of someone wanting her — of someone wanting her enough to touch her like that, in public. All of this Alpha posturing, this possessiveness, even the social implications of just having an Alpha treat her like this...

On a very pragmatic, social-climbing level, being an unbonded Omega — an Omega who can never bond — is near the bottom. She's respected for who she is, for her mind, for her academic achievements, but that only goes so far.

Having an Alpha set would lift her up a few rungs on the ladder — but getting halfway to having an Alpha set then having them drop her would make everything infinitely worse. Not at work, but back home, back with her family's social circle and people she'd meet in academic circles outside of her university.

And she'd be able to live with that — but not if she lets it break her heart, too.

So she can't let herself get too attached. It won't end well if she does.

"Everything good, sweetheart?"

"I'm good," Kara says brightly, glad now that he can't scent her like this. "I—oh, whoopsie daisy." She softens her knees as a little kid going the wrong way comes skidding into her, reaching down to catch him before his skate can hit her. "Hey, baby, you want to be going in the other direction."

"I couldn't stop," he says, trying to stand up again. His feet slip and slide under him, and she catches him by the arm before he can crash headfirst into the barrier. "And I keep falling."

"Did anyone ever show you how to stop?" she asks.

He shakes his head, chewing on his lower lip in a way that makes her a little nervous. The last thing any of them need is him putting his teeth through his lip while faceplanting on the ice.

But what she can change here is the fact that he doesn't know how to stop, so she says, "What you want to do is press down really hard on the ground with your feet and then push them out, like you're pushing all your wanting to stop *down* and *thataway*."

The kid does that once, then again, and when it works he stares open-mouthed at her to say, "That's *magic*."

And then he takes off in another direction and immediately smashes into another wall.

Kara swallows a laugh, turning back to look at Jason to say, "Sorry, habit."

She can't tell exactly what look is on his face, but he swallows it away to ask, "Did you teach?"

"All through high school. Group classes, mostly." It's close enough to childcare that they want Omegas for it, when they can find them, so she was in hot demand. "They were cute, if menaces."

"You were good with him."

"If I were better, he wouldn't have immediately gone and crashed again."

Jason laughs at that, pulling her forward. "He would have, and we both know it. Or did you not spend your childhood running headlong into every wall you could find?"

"That sounds like a metaphor."

"We consultants love our symbolic language." He pulls her toward him to plant a chaste kiss on her lips, then tugs her so they push forward again, picking up the pace to skate past the slower people on the rink.

It feels a little bit like flying, and she pulls away to do a few turns, just because she can. She ends up skating backward, doing crossovers around a corner, and with a few long strides Jason catches up to her.

"I think you'd like Cassie," he says to her once they're keeping apace again. "My sister. You get the same smile when you're skating."

"Is she in the DC area, too?" Kara asks.

"She wishes," Jason says, but he's smiling indulgently, like just thinking about his sister makes him happy. It's an unexpectedly sweet look coming from an Alpha. "No, she's still out in Illinois with my parents. She's only seventeen."

"Wow," Kara says, eyebrows going up. "Big age gap."

Jason laughs, gently moving her out of the way of a kid skating behind her. She saw them when she looked back, but she appreciates his thoughtfulness anyway. "My parents have never said if I was the accident or if she was, but all signs point to it being me, and then they waited until they were ready before having their intentional kid. Not that they were bad parents to me, but they were pretty young and still trying to get their feet under them when I came along."

"So she's the baby of the family, then?"

"Oh God, like you wouldn't believe. Youngest, daughter and an Omega."

"Poor kid."

"Poor *me*." He makes an exaggerated face of dismay. "I growled — *growled* — at some weirdo for looking at her too long last time I was there."

"The trials and tribulations of an Alpha," Kara says with no sympathy, and Jason barks out a laugh. She remembers being that, a teenage Omega, scared shitless of life to come. She was lucky that she found her space in college, but it wasn't easy. "If she's ever down here, you should introduce us. I can give her tips on scaring weirdos away herself."

Jason's entire face lights up. "Yeah?"

"Yeah."

"We got so lucky finding you," he says, then leans down and kisses her, which is a lot easier when they're not both on ice skates.

But fortunately they both end up smushed against the barrier wall instead of crushing a small child, Jason pressing her back against the clear plexiglass and almost lifting her up off her skates to press kisses to her lips again and again.

This close, Kara can smell him despite the cold, the heat of his scent filling up her nose and her mouth until it's the only thing in her lungs. She *wants* him, desperately, embarrassingly, wants to feel skin against skin, wants to taste —

Ice sprays against her ankles, and Kara flinches back from him just as a woman says, "Keep it off the ice, please — we have kids around."

"Sorry, ma'am," Jason says, pulling back from her and letting her get a solid footing on the ice again. "Got a little carried away."

"Just keep it clean," the safety guard says, then skates away again.

Jason makes a face at Kara, half sheepish, half something else. "Whoops."

"A few more laps and then we'll get off?"

Jason's expression turns into a smirk, and Kara pushes at his shoulder and skates away before he can make whatever joke he's clearly thinking of. He follows after her, looping his arm around her waist so they can move together.

Off the ice, they both wipe their skates down, then put on blade guards before untying them. It's muscle memory as much as anything else at this point, the number of times she's done this, and she can tell it's the same for him from the way his hands move.

"So," he says once they head out of the rink. "Dinner? Or a quickie first?"

"Are those allowed?"

"You're allowed to do whatever you want."

"I think arson is still illegal."

Jason laughs, crowding against her. "Okay, *most* things that you want. But you can have any of us, or none of us, whenever you want. We don't need anyone's permission."

"Do you always operate like this? With every Omega, I mean?"

Jason looks over at her, like he's not sure how to answer or isn't sure he wants to, but she just waits.

She's not jealous of whoever they were with before. She doesn't expect them to have come to this relationship untouched.

If they're touching other people *now…*

"Eric and I usually are with people together because we're usually with *each other* together, but it's not a rule by any stretch of the imagination. And Damon's been with everyone from here to Delaware. All in all, maybe forty, fifty percent of the time, it's at least three of us in bed together with someone."

"Is that what you're expecting with me?"

That gets another hesitation, one that lasts all the way to his car. But before he gets in, he says, "I'm trying to figure out how to answer you. Not because it's a problem but just because I want to make sure I say it the right way."

Kara can respect that, even as her anxiety builds a little. They haven't had a lot of real conversations about what they expect this to look like, and she's realizing that she wants to know.

She doesn't know what she wants, but she's pretty sure she'll be able to tell if there's something she really doesn't want.

Once they're both inside his car, he turns to drop his skates in the backseat, then takes the opportunity to nose up the side of her neck. "You smell so fucking good I can hardly think," he says against her throat. "I just want to lick you all over."

"Maybe later."

"I'll hold you to that." With a sigh, he pulls away, though he grabs her hand and holds it up to his lips like he can't bear to be too far from her scent. It's flattering. "I don't mean to sound like I'm avoiding your question, but our expectations with you are that you tell us what you want and then we give that to you as best we can. We want an Omega who wants to have sex with us, but if it's one of us, or one at a time, we'll figure it out."

"And if I don't want sex?" She does, but she wants to know the answer, too.

Jason drums his fingers on the steering wheel, humming under his breath, then says, "If it's a never, I think that's probably a more fundamental incapability than we can get past. But there are four of us — we can entertain ourselves whenever you're not interested."

"But you're not planning on finding other Omegas, right? Or Betas?"

"Are we —" He turns and blinks at her, then frowns. "No, we're not planning on cheating on you."

"Damon implied that I could potentially find another lover."

"Damon would have promised you the moon if he thought it would get you to hear us out." Jason presses his lips to her hand, humming. "If you want to take other lovers, we can talk about it, all of us. I'd — I don't love the idea, but we're — we can talk about it."

He sounds so earnest that she gives in and puts him out of his misery. "I'm not looking for another lover. Four is more than enough. It's about four more than I've had in…a few years."

But the fact that they're willing to talk about it, even — it means they're less obnoxiously possessive than three-quarters of the Alphas out there. Or it means they just aren't invested enough to care.

"So," Jason says, when she doesn't say anything else. "How about that quickie?"

Chapter Five

They end up grabbing dinner at a ramen place nearby, Kara batting away Jason's hand as he tries to steal her *naruto*. She eats it just because he's trying to get at it, even though it's not her favorite, patiently not commenting when he gives her his extra *chāshū*.

She eats it, though.

Alphas get kind of weird about food—it's traditionally an Omega's job to cook but an Alpha's job to provide the food. They'll try to steal food when courting to see if the Omega is willing to give over their food to them, but they also try to give Omegas food. It's one of the most common courting gifts.

She's heard that some Alphas like to hand-feed their Omegas, but nobody has ever done that for her. It sounds messy.

"We have a few options," Jason says as they head out. "I can take you home and kiss you goodnight, and we can call it a night. You can invite me in, and we can have some fun. We can head back to my place, and we can have fun with as much of the set as you want. Or we can get a hotel room and have some fun there."

"I see a theme in your suggestions."

"Hope springs eternal."

Kara feels like she should go for the first option, for propriety's sake—but fuck propriety. She's been on the edge of *something* since he kissed her on the ice, and she doesn't think it'll be sated by her fingers or some toys.

But she doesn't want him to see the mess of her apartment or her shitty nest.

"A hotel seems a little…indulgent," she says, because she feels a little guilty just thinking about it. "We should—I mean, we—going back to your place makes the most sense, I guess."

"Is that what you want to do?"

Not really—not for something like this, where she wasn't planning on having sex with more than one of them. "I—"

"Great," Jason says. "A hotel it is." He gets his phone out and dials a number, wrapping an arm around her shoulders as it rings. "Hi! I—yeah, good evening. Do you have any rooms available for the night? Wonderful. Please make a reservation under the name Jason Alva for the night. We'll be there in about twenty minutes. Yes—yes, thank you."

When he hangs up, it's to lean down and press a fleeting kiss to the tip of Kara's nose.

"You really didn't need to do that," Kara says, even as her chest flutters at the thought of the pure *indulgence* of spending a night at a hotel with one of the most attractive Alphas she's ever met. "It must be so expensive—"

"We have so much money," Jason cuts in. "Sorry for interrupting, but I want to make this clear—money is not an issue here. We have an ungodly amount of money. We could fly out to anywhere in the world and get a hotel there for one night, and it wouldn't make a speck of difference in the amount of money we have. So if you will, please, sweetheart, put the cost out of your mind for a night and let me spoil you a little."

Kara makes a face. "I don't want you to think that I'm with you for the money."

"Sweetheart, it's okay if you're with us for the money." He turns so they're facing each other, so he can look her in the eye. "We know that we're asking for a lot, for you to open yourself up to scrutiny and questions for a relationship with four Alphas you don't know. And you're giving us a chance — maybe our only chance — to have a relationship that's equal across all four of us. If what you're getting out of it is some fraction of our money, great. Now can we go have fun?"

"Yeah," she says. "Let's have fun."

She expects a decent hotel as they drive into DC, maybe a Marriott or something, but instead they stop in front of what might be the fanciest goddamn hotel in the entire city. It's all stone, an iconic, classic DC building with arches and columns and a surfeit of flags.

A valet opens her door before she can get her wits about her, and she is very conscious of the fact that she's in leggings and an oversized sweatshirt in front of a ridiculously nice hotel.

But Jason isn't dressed much better, and he strides around the car to wrap his arm around her and lead her inside.

He leads her right to the reception desk, which is unsurprisingly empty given the time of day, where a smiling Beta receptionist asks, "How can I help you?"

"We're here to check in," Jason says. "I called fifteen, twenty minutes ago."

"Mr. Alva? I'll need to see ID and—ah, yes, thank you." She takes the ID and credit card she hands him, then types a couple things into her computer. "I see that your standard suite was available, so we were able to put you there. Should we expect anyone else from your set to be staying with us tonight?"

"Just me."

The Beta glances at Kara, and she seems to have mastered the look of polite non-judgment, because there's nothing but professionalism in her eyes when she asks, "Would you like two key cards?"

"Yes, please."

"Of course." She hands back his cards, then hands over two key cards in a tiny card holder with a beautifully written room number on it. "Please let us know if you need anything."

"Thanks."

Once they're—hopefully—out of the receptionist's earshot, Kara asks, "Is *that* what being rich gets you?"

To her surprise, Jason flushes a bit, a delicate pink touching his cheeks and the tips of his ears. "It's only because my name is associated with Damon's in the system."

Kara is delighted by the look on his face. "So that's a yes, then."

"Don't tease, Omega," he whines.

Kara grins at him. "Is the rich little Alpha upset that someone's calling him on it?"

"I don't know why you're being so mean to me." He presses his fingers up her shirt as they step into an empty elevator, dragging hot skin against skin. "Omegas should be nicer to their Alphas."

"You're not my Alpha yet."

"We could pretend I am." He ducks his head down to press his face into her hair, scenting her. "You could be the Omega who's spent all day with slick panties, thinking about how she could please her Alpha."

"And who would you be?" Kara's voice comes out a little hoarse, and she can *feel* herself getting slick just from what he's saying. The entire elevator smells like lemon meringue pie and Alpha heat.

His hand spreads flat across her stomach. "I'd be the devoted Alpha who's spent just as long imagining how good it'll taste when I get my face between your legs."

Kara feels a *rush* of slick between her legs, soaking through her panties, and all she can hope is that there isn't a wet spot on her leggings. And that Jason will get that face between her legs sooner rather than later.

"Fuck," he breathes into her hair as the elevator door opens, letting in a wave of air that smells of something other than them. "Fuck, sweetheart, you smell so good, I want to take you right here."

"We have a room," she reminds him, even though everything in her is screaming for him to get inside her, right fucking now.

"Right," he mutters. "Yeah." He hurries her forward, fumbling with uncharacteristic clumsiness to get the key card out and unlock the door.

He crowds her into the room—then she breaks away, hurrying over to the window, because out of it, she can see the Washington Monument and the White House, lit up in the evening's growing darkness. It looks amazing from up here.

Then Jason's dragging her sweatshirt up and over her head, and she gets back with the program, spinning almost before the sweatshirt is off to press up against him. He's too goddamn tall, though, and she herds him toward the bed. He goes easily, pulling off his shirt as they go.

There's a scar high on the right side of his chest that she didn't notice in that frantic night after she agreed to their courting, and she reaches up to touch it—

But he grabs her hand instead, using it to help pull her up on top of him as he sits down on the bed. She lands in his lap, the rigid line of his erection pressing up against her pussy, and she grinds down before she can help herself.

"Sweetheart," he groans, tugging her up his chest. She ends up straddling him, legs on either side of his ribs, as he props himself up to unhook her bra and pull it off her. Then his lips are on her nipple, tongue laving it into aching stiffness, and she loses track of everything but the bolt of heat it sends through her body and the feeling of electric need running across her skin.

The whole room smells like them, her arousal mixed with his, and she shoves one hand down her panties just to get a little bit of relief, fucking herself with two fingers that slide in easily with how wet she is.

"Fuck," Jason mutters around her nipple. He lets it slip out of his mouth with a pop to ask, voice shot, "Can I taste your fingers, sweetheart? Just a taste, to tide me over? The things I would do, to put my mouth on you, to put—"

She slides her fingers out of herself, whimpering at how empty she feels as soon as they're gone, to offer them to him, and he sucks them into his mouth, dragging tongue and teeth over both of them. "Do I taste good?" she asks, half aware of what she's saying.

"You taste like heaven." He lets her fingers slip from his mouth—but then they're moving, and she finds herself blinking up at him before she even knows what he's doing, half-drunk on the smell of both of them. "Up, sweetheart, let me —" She lifts her hips, and he jerks her leggings down and off her legs, pushing both her shoes off so they go flying somewhere.

Then there's heat against her pussy, moist heat through the thin layer of her panties and teeth against her inner thigh. "Jason —"

"May I?" He tilts his head up so he can look her in the eye, but one of his hands is brushing *so close* to where she needs it, and she can barely keep her eyes open, barely keep from humping the air until she finds some pressure, some friction, *something*. "I'll make you feel so good."

"Please."

"Please, what, sweetheart?" he asks. He sounds ragged, but also smug, like he knows exactly what he's doing to her.

But she can't *think*, so she just shoves her hand down her panties again to try to get some relief, or tries to, but it's caught by his hand, pressed down against the bed. She lets out a cry, desperate with need.

"*Anything,*" she gasps out, "please, anything, please."

"Anything," he repeats, then her panties are being shoved down and his mouth is between her legs. Her head goes back and she presses up against him, and that's the only thing there is, heat and need and slick between her legs. His tongue feels like it's everywhere, against her clit and sliding inside of her and making the most obscene noises, and it's like everything is gone except pleasure, so much pleasure, drippy, wet, needy.

Everything smells of them, intertwined and sweet, like something heavy on her tongue and she swallows, then swallows again as he slides two fingers inside of her, then a third. She might be begging but she can't hear over the rushing in her ears and the sounds of his mouth on her.

"You taste so good," he groans, the sound vibrating through her. Her hips jerk up, looking for that last little bit of friction that will tip her over the edge, and he lets out a low, rough noise. "Kara, sweetheart, can I fuck you?"

Having him inside of her sounds like heaven right now, and she reaches down for him to get him up toward her. He moves, and she mourns the loss of his tongue and his fingers, but only for as long as it takes her to get them rolled over again so she can straddle him and sink down onto the hot length of his cock.

"*Fuck*," he breathes, or she does, then she's riding him, one hand braced on his chest as she shoves her mass of hair out of her face so she can look at him.

There's a flush all the way up his chest, and his gland is swollen, and his eyes are closed, his head thrown back so she can see the veins tracing up his throat.

She wants to bite.

She wants to bite and bite and bite, marking him up so people will be able to see it, high above his collar, and he'll show them off—

His hands grab onto her hips, digging in deep, and she moans as he holds her, at the dual heat of his hands and the throbbing of his cock inside of her.

"That's it," Jason says, one hand sliding up to drag against her gland, scenting her as though he isn't already marking her from the inside out. "Fuck, Kara, you feel so good. That's it, you—" His other hand lets go of her hip to move between her legs, finding her clit, and her eyes slip closed as clever fingers drag just right over sensitive skin, and she comes.

He follows her over that edge, then he's tipping her over so they're side by side as he slips out of her.

The bedspread below them is soaked through. They never even got down to the sheets.

Kara laughs, even as she gasps for breath. Her heart is beating so fast that it feels like it's going to come out of her throat, and she can feel little aftershocks going off between her legs.

"Hmm?" Jason asks.

"We just," she gasps out, "absolutely defiled this very expensive hotel room."

Jason laughs too, leaning over to kiss her, slow and dirty and tasting of her slick. "The hotel room has seen worse," he says once he pulls away. "You're beautiful."

"I'm still wearing my socks," she realizes, though she doesn't reach down to take them off. It seems like too much energy right now. "So are you."

"The only way I have sex," Jason says. "When all of us are still ensocked."

Kara's mouth drops open—then she sees the smirk on his face and leans over to bat a hand against his chest. "That's not even a word."

"It could be."

With a groan, Kara levers herself up to go pee in the fanciest bathroom she's ever seen in her life. Afterward, she looks back out into the bedroom. Jason is still lying on the bed, on top of the covers.

"Want to conserve water by sharing with me?" she asks.

"We have to do our part for the environment," he says with a grin, and rolls off the bed to head over to her.

* * * *

Kara wakes up in one of the most comfortable beds she's ever slept in, with an entire person on top of her and the smell of Alpha in her nose.

Jason's still asleep, or at least he smells like it, that soft warmth of calm dreaming. She presses her nose into his wrist, and it's like the warmth of a sunbeam on a spring day, *safety warmth protection.*

She doesn't want to get up and move.

But this can't last forever, this fantasy moment in this expensive hotel, hidden from real life. She's going to have to get up and go back to her shitty nest in her lonely apartment, where it won't be as easy to convince herself that this is all going to go well and she's going to get a relationship at the end of it.

That they really will decide at the end of the day that they want to tie themselves to someone who can never give them a bond or a biological child.

"Why do you smell sad, sweetheart?" Jason mumbles against her temple.

"It's nothing," Kara says, pressing her nose more firmly against his wrist. "What time is it?"

Jason groans, then shifts a little and says, "Nine-ish." His hand slides down to settle on her hip, then starts to worm its way under her, between her legs. She shifts obligingly so he can get his hand there, gasping when his long fingers find her clit. "We have time to play around some more, if you want."

Kara does want—but she's already going to reek of sex and arousal, walking through this ridiculous fancy hotel with last night's slick-drenched panties, and this would just make it worse.

So she rolls away, and Jason obligingly moves his arm so she can prop herself up on one arm and look at him. He looks half-asleep still, with whatever the nine a.m. version is of a five o'clock shadow, eyes half-lidded as he smiles at her.

"You look beautiful," he says.

"This entire room smells like sex," she blurts out.

Jason snorts out a laugh, rolling over onto his back and throwing a muscular arm over his head. He looks so good that she wants to climb on top of him and make out until the entire world goes away, but she satisfies herself with just looking.

"You don't have a romantic bone in your body, do you?"

"I do," Kara protests. "I just keep getting distracted by the fact that everyone and their mother is going to be able to tell what we spent last night doing, because I'm going to have to put yesterday's clothes back on."

"I wouldn't mind that," Jason says.

Kara groans. "Ugh, Alphas." When Jason laughs again, she rolls off the bed and gets to her feet. "I'm going to go shower again."

"I'll order food," Jason says, dragging himself up to sit against the headboard. The sheets pool around his waist. "What do you want?"

"Something with fruit, if they have it."

"Fruit," he says. "Roger."

Kara takes longer than she planned in the shower but finally pries herself out of it, wrapping herself up in the plush bathrobe and leaving her hair down to air dry because she's too lazy to spend the time blow-drying it. When she leaves the bathroom, it's to the sight of two covered plates at the table in the part of the suite they never made it to last night, a bag with unreadable fancy cursive on a chair and Jason standing shirtless by the window, playing with his phone.

"I'm all for you eating — and doing everything else — dressed just as you are," Jason says, turning to look at her, "but the bag's for you if you'd rather change."

"Please tell me the hotel's room service doesn't also deliver clothing." Curious, Kara heads over to the bag, which has a pile of folded-up clothing inside of it in between that delicate tissue that every fancy clothing store seems to use. When she pulls it out, it unfolds to a soft blue piece of fabric with sleeves — a wrap dress. Underneath it is a pair of black lace-trimmed panties. "Oh, God. *Please* tell me the hotel's room service doesn't also deliver clothing."

Jason laughs. "If they do, I've never asked. I asked Shannon to pick something up for you."

Kara freezes, halfway through pulling the panties out of the bag. "Who's Shannon?"

That gets a face — the same expression he made when she teased him about the way the hotel concierge treated him. "Our PA. Technically, she's the set's PA, but Damon has his own, and then there's a house manager who deals with managing all of the household staff."

That's…a lot, so much that Kara doesn't want to think about it right now. The kind of rich they are is hard to conceptualize.

But what she does ask is, "You made your PA buy me underwear?"

"Shannon's last boss used to make her fly to France to buy them bespoke sex toys. And she makes a very solid six figures."

Well, Kara decides, if she's going to be with them, she can't let herself be too weird about this, or it'll never work. So she takes a breath, steels herself and puts on the panties.

They're very comfortable. Shannon has good taste.

Kara puts on her own bra, then ties on the wrap dress. None of the clothes have any tags on them, and she decides she doesn't want to know how much they cost.

When she looks up from securing the tie, it's to see Jason watching her. She can't tell what's on his face or what's in his voice when he asks, "Do you like it?"

"It's very comfortable," she says honestly. "Tell her thanks for me, will you?"

"Will do," Jason says. "Now, let's eat."

Chapter Six

Before they leave the bedroom, Kara realizes that, while the new clothes might have fixed *her* scent issue, they didn't fix *Jason's* scent issue, because he still smells very well fucked. And him walking through the hotel is one thing, but going back to the rest of the set smelling like that…

"Are you sure they won't be jealous?"

"Oh, they'll be jealous," Jason says smugly. "They're going to be all over me, trying to get some of your scent onto their skin. I see some aggressive cuddling in my future."

"I didn't think Alphas did that with each other."

"Touch between Alphas generally isn't the same as between Alphas and Omegas," he says, leaning over to press an illustrative hand to the small of her back. "But we have our ways that we touch. It's just a little more…competitive."

"Competitive touching?"

"Well," Jason says with a laugh, "Eric and I like to play 'who can make the other come first.'" He slides a hand around to Kara's stomach, fiddling with the edge of her panties. Her muscles clench, and she bites her bottom lip to keep from making a noise. "But it's just...a little rougher, maybe, between Alphas. At some point I'm sure you'll see us all piled on top of each other."

There's something that sounds so nice about casual contact like that. So much of touch with Omegas is wrapped up in other things, in courting and nesting and ownership and *sex*.

"Do you like that idea?" Jason asks. His hand slides a little lower, to brush the edge of her curls. "You like the idea of four Alphas on top of each other, fighting to get a little bit of your scent for themselves?"

She *does*, shamefully, voyeuristically — but Jason seems to like that idea, going by the heat of his fingers playing between her legs.

"It's a game I've heard some Omegas play," he tells her, and his voice goes even lower as the tip of his finger brushes against her clit. She shudders, pressing back against him. They shouldn't be doing this again — she's going to be walking through this hotel smelling like slick and sex even in these new panties — but it feels so good. "They only let one Alpha touch them, while everyone else watches, and the other Alphas all fight to get a little bit of that scent on them, to carry with them for the day."

"That seems — *ah* — mean."

He drags the tip of his finger around and around her clit, and her panties fill with slick. She can smell herself in the air — can smell both of them in the air. They're going to have to de-scent this entire room. "I think Omegas should be allowed to be a little mean to their Alphas, sometimes, as a treat." He pulls his hand out of her panties, and she hears him slip them in his mouth...tasting her. "But sometimes we Alphas like a tease, in a set—and we like fighting for our Omega, impressing our Omega."

Kara leans back against him, trying to catch her breath. "Is it always like this, between Alphas and Omegas?"

"When we're this good a match, it is." Jason leans down to press one last kiss to her throat, then steps back. He says, "If we keep going, we might never leave."

When Jason drops her off at her place, he lets her open her door for herself—but he walks around to help her get out, holding on to her hand as she stands. He leans down to press his lips down to her wrist. "Eric next," he says as he straightens. "But if you want to come see us, if you want to stop by or just spend time with us, please let us know." He gives her a toothy grin. "Or if you want to have some fun."

"You really have a one-track mind," she teases, then rises up on her toes to give him a quick peck on the lips. Before he can deepen it, she pulls away, darting inside. When she looks back, he's grinning.

* * * *

Sunday brings real life with it, and Kara spends a few hours doing her laundry and deep-cleaning her mess of a bathroom. Her nesting instincts might be iffy on the best day, but every couple weeks she does an aggressive clean of some part or another of her apartment, and even her having cleaned it a few days ago doesn't mean she's willing to give up the full deep clean.

That gets her through most of the day, at which point she gives up and orders half a tandoori chicken and two mango lassis from the local Indian place.

When she gets back from meeting the guy at the apartment entrance, because the system is on the *don't open for anyone* side of its too open-not open enough oscillation, it's to two texts on her phone.

From Jason: *I'm the most popular Alpha in the set <3 miss you already*

From Eric: *Wednesday night?*

Kara's weeknights all consist of basically the same thing—watching a cooking show or a docuseries or hockey or poking around JSTOR—so she sends back a quick thumbs up to Eric before setting up her food.

The first of the lassi goes in a glass and the second goes in the fridge, and she sticks the naan in her toaster oven because it never shows up quite hot enough. The chicken goes on a plate because she likes to pretend she's an adult before eating it with her bare hands.

Once that's all done and the naan is heated up, she sees another text on her phone—a selfie from Jason, sleepy-eyed and smug and shirtless, with Eric with his nose jammed all the way against Jason's throat and Damon behind him and Ry sprawled on top of him. They look soft in a way that makes her chest ache.

She wants that. She wants it so much—*too* much. Wanting something this much means it'll hurt all the worse when they change their minds.

And they will. Things like this don't happen to her. People like her don't get fairytale endings—at best, they get the lives they build. But she wants it, what they're offering. Damn her, but she wants it.

* * * *

"How did you decide the order of the dates?"

"We drew straws," Eric says.

Kara presses her earbud into her ear, asking, "Really?"

Eric laughs, but it's a *with her* laugh rather than an *at her* laugh. "We used a random number generator, actually. There was a fight about whether Damon should go last, because he met you first, but we ultimately decided random was fairest."

Kara lounges back against one of the pillows on her loveseat, laughing too. "That's such a nerdy way to do that."

"Aww, thanks. I — *ooph*."

"Eric?"

The tenor of the background noise on the call changes, half a second before Jason's voice says through what is clearly now speaker phone, "I couldn't let him hog talking to you."

"Hi, Jason," Kara says with a smile.

"Hi, sweetheart."

"Get off me," Eric grumbles, and there's what almost sounds like wrestling.

But it's Jason who seems to win, because he says, "We're *cuddling*, you heathen."

"Cuddling, my ass."

"I'm happy to cuddle your ass." Then Jason says, a little slyly, "You're welcome to come here and cuddle his ass, too."

Kara laughs. Jason and Eric don't.

"I don't want to bother you," she says, stammering a little. "You didn't—I mean—I don't want to intrude." Alphas get weird about people being in their territory, and if Damon and Ry aren't expecting her…

"You wouldn't be intruding," Eric says. "Seriously. Come over, if you want to. Whenever you want to."

Kara hesitates—but then she stops hesitating and says, "I'd love to, though you'll need to text me your address."

"I can come get you," Jason says.

"That will take at least twice as long," she reminds him. "I can just Uber over."

"You shouldn't have to—"

"I can afford a ride," she says, a little exasperated. "I know I don't have as much money as you, but I can pay for that."

There's silence after that.

Fuck.

"Sorry," she mutters, dropping her arm over her face. Alphas don't like being reminded of the fact that Omegas have actual financial independence now.

Jason sighs. "I know you can pay for a ride," he says. "I just want to be able to do things for you."

"Sorry," she says again.

"You don't need to apologize," Jason says, "and I'm not just saying that because Eric is poking me in the side. We're figuring each other out. We'll set each other off sometimes. Eric and I have set each other off about a thousand times. I'll send you the address. You should have it, anyway. And the gate code."

Kara chews on her lip, then asks, "Do you want to come pick me up? If you're still—if you still want to?"

"I'd love to," Jason says brightly.

"And I'd love for you to get him off me," Eric puts in.

"You love me," Jason says.

"I do," Eric says, and there's a sound like them kissing. "Now get the fuck off me."

* * * *

It doesn't take too long for Jason to get there, and this time she's outside waiting for him so she doesn't run late again, pen all over her. He greets her by scenting her wrist, then gestures exaggeratedly at her door and says, "Your door is your own, sweetheart."

Kara grins and opens the door herself, climbing in.

There's more traffic this time, and Kara relaxes into the drive. It's nice to be in his car instead of a taxi, even if giving in still smarts a little.

But it's a stupid reason for a fight or to make herself miserable, and she hasn't gotten this far in life by letting her pride get in her way.

"What time are you usually done with work?" he asks as they slow to a stop in yet more traffic.

"It depends on the semester, but I managed to mostly do morning classes this time, so Monday through Thursday I'm done with my classes by one, and then I run office hours from two until four on Mondays and Thursdays. My timing for grading, research, paperwork, all the other shit, that's a lot more flexible, so I'll do that on evenings or weekends a lot, or whenever I talk myself into it. It gets *way* worse during finals."

"Maybe you can come over for dinner sometimes, then. You can come straight from work, if you want."

"I'd like that." They move forward a little, then stop again, and Jason sighs. "What do your hours look like? You at the normal nine to five?"

Jason laughs. "I don't think any consultant has worked nine to five since the dark ages. I start at eight-thirty, three days a week, and a truly godawful seven the other two days, because my clients are like that, and then I usually do eight and a half to nine hours in the SCIF, and then a few hours a week outside of one. Which also means that, and I realize I should have told you this earlier, you're basically never going to get me on the phone during the day on weekdays. But I'll always get back to you once I'm back on my phone."

"Yeah, of course." Kara's heard stories from people who had to work in SCIFs because their work was classified, and it mostly sounds like a windowless, cellphone-less nightmare. She hesitates, then asks, "Dare I ask who your client is?"

"You can ask," Jason says, but doesn't elaborate.

Which is fair enough.

The traffic stays stop-and-go, and Jason sighs again. He lets go of the wheel with one hand to take her hand in his, pressing his lips to the nail of her thumb, her pointer finger, each of her fingers in turn. "You smell so good," he breathes. "God, my whole car is going to smell like you for days." He glances over at her, giving her a sly little look. "We could make it smell even better."

"I'm not having sex with you in your car in traffic."

"Not yet, you aren't," Jason says with confidence, then kisses her palm when she laughs. "One day, maybe I'll convince you."

The traffic finally opens up in front of them and the rest of the drive goes quickly. Jason doesn't let go of her, though, resting their intertwined hands on his thigh.

As they get close to the house, Kara asks, "Do Damon and Ry know that I'm coming over?"

"Ry's not around," Jason says, a little too fast, like he's trying to say something else or not say it at all. "And I texted Damon but he's in back-to-back-to-back meetings that he has to pay attention to like a real boy, so he won't check his phone until he's done, most likely."

"But they won't mind?"

"They really, really won't mind," Jason reassures her.

They slow as they head up the driveway, then stop. Kara climbs out, stretching up toward the sky. It's a little damp out, just at that point where it's not quite ready to rain but it feels like water will start gathering at every joint if she stands outside for too long.

Jason's arm settles around her waist as she finishes her stretch, his body warm against hers. He says, "Another drive here, and yet again, you weren't murdered."

"The night is still young." Kara turns in his arms to press a kiss to the side of his jaw. "I also have to warn you that I will probably get hangry at some point if I don't get something to eat, because I haven't eaten dinner yet."

"Oh, don't worry, you are not alone in that." Jason plants a kiss on her nose, then herds her into the house. "If you can wait, we generally don't eat until Damon's done with his meetings."

"Yeah, of course. Does he usually work this late?"

Jason huffs out a breath. "He is wildly bad at setting boundaries with work, so...yes."

"Have you considered—"

"Yes."

Kara laughs. "I was going to say tying him down and making him take a break."

"Is that the sort of thing you're into?" Eric asks, emerging from one of the nearby rooms. He holds his hand out to her, and when she gives him her hand, he scents her wrist, the way they all seem to. She's never had that happen to her so much in her entire life before this.

But he holds on to her hand instead of letting go, dragging one callused thumb down the entire length of her palm. The sensation sends a frisson of pleasure down her spine, and she shivers against Jason.

"So?" Eric asks. "Is it?"

"Is what?" Kara asks around a clumsy tongue, too distracted by that one point where Eric is touching her and by the wave of their scents surrounding her.

"Is tying people up what you're into?"

"I—" Kara blinks at him, then remembers the comment that she made before he distracted her. "I mean. I've never tried it."

"Well," Jason says, sliding a hand up the back of her shirt. He does it slowly, like he thinks that'll keep her from noticing. "That might keep Damon from work for at least a little while."

Eric rolls his eyes. "Knowing Damon, he would figure out how to get out just so he wouldn't be late for his next call." He leans down to kiss the inside of her wrist, the bristles of his five o'clock shadow scraping over the sensitive skin there. "I'm always up to give it a try, though."

"What I would like to give a try," Jason says, now toying with the clasp of her bra, "is making out on the couch."

Kara snorts out a laugh at that, twitching away just as it seems like he might undo one of the hooks. "I'm not sure it's big enough for all three of us to make out on," she says, but it's not a *no*.

"That's what experimentation is for, isn't it?" With a hand on her back, Jason leads her into a living room area. As they pass Eric, he reaches out and strokes a hand against Eric's hip, like he can't go without touching him, too.

There's a massive couch in the living room, and Kara has just enough time to consider that all three of them *might* be able to make out on it before Eric tugs her to face him, cupping her cheek in one large hand and lowering his head to give her a kiss. It's a long kiss, his tongue brushing against her lower lip again and again until she opens for him, then it's all tongues and lips and a little bit of teeth. By the time he pulls away they're both gasping for air, and she's on her toes to chase his lips with hers.

Behind her, pressed against from thighs to shoulders, Jason asks, "Top or bottom?"

Kara's not sure if he's talking to her or Eric, and she doesn't care, because she finds a spot right next to Eric's gland where it tastes like the essence of him, and she chases that with her tongue and her teeth, worrying the spot until she practically feels the blood blooming under his skin. People should know that he's hers.

"Oh, fuck," Eric gasps under her teeth, his throat vibrating against her. His hands settle on her hips, pulling her even closer. "Oh, *fuck*, Omega, you feel so good."

"Top it is," Jason says, sounding amused, then Kara and Eric are both being pushed. It's a soft landing on the couch, and Eric pulls her on top of him so she's straddling him, her head still right where it needs to be to worry another bruise next to the one she's already managed.

She loses track of Jason for a bit there, with Eric's hands everywhere on her, getting her shirt unbuttoned and off her then sliding up her stomach, up her back, digging blunt nails into her skin when she bites down on his collarbone.

She can smell her own arousal, not just all over her but all over him too, and it's a heady mix, like two puzzle pieces that slot together just right. And as she rises up to kiss him again, his scent spikes — and so does Jason's, heat and spice and Alpha washing over her.

"I could watch you two all day," Jason says, dragging a hand up her back. "Absolutely gorgeous."

"Lazy," Eric murmurs from underneath her with a smirk. "You see this, Kara? We have the laziest Alpha here with us."

"I'll show you lazy," Jason says, and leans down to kiss Kara's neck. She turns her head obligingly, and he gives her a kiss, sucking the taste of Eric off her lip. "I could get you off while you're on top of him," he says against her mouth. "Leave you both smelling like slick for hours. Do you want that, sweetheart?"

Kara kisses him back, then says, "It might be a little early for that." She brushes a hand against his cheek to soften it, and he smiles. "I am enjoying this, though."

"I can't complain either," Eric says, wiggling suggestively under her. He's hard, but there doesn't seem to be much urgency. She appreciates his patience.

She slides a hand down his stomach, and he trembles, then grins up at her.

"We can play, if you want," he says. He doesn't seem to mind that she can see his need, that she can smell it. Instead, he arches up against her touch, the muscles working in his core. "I'm always up for playing with a pretty Omega."

"I'm not trying to tease you," she says, even as she leaves her hand where it is.

His grin grows, and he presses up into her hand, even as it makes his abs shake. "It would be okay if you were."

"Alphas can put up with a little Omega teasing," Jason adds. He pushes her hair out of the way so he can get to her throat, laving kisses on it. "And Eric likes to be teased, sometimes."

Eric relaxes back down on the couch, but only so he can tuck a hand around the back of her neck and tug her down into a kiss. Jason goes with her, so she's blanketed between them. "It's your right to say no," Eric says into her mouth. "Or to tease, or to play. I want to know what you want from me."

"From us," Jason says.

Kara doesn't know what she wants, not really, so she leans down and kisses Eric, and he seems satisfied with that for now.

* * * *

They're cuddling on the couch, the whole room smelling of arousal, when the door opens and Damon calls, "I come bearing food."

"In the living room," Jason shouts back.

Damon appears in the doorway to the living room dressed in a full suit, already loosening his tie like he can't bear to have it on a moment longer. In the hand not loosening his tie, he's carrying two very full plastic bags of what look and smell like Chinese food.

"We have soup," he tells them, setting the bags down on the table. "We have so much soup they think we only consume soup." He kneels before Kara, scenting her wrist, and she reaches out to brush a hand against his hair, thrilled at the ability to touch someone who looks so together.

"Please tell me we have something other than soup," Jason says.

Damon adjusts his glasses, then stands, grabbing the bags to start emptying them out. "We have Peking duck, we have chicken fried rice, we have lo mein, we have — honestly, it would be faster to list what we don't have."

"And it's from the good restaurant, right?"

"No," Damon says sarcastically, "I got the shitty Chinese food."

"I was just asking." Jason kisses Kara's temple, then gets up and heads out of the room, saying, "I'll get the plates and bowls."

"Can I do anything?" Kara asks.

Damon hesitates, then says, "If you could help Jason?"

Kara stands and follows Jason into the kitchen, gathering up glasses that he hands her. It's a little awkward to carry four at once, but she has enough experience from family holidays to manage not to drop any of them as she carries them into the living room.

When she gets there, it's to hear the tail end of Eric saying, " — bring him some later."

It seems like something they don't want her to hear, and she doesn't need to pry when it's none of her business, so she just says, "I have the glasses, though they don't have any actual liquid in them, so I don't know if they'll be much help."

"I'll get water," Eric says, and heads into the kitchen.

"See?" Damon says as he keeps taking containers out of the bags. "Set teamwork at its best."

"I'm very impressed."

Damon leans over to give her a quick kiss, then says, "I'm glad you came."

"How were your meetings?" she asks.

He makes a face. "It makes me wonder why I haven't retired."

"Why *haven't* you retired?" she asks, genuinely curious. "It's not like you don't have enough money."

Damon shrugs. "I'd be bored, I think. And it's — well, it's mine, and I'm not very good at letting go of things that are mine."

"That's very Alpha of you."

"As though Omegas are any better at it," Damon says, and Kara shrugs, conceding the point. They're not, even if they're a bit different in the ways they go about it. "Anyway, I like my work, most of the time. Or, well, some of the time. I like it conceptually."

"That was very convincing."

"Maybe one day I'll retire to live a life of leisure," he says, though he doesn't sound convinced of it himself. "Anyway. Soup. Please tell me you like soup."

It's an obvious change in topic, but she goes along with it anyway. "I do like soup."

"Perfect." He tugs his tie off, tossing it on the couch, then unfastens the top button of his shirt. "One day, I'm going to go to a meeting in jeans and a T-shirt. Mark my words."

"Bullshit," Jason says, clinking the plates he's carrying pointedly. "You're going to be eighty and still wearing these stupid suits in your stupid meeting."

"These stupid meetings are keeping us in our lifestyle."

"A few very good accountants are keeping us in our lifestyle."

"Point." Damon gestures expansively at the array of soup containers on the table. "What's your soup of choice?"

"Hot and sour," she says, "if you have it."

"Boy, do we have some hot and sour soup," Damon says.

Kara laughs. "You really weren't kidding about the volume of soup."

"I never kid about soup."

They get the soup parceled out, then Eric comes back with water. They eat sitting on the couch, with Damon lounging on the floor with his head near her knee. He looks unconcerned about sitting on the floor eating in his no-doubt wildly expensive suit.

"This is good soup," Kara says when she's done inhaling most of a bowl of it. "What's the restaurant?"

"It's this hole-in-the-wall place that Eric found a couple years ago," Jason tells her around mouthfuls. "They speak basically no English, and they don't have a website, and they make the best Chinese food we've found in the DC area."

It's *very* good soup, just the right balance of flavor and heat, and Kara could eat another pint of it. "Well," she says, "good find."

"I do my best," Eric says humbly.

Kara drinks the last few drops of soup, then leans back on the couch, nudging her knee against Jason's. "Thank you for inviting me over," she says. "This has been lovely."

"We're happy to have you," Damon says, turning to look up at her. "We are always happy to have you here.

Chapter Seven

On the day of Kara's date with Eric, out of fear of being late, Kara ends up half an hour early to the café where she and Eric decided to meet. It's a decent size, half-filled with people on laptops, most of whom have the desperate look of graduate students with an upcoming deadline.

Kara orders a cappuccino and takes a wobbly metal pole with a black eight on it, then heads over to a table within easy sight of the door. It's one of those round tables that's great for chatting and terrible for laptops, so she doesn't feel bad for taking a table from some other poor graduate student who might come in.

She has an article that Yelena, the Insurgency-Counterinsurgency professor, sent her about tactics in Yemen downloaded on her phone for a bit of light reading, so she pulls that up, taking out the little notebook and pen from her bag so she can take notes as she reads. If she's going to sit here, she might as well make the most of her time.

At some point, someone drops off the cappuccino and takes the wobbly metal pole, but Kara honed her ability to read academic articles through anything during her PhD days so doesn't even look up.

She does look up, though, when someone places a plate in front of her, saying, "Sorry, I think you've got the — *oh*."

Eric, standing across the table from her, reaches out to take her hand. He bends so he can touch his lips to her wrist, skimming them against the thin, sensitive skin there. She shivers.

His lips spread in a slow smile, and he says, "You smell absolutely amazing. I'm sorry if you've been waiting long."

"I was just reading," she says. "And I was early. How was your day? Did you have a shift?"

Eric sits, nudging a plate with a massive muffin on it over to her. When she pulls a piece off, it looks like it's lemon poppyseed.

"I wanted something that would taste like you," Eric says with a smirk. "I can't get enough of you on my tongue."

Kara's entire face goes hot, and she hisses, "You can't say something like that out loud, in *public*."

"I think you'll find that I'm very good at saying things like that out loud, in public." Eric drags a finger across the back of her hand, breathing out a laugh when her fingers twitch. "You're hot when you're being studious."

Kara rolls her eyes, even though she can feel how hard she's blushing. "I'm an academic. My entire life is me being studious."

"Ipso facto."

"I'm not sure you're using that right."

"I studied Latin when I studied medical shit. I save lives, you know."

"So I've heard."

Eric grins at her. "Oh, have I mentioned it?"

"Once or twice." Feeling bold, Kara turns her hand over, letting Eric's fingers settle on her palm. He doesn't take her hand, just drags his fingers up and down across the lines of her palm.

This close, she can smell his scent, peeking through the scent blocker he must wear to work. He smells like heaven.

With a crooked smile, he pops a piece of muffin in his mouth. His eyes close like he's savoring the taste. Once he swallows, he says, "The real thing tastes better."

"Oh my *God*." Kara tries to pull her hand away to bury her face in both of them, but Eric grabs on, laughing, his fingers tangling with hers. "*Eric*."

"I licked all of you off of Jason, every inch I could reach, fought Ry and Damon for it. You tasted so good against his skin." He lifts her hand to his mouth again, and she knows she could pull away, she *should* pull away, but instead she brushes her fingers against the stubble on his chin until he shivers.

"You really shouldn't be saying *that* in public," she says, a little shaky.

With a wink, he says, "We can fix that."

"Despite what it may seem," Kara says, even though she's undermining herself as she speaks by stroking her fingers against his chin, "I'm not usually the type of girl who puts out on the first date."

Eric presses a kiss to her palm—then lets go of her hand with a smile. "Well, then," he says, "what were you reading about?"

Kara blinks at him. Her hand is still against his cheek, just sitting there, and it takes her a second to pull it away. When she raises it up to her nose, before she can stop herself, it smells of his sharp heat.

Then she realizes what he asked. "It's not that interesting," she tells him. She's pretty sure he doesn't want to hear about insurgency tactics in Yemen. And she's even more sure it's not the sort of thing an Alpha wants to hear about from the Omega they're courting.

Something shifts in his expression, turning odd. He asks, "Do you find it interesting?"

"Yeah?"

"Then it's interesting." Eric leans back in his chair, surveying her. "What were you reading about?"

Kara hesitates—but Eric is just watching her, munching on a bit of muffin, so she says, "It's an article about tactics being used by both sides in the war in—"

Her phone goes off, buzzing against the wood of the table, and she glances down at it. The screen reads *Mom*.

"I don't mind if you pick it up," Eric says.

Kara hesitates, not wanting to be rude even if Eric said it was okay, then picks up her phone and answers it. "Hey, Mom," she says. "Now's not the best—"

"I heard from Anna Winter that you were out skating with an Alpha."

Kara leans forward and puts her forehead directly on the table. "I'm not fourteen, Mom. Why is Anna Winter telling you who I'm out *skating* with?"

Across the table, Eric huffs out a laugh, and Kara lifts up her head to glare at him. He grins.

"Her daughter skates at that same rink, you know. She's a wonderful skater, though not as good as you were at that age."

"Mom."

"So, tell me about this Alpha. Where did you meet him?"

"*Mom.*"

"I just want what's best for you," her mom says. "Are they—does he know? Did you tell him?"

Kara scrubs her hand across her face. She doesn't want to be having this conversation, and she wants to be having it even less with Eric sitting across from her, watching her with a little smile on his face.

But there's not an easy way to get rid of her mom without finishing the conversation or just flat-out hanging up on her, neither of which are great options, so she says a little flatly, "Yes, Mom, they know."

"Is it just a fling, then? Tell me they haven't made promises to you. Alphas do that, you know, they make promises and then take what they want, and when they're done they leave you—"

"What, pregnant?" Her mom's rant falters, and Kara pushes on, genuinely irritated now. "It's not the nineteenth century, and there isn't a line of Alphas just aching to take me so long as I don't end up defiled and abandoned."

Across the table from her, Eric's eyes narrow.

"All Alphas want is a bonding," her mom says, because she still hasn't gotten over that one bad Alpha boyfriend she had in college, a million years ago. "I just don't see why you can't settle down with a nice Beta who isn't going to care about your…disability."

"Well, when they inevitably leave me, you can say 'I told you so.' In the meantime, tell Anna Winter to stop informing on me."

"Kara—"

"*Jesus,*" Kara mutters, ending the call. "Sorry. My mom is convinced that I'm destined to be alone forever unless I find a Beta who will overlook my little..." She gestures toward her useless gland. "Issue."

"And you?" Eric asks. "What do you think?"

"I wouldn't be here eating a muffin with you if I thought I should find myself a Beta boyfriend."

He still doesn't look convinced, though, so she reaches out to touch his hand again. It flexes under hers, then relaxes, and he turns it over to intertwine their fingers. She still can't tell what he's feeling, not under the scent blocker that's still clinging around, and she feels nose blind right now.

She doesn't know how Betas do it. They don't put out the same level of pheromones, but they can hardly smell Omegas or Alphas either, so they have to go through life relying just on what they can see and hear to tell what people are thinking.

"We could meet her," he says. "Take your family out to dinner."

Abject horror rushes through Kara, and she says hurriedly, "No, that's okay. We're not—I mean, she probably wouldn't like you. Or she'd be weird about the money. Or about—I don't know, she thinks all virile young Alphas want to do is knock some Omega up, which clearly is not going to happen in this case."

His fingers tighten around hers. "Do you imagine us never meeting her then?"

Kara hadn't thought about it. "I mean, if we get, you know—"

"Married?"

That. "Then obviously you'll have to meet my family." She rubs at her forehead with her free hand. "I feel like I'm giving you the wrong impression. My family is—they're good, you know. They're just all Betas, and there's very much this idea of, you know... Not that if you date you have to get married, they're normal about stuff like that, but they thought it was special or whatever to have an Omega in the family, it raised their social status, and then they found out that my gland's all fucked up and I'm never going to be an *Omega*-Omega. So they think—my mom thinks—that that means that I'm basically a Beta. And she's not necessarily...wrong, you know? Me versus a Beta is basically a distinction without a difference at this point."

Eric grabs both of her hands in his, leaning down to press his lips to her fingers. She twitches in surprise but doesn't pull away. "It's not the same," he says passionately. "*You're* not the same. Having a non-functional gland doesn't change your dynamic. Nobody but you gets to decide what your dynamic is."

Kara doesn't know what to say—because nobody has said that to her, not like that. People have reassured her that she's still an Omega, that the way that they see her hasn't changed, but nobody ever said that it's *her* that gets to decide it.

And she does still think she's an Omega. She *is* an Omega.

"Come back with me," Eric says suddenly. His eyes are very wide now, fixed on her, and she can smell a hint of something that is warm and solid and doesn't smell much like lust at all. "Not for sex." His lips twitch up into a smile. "I mean, it can be for sex. But I want you to give us a chance to show you how we see you. How much we want you."

Kara shouldn't, she knows she shouldn't—but right now, she can't think of a good reason why not. So she says, "Yeah. Let's go."

Chapter Eight

Eric's scent fills the car as they drive. His blocker is wearing off now, or maybe entirely worn off, and the scent of *want* and *need* and *heat* rises off of him in waves, leaving her wet and squirming despite herself.

And he can smell it too, based off the growing smile on his face, but instead of commenting on it he keeps her explaining her research to him, the research she's been doing on how insurgency tactics change with foreign state support.

He seems genuinely interested, too, not just fake-listening the way a lot of non-academics do when she gets going.

Finally, he asks, "How did you get into this? I can't imagine there's a straightforward path to it."

"You mean for an Omega?"

"I was thinking more someone who wasn't in the military, but that, too."

She forgot that he was in the military. "Would you believe me if I said my original major was biomedical engineering?"

Eric barks out a surprised laugh. "That's not what I thought you were going to say."

"It's never what people think I'm going to say. But I wanted to help people, and I was good enough at the math. But it became pretty clear pretty fast that I wasn't good at the squishy bits. The people-y bits."

"Can't relate."

Kara laughs, shifting in her seat as she feels the slide of slick-on-flesh that she's doing her damndest to ignore. "So anyway, I needed to find something else to study, and for some reason I decided to take an international relations class when I was trying to figure out the rest of my life at nineteen. I hated the theory, but I liked the security side. And thus started my path to becoming a professional academic. How about you? Why did you go into nursing?"

"To piss off my parents, mostly." Eric grins at her. "I'm from an Alpha-Omega family, and my dad was career military, but he had pretty specific ideas about what military Alphas should be. Officers, spend a few years on the front lines, rise up the ranks, aim for Colonel at the minimum. So I enlisted, decided to try for medic. I had taken first aid before I got in, but it was…different."

Kara can imagine, but she's not going to ask.

"And it got me Jason," he adds. "I had to save his ass when the idiot got hurt, and then he wouldn't leave me alone. Like a lost puppy."

"So not all bad, then."

"It has its perks. And by the time I got out, it was the only thing I knew how to do, so I got my nursing degree, and here I am."

"Are your parents still mad about it?"

"A month into basic training, my mom told my dad to get his head out of his ass and call me. We talk pretty regularly now, though they live in Vermont, so we don't see each other much."

"Did you grow up there?"

Eric shakes his head. One hand leaves the steering wheel to land on her thigh, just sitting there, and she feels another rush of slick between her legs. She could push him off, she knows, and he would go.

She doesn't move.

"I grew up in New York. Westchester County. But my mom likes the cold, so once they were an empty nest, they moved farther north." On the last word, he slides his hand up, just a little, just enough for her to be very aware of it. It's teasing, she knows, a step up from casual Alpha teasing, *touch and see what the Omega does*.

Kara could push him away. Maybe she should.

She spreads her legs, just a little.

Eric sucks in a breath, his gaze darting over toward her. But she doesn't give him the satisfaction of saying anything, because there's not much power that Omegas get but to leave Alphas a little off balance.

Omegas get the reaction, the need. They get the scent sensitivity and the slick. They get little pieces of their control picked away, inch by inch, everyone around them able to smell when they're wanting, when they're needing.

But there's something in Alphas that makes them want to protect Omegas, to please them. To own them, yes, but to give them so much pleasure that they forget everything but their Alpha.

Even her, despite everything.

"We can make you feel so good," Eric says. There's a touch of desperation in his voice that wasn't there before, a hoarseness. "We can make you feel so good."

Kara is so wet between her legs, throbbing, and it would be so easy to let him open up her pants, let him slip a hand inside and slide *wet hot* inside of her, take the edge off her need.

But it's an Omega's prerogative to say no — and more than that, it's almost expected, to draw boundaries and push and pull until they decide whether who they are together works.

So she says, "I can make myself feel good, too, but you don't hear me bragging about it."

Eric chokes out a laugh, his hand curling around her thigh. "You should," he says. "We'd love to hear you talk about how you get yourself off."

"I'm sure you would."

Pulling up to the house, Kara is struck once again by how *big* it is. How it was a house built for an entire set — and children, probably, little ones running around their massive yard.

They don't let single Omegas adopt, so she's never let herself think —

And she won't let herself think that now.

She gets out, taking Eric's hand and letting him lead her into the house.

As soon as the door is closed behind them, Jason's voice shouts from somewhere, "I thought you'd still be at your date with —" He appears from another room, barefoot and shirtless in a pair of low-slung sweats. "Oh."

"Hey," Kara says, not sure whether she should be here at all. Eric invited her, but maybe he shouldn't have. She doesn't want to interrupt everyone's time to themselves.

Jason strides over to them, pulling her up into his arms. "You smell like heaven," he breathes, burying his face in the crook of her neck. Then he pulls back to ask, grinning, "Your date go so badly you need the rest of us to salvage it?"

"I thought I'd be generous and share," Eric says, his hand settling on the small of her back. "But if you're not interested, I'm sure we can find some other way to entertain ourselves."

"And what about you?" Jason asks, smirking down at Kara. "You want to be shared?"

"Why don't you convince me that I do?"

"Well, okay."

"Where are Damon and Ry?" Eric asks. He leans forward to press a kiss to Jason's lips, then starts to herd both of them toward a nearby room. Not the kitchen.

"Ry decided he just had to have some special mushroom or something, and he didn't want to bother Shannon because Annamarie is sick, so he's out at that weird specialty grocery store he loves. He should be back sometime in the next year."

"And Damon?"

Jason rolls his eyes. "He's still on a meeting that was supposed to end"—he checks his watch—"an hour ago."

"Did you tell him to tell them to fuck off?" Eric asks.

"Yeah, and he told *me* to fuck off." Jason stops their slow progression to wherever they're going to look down at Kara and say, "You know, he probably wouldn't tell *you* to fuck off."

Kara can see where this is going. "I really shouldn't be getting in the middle of whatever meeting Damon is on."

"Oh, you absolutely should be." Jason leans down to touch his forehead to hers, even though he's too tall to be doing that comfortably, then says, "When you're our Omega, our b—married Omega, it'll be your job to keep Damon from losing himself in his work like that."

He almost said bonded Omega, she can tell, but he doesn't comment on it, so neither does she.

And the thing is that he's right. It is the job of the set's Omega, if they have one, to maintain the wellbeing of the set. Most people interpret that to mean cooking and cleaning and homemaking, but there's a reason why Omegas are sometimes called the Heart of the Set.

So Kara asks, "Where's his office?"

Jason smiles. "All the way at the end of the hallway."

The hallway has a few rooms leading off from it, but there's one door at the end of it, closed and nondescript. When Kara gets close, she can hear voices coming from it, but they're all muffled like they're coming through a computer speaker. Nothing from Damon, and that's how she works up the courage to turn the knob and open the door.

Damon is sitting at a desk that faces the door, a laptop and two monitors sitting on a beautiful wooden desk along with a notebook and a couple of pens. But Damon himself is facing away from his computers, his chair turned so he's looking out one of the massive windows next to him.

"If you're here to yell at me, Jason," he says over the sound of someone saying something in what sounds like Chinese, "I'm going to tell you the same thing I told you half an hour ago."

"I wasn't planning on yelling at you," Kara tells him, and Damon shoots out of his chair so quickly it goes spinning into his desk. His microphone must be muted, because the person keeps speaking.

Damon is in a full suit, even here in his house, though his tie is crumpled in one hand before he drops it down on the desk. "Kara. I—sorry."

Kara heads across the room to him, ignoring the new person who's now saying something in English about revenue and growth. "I heard you were supposed to be done with this meeting an hour ago."

Up close, Damon looks tired, his hair mussed up like he's been running his hands through it. Kara itches to smooth it down, to help put him back together. To make him look a little less exhausted.

"My CFO has never run a short meeting in his life." When Kara gets close, Damon reaches out and takes her hand to skim his nose over the sensitive skin of her wrist, the way he always does. As he inhales, his shoulders go down, and he relaxes like something is uncoiling inside of him. "Did Jason send you?"

"I sent myself." Kara leans up to press a kiss to the corner of his lips, more comfort than anything else, then says, "Aren't you in charge? Can't you just end the meeting?"

Damon opens his mouth—then closes it and pulls away to round his desk. He presses a button, then cuts off whoever is talking to say, "Gentlemen, ladies, I have an Omega waiting for me. If there is anything else that I need to know, you can email it to me."

Then he clicks on something, and all of the noise cuts off.

Damon sags, stripping off his suit jacket and draping it over the back of his chair. Somehow, he looks even more tired now that the call is over, as though it was the only thing keeping him going.

"Are you okay?" Kara asks.

"We haven't been sleeping well," Damon says. "And I've been in calls since six this morning. We're having issues with our office in Shenzhen so I've been putting out fires on that for the last couple days."

"Anything I can do to help? Not with your office, but—"

Damon smiles, walking back around his desk to her. "Just you being here helps." He tugs her close, touching his forehead to hers the way Jason did. Then he pulls away, demanding, "Weren't you on a date with Eric? Did I—that was in my calendar."

"You put other people's dates with me in your calendar?"

"I put everything in my calendar." He slides his hands up the back of her shirt, smoothing then against her skin. He still smells stressed, but the scent is easing into something a little more even. "Have you eaten?"

"I'm fine." Standing here in his arms feels good, like she's actually doing what she's supposed to be doing and an Alpha is recognizing her for it, satisfying some innate need deep in her.

She thought she had given up all possibility of being an Omega like this the day the doctors told her that she would always be heatless.

Damon pulls away to say, "You need to eat. Are you hungry?"

"I'm fine," Kara says again, laughing. "Though I did leave Eric and Jason alone...somewhere in your house."

"We can't have that," Damon says. He wraps an arm around her waist and starts leading her out of the room. "Where's Ry?"

"Apparently he wanted a special mushroom?"

"Of course he did."

Damon's hand stays chastely on her waist as they walk, but underneath his exhaustion, she can smell the smoky undertone of his arousal. He doesn't mention it, though, so she ignores it.

When they get back to the living room, Eric and Jason are sprawled out on the couch, Jason's hand high on Eric's thigh like a tease.

"Our fearless leader," Jason says when he spots them. "I see you've been dragged out of your cave."

"Thank you," Damon tells him.

That gets a sloppy salute from Jason before Eric catches his hand, pulling over to his lips to kiss his knuckles. It looks like an absent gesture, like Eric has done it so many times he hardly thinks about it anymore.

Kara wants that, one day.

When she's here with them, she can't help but think it might even be in their set that she'll find it.

She asks, "Are you?"

"Am I what?" Damon asks.

"The leader."

"Yes," Eric says at the same time Damon says, "No."

"*No*," Damon repeats more firmly, giving Eric a look. "We don't have anyone who's 'in charge' of the set."

Eric rolls his eyes good-naturedly. "And yet, Damon does most of the providing, most of the organizing, and he's the one who brought all of us together."

"And we do live in his house," Jason adds, smirking at Damon.

Damon flips him off, herding Kara over toward the couch. He pulls her down next to him, cuddling her against him. She's between him and Jason, but almost a foot away from Jason. From the look on Damon's face, she's pretty sure the distance is pointed.

"It's our house," Damon says once they're settled on the couch. "Want to watch something until Ry gets back? *Not* soccer."

That sounds directed at someone — and sure enough, Eric says, "At least it's not the country's worst football team."

"I'm just supporting my local team," Damon shoots back.

"Not even the locals support the local team." Jason drapes his arm across the back of the couch, his hand settling on the back of Kara's neck. A thumb sweeps across the nape of her neck, sending shivers all the way down her spine.

When she looks at him, Jason is smiling.

"Do you usually watch sports?" Kara asks.

Jason barks out a laugh. "Hardly. At least not together. Eric's obsessed with some German soccer team. Ry and Damon watch football together, like red-blooded American Alphas. And I follow hockey, mostly."

Kara perks up. "What did you think about last year's Stanley Cup?"

"Please don't get him started," Damon says, voice muffled as he presses his mouth to her hair. "He can go for hours."

"It was a *travesty*. The ref —"

"He wasn't wrong."

"He was absolutely wrong," Jason says. "When a player bites someone —"

"He didn't *bite* him."

"Okay, what do you call putting his mouth around someone's wrist and inserting his teeth into the other person's skin —"

"That's a little overdramatic."

"A little over — there was *blood*."

"It's *hockey*."

"Oh my God," Eric breathes. "There's two of them."

"Sorry," Kara says, catching herself. "I have opinions about hockey."

"So I guess the consensus is not watching sports," Damon says, amused. "What kind of movies do you like?"

Kara makes a face. "Is it terrible if I admit I don't watch many movies?"

"Too busy watching hockey?" Eric teases.

"Okay, okay." Kara holds up her hands in mock surrender. "If I'm going to watch something, it's usually a documentary or a docuseries. Or a cooking show. I don't have a particularly exciting home life."

Damon leans forward to grab a remote from the ottoman, and whatever button he presses makes a massive television reveal itself from inside what looked up until this moment like a decorative cabinet. "We could watch one of those documentaries that's just some British guy describing pretty shit. That way we won't miss anything if we start making out halfway through."

"Pretty confident, are you?" she teases.

"Think of it as an aspiration." Damon turns on the TV, clicking through what looks like every streaming service in existence.

"I vote for one about space," Eric puts in.

"Fuck yeah," Jason says. "Space."

Damon does in fact find one about space, and soon the room is filled with the dulcet tones of a British man describing space.

It's more engaging than Kara expects, and soon she finds herself entranced by the description of the Helix Nebula. The remnants of a dying star, like the whale fall of some old god, something that matters because it is not what it once was. They're watching something dying, she thinks. Their children will watch it die, and their children's children, and it looks back at them as they look at it.

It's beautiful.

The door opens, and Ry walks into the room, saying, "I—oh." He's not looking at her but past her, and she turns to see Damon with his head tipped back against the back of the couch, eyes shut and mouth open.

Oh, she thinks.

The sight of him sleeping stirs something in her, not the instinct that Alphas have but something different, to make sure nothing wakes him until he's gotten the sleep he needs, until he doesn't smell of exhaustion anymore.

"We haven't been sleeping well," he said, and she wonders suddenly who *we* is. Because neither Jason nor Eric has that same dragging bone-deep exhaustion scent clinging to them. For Eric, it could be the scent blockers, but looking at Ry's face, at the sharpness of his cheekbones and the bruises under his eyes, she thinks it's not them. Or it's not about them, at least.

Kara's not close enough to pick out Ry's scent over all the others in the room, but she thinks he probably smells like exhaustion too, or something worse.

She wants to coax him over to the couch, to curl up between him and Damon until he sleeps too, softening her scent until it's rich with *stand down you've done enough sleep sleep sleep.*

On the other side of her, Jason yawns.

"Having a slumber party?" Ry murmurs.

"The pillow fight is at ten," Kara says quietly.

Ry grins. "Count me in. You staying for dinner?"

"I don't want to impose or throw off your plans."

"Ry has yet to figure out how to cook for fewer than ten," Eric says. "You will definitely not be inconveniencing us to stay here."

"And even if you were," Ry adds, "we'd still want you to stay."

"You want any help?" Kara stands, easing Damon's arm down to try to keep him from waking up. His breathing hitches, but then he settles again.

When she looks back at Ry, he's smiling, a secret little half-smile. "I'd love that."

"I'm not as good as you or Damon," she warns as she follows him into the kitchen. Jason and Eric stay on the couch, and she sees Eric's hand creeping up Jason's thigh as she passes.

"I'd love for you to just join me in the kitchen," Ry says. "You're welcome to just sit there and look beautiful."

"No, no, I'll help. I just don't know how to do anything fancy like...brunoise or whatever."

"Well, no brunoising necessary." Ry sets down the bag on the kitchen island, then turns to look at her. He reaches out to touch her hand, fingers barely hovering against the pads of her fingers. "May I?"

She rejected him doing that when they first met, after he rejected her first—but doing so now feels cruel. So she nods, and he lifts her hand to skim his nose against her wrist. When he inhales, it's like a benediction.

So when he starts to pull away, she wraps her hand around the back of his neck and pulls him to her. He gets with the picture fast, wrapping his arms around her lower back so he can press her against him, his lips skimming against hers once, twice, before he deepens the kiss.

His mouth is dry, his lips firm as they part hers. He kisses like he knows what he's doing, pressure and breath and touch in all the right places to send heat running up and down her body, trembling where she's pressed against him.

"Thank you," he whispers when he lifts his head away.

"Any time," Kara whispers back.

His face lights up, and he looks so much better like this. He looks almost healthy like this, and she hates to think that, to think of him in terms of his health, but right now that's all she can think. That she wants to see him like this more.

Then he coughs and steps back and says, "Damon's going to get hangry if we don't eat soon."

"Put me to work, chef."

"Can you cut things without injuring yourself?"

"I'm not that bad," Kara says, laughing, half-offended.

Ry laughs too, heading around to open a pantry door. He pulls two aprons off a hook in the back, handing one to her to put on. "You'd be amazed at how bad Jason is at cooking." Kara raises an eyebrow at him, and he says, "Let's just say it's a good thing we have a nurse in the set."

Oh dear. "Well, I can cut things, and I can cook them. I'm just no gourmet. There's a lot of salads and pasta in my life."

"None of that tonight, at least." Ry starts bustling around the kitchen, taking out various things from the fridge, and Kara stands back and watches. He's clearly in his element here. "We'll be having shredded beef with morel mushroom sauce, mashed potatoes and zucchini. No chestnuts or eel in sight."

"My desire not to have hives thanks you." Kara steps forward, brushing her hands against her apron. "What can I do to help?"

"Would you mind terribly if I asked you to peel potatoes?"

"Peeling potatoes is one of my specialties," she says. It's one of her standard Thanksgiving jobs, when there are a hundred people in the kitchen and everything needs to get done all at once. She washes her hands with their fancy touch faucet, drying them off on her apron, then starts washing the literal dozen potatoes he sticks on the counter next to her. "You think this is enough potatoes?" she jokes.

"Do you think it's not?" Ry asks, not joking. "We have more, if you think we need another couple."

"I don't think we need more potatoes." Kara finishes rinsing all of them, then starts peeling onto the layer of paper towels Ry put down. "Do you usually cook this much food?"

"If not more." Ry starts cutting up some zucchini, standing far enough away at the island that they won't get in each other's way. "Leftovers become lunch, so there's always food to eat."

"And I'm not messing up your calculations?"

"You're really not."

They work around each other for a bit—Kara peeling then cutting up potatoes, Ry prepping everything else. It's the absolute biggest kitchen Kara has ever cooked in, and they can stay out of each other's way, but every couple of passes, Ry's hand will brush against her back, just the briefest touch, like he can't help himself.

Finally, they have the potatoes in a pot of water with a good helping of salt and some garlic, Ry has a sauce started and the kitchen is starting to smell absolutely amazing. Kara thinks, *this is what I've been missing*.

Because the way she lives, alone, nobody coming over and her going almost nowhere—she likes the independence, not being reliant on other people the way so many Omegas are, but it's also so, *so* lonely sometimes.

Nobody is built to be alone—but Omegas, most of all, aren't built to be alone. And that's not to say that Omegas shouldn't live alone, shouldn't *be* alone, but her life has shrunk and shrunk and shrunk until it's just her.

She shrunk her life until it's just her, piece by piece, cutting away everything that reminded her of those things she couldn't have.

She isn't supposed to be able to have this. Heatless Omegas don't get this. Erin Overly lives under her Alpha brother's guardianship, trapped in an old traditionalist family that won't let her work or marry because Omegas only bond. Maurice Ellis was kicked out of his family when they found out. Kieran Reilly is a spinster and pretends to be happy about it.

A couple are married to Betas, which isn't unheard of in Omegas as a whole, though it's not particularly common even now. Kara's considered it, more than once.

It's never felt like anything other than failure.

"What's on your mind?" Ry asks.

"Just how nice it is here. You keep a gorgeous house," she says sincerely.

"Thank you." He grins. "You're not too bad yourself."

"You only say that because you haven't seen my apartment." And if she has her way, he never will. "What do you — no, sorry, ignore me."

Ry lifts an eyebrow at her. "What could you possibly want to ask that's so inappropriate? If it's about my favorite sex position, I'm more than happy to answer in great detail."

Kara feels her face go very hot, and she says, "No, no, not — I was going to ask what you do all day."

"Beyond lounging in decadent repose?" Ry turns to stir the sauce, but he keeps his face toward her as he seems to consider the answer. "I wasn't joking when I called myself a house-Alpha. We have a number of household staff, because that's what you have when you're rich and trying to manage a place as big as this. I manage our finances. I cook when I want to. And I spend the rest of my time lounging in decadent repose."

Kara laughs. "That doesn't sound like a bad life."

"I'm lucky that it's a life I can have." Ry shakes his head, looking back at the sauce. "I'm not sure where I'd be if it weren't for Damon."

"You've known each other for a long time, right?"

"Since preschool." Ry gives the sauce one more stir, then turns the heat on low. "He's the first person I remember existing in my life, other than my parents. When things went to hell in my life, Damon was the one who stuck with me."

"Aww," Damon drawls from behind Kara, making her jump and look to see him standing in the doorway. "You're going to make me blush."

"Go back to sleep, asshole."

Damon heads over to them, draping himself over Kara so she's getting his warmth and presence without much of his weight. "No, no, I want to keep hearing about how amazing I am. Keep selling me to the Omega we're courting."

"He doesn't pick up his socks," Ry says flatly, though Kara can see the ghost of a smile on his lips. "We end up with suit jackets absolutely everywhere because he takes them off and then forgets where he puts them—"

"We do *not*."

"We very much *do*." Ry drums his fingers on the counter like he's trying to think about what else there is to say about Damon. Next to her, Damon is grinning. His hair is all mussed up now, and he's a little sleepy-eyed. "He buys into his rich people bullshit a little too much."

"You're a rich person, too," Damon protests, though he can't quite hide the laughter in his voice.

"I'm a rich person's house-Alpha."

"Does a rich person's house-Alpha have a quarter-billion dollars in their personal accounts?"

"I'm a well-kept rich person's house-Alpha," Ry says, at the same time Kara breathes, "Oh my God."

"Damon has about seven billion in his personal accounts," Ry adds.

Kara gapes at Ry. "Oh my *God*. What do you do with all that money?"

"Fund medical research, mostly," Ry says with a shrug.

Damon groans. "Which I've told you to do from the set's money. You don't need to spend your personal money on that."

Ry rolls his eyes, turning back to the sauce to give it a stir. "This is the real downside of joining our set," he says to Kara. "Damon hounding you about taking more money than you could possibly want or need in a lifetime."

"I just want to make sure that, if something happens, you're taken care of." Damon huffs out a sigh, then presses a kiss to the side of Kara's head and pulls away. "Either of you want anything to drink? We have a sauvignon blanc chilled if you'd like some."

Kara is absolutely not going to touch whatever that last conversation was with a ten-foot pole—*seven billion dollars, what the* fuck—so she just says, "That would be great."

"Ry?"

"We're having beef, so I'll take a red."

"Are you hiding the beef somewhere?" Damon asks as he busies himself getting out and pouring the wine. "Is it secret beef?"

"It's in the slow cooker."

There's noise behind Kara, and she turns to see Eric and Jason standing in the doorway. Jason's arm is draped around Eric's shoulders. "Oh, shit," Jason says. "Is that the fancy shredded beef?"

"It sure is."

"Fuck yeah."

* * * *

Dinner passes like a dream, amazing food and conversation that manages to be fun without being trite—except by the end Kara can remember all of it, softened as it is by a couple glasses of wine, with the certainty that this is *real*, that there is something here that might actually work.

"You can stay," Eric tells her once they're done with dinner. "We have a nice big bed that you're welcome to share."

"I wish," Kara says, and means it. "But I have a lecture tomorrow morning that I do need to teach. I'm just going to call an Uber to head home."

"And deprive me of the opportunity to drive you home?"

"You don't need to do that," she tells Jason.

Eric knocks his shoulder against Jason's. "Jason has never passed up an opportunity to drive a beautiful woman anywhere in his life."

Jason laughs. "You don't need to make it sound like I'm just waiting around where women are to drive them places. But I would like to drive you home. Maybe even kiss you on your doorstep, if you'll let me."

"Right now, though," Eric says, "is my turn." He swoops over to give her a quick kiss, which turns into a longer kiss, his tongue parting the seam of her lips until she's gasping. When he pulls away, it's to press his forehead against hers. Both of them are breathing hard. "Thank you for the date," he says.

"It was my pleasure."

"It could be *more* your pleasure," Eric says with a grin, pulling away just enough to peck another kiss on her lips.

"I need to go," Kara says, even though staying is much more appealing at the moment. But she knows she'll regret it if she has to get up at fuck-off early in the morning to be able to be home before her class starts — especially because it would require being in traffic during rush hour, which she hates more than anything. "Let me just say goodbye to Damon and Ry before I go."

Back in the kitchen, Ry's sitting at the island, drinking a glass of water as he watches Damon fill the dishwasher. The entire kitchen still smells like dinner, which means that even when she's almost right behind Ry, she can't smell anything but the barest undertone of his scent.

On the other hand, he doesn't seem to be able to smell her either, because he startles aggressively when she asks, "All this money, and you still wash your own dishes?"

"You'll find," Ry says, "that Alphas don't like having too many people in their space."

"What Ry means is that he almost made the singular kitchen staff we had cry," Damon tells her. "There's a reason we have a reputation for being reclusive."

Kara feels a wave of guilt. "Does it bother you to have me here?"

Damon whirls to look at her, soapy water splattering from his hands onto the floor. "Have we made you think that?"

"No, no, I just—I'm just crowding up your space."

"You're not—" Damon takes a step toward her, then stops, looking down at his hands in frustration. He wipes them off on his apron impatiently, then strides over to her to take a hold of her upper arms. His hands are still wet. "The exception to Alpha territorialism is Omegas and kits. Especially Omegas that we want."

"You're always welcome here," Ry adds.

But Kara's still distracted by Damon—not just his proximity, but his use of the word *kit*. It's an old, *old* word for children of Alpha-Omega relationships, the kind that she'd only expect from the most traditional of traditionalists. The kind that still wants Omega ownership rights.

He's never indicated that he wants that, never treated her the way that traditionalists treat Omegas — much less heatless Omegas.

But it's just not a word she expected to hear from him.

"Kara?"

"Sorry," she says, slipping out of Damon's grasp. "I just remembered something I have to do before my lecture in the morning."

"Of course." Damon smiles at her, then leans down to give her a brief kiss. "Thank you for coming for dinner."

"Thank you for feeding me dinner." She makes herself smile at him and at Ry, then says, "I need to go."

* * * *

To Sue Ann: *how much of a red flag is an Alpha using the word kits?*

Less than thirty seconds later, Kara's phone rings. "Why are you hanging out with Alphas who use the word 'kits'?" Sue Ann demands as soon as Kara picks up.

Kara groans. "That much of a red flag?"

"I'd put it at sort of sunset orange," Sue Ann says. "Who do you know that calls someone a kit? Was it one of those assholes at your university?"

Swearing always sounds funny in Sue Ann's accent, an accent that is self-described as "*Tennessee by way of Oklahoma.*"

"He didn't call anyone a kit, he just used the term, and I don't think he meant a group of pigeons."

"All the ways the term kit is used, and your first thought is 'pigeons?'"

"Foxes, ferrets, whatever. He was definitely talking about human children. But more in the conceptual than in the concrete."

"So then we get back to my original question — why are you hanging out with Alphas who use the term kits to refer to human children? And also, is he rich? Because that changes my answer."

Kara takes a deep breath — then says in a rush, "It's one of the Alphas that's courting me."

"Oh my God," Sue Ann breathes. "Oh my *God*. You absolute asshole, when were you going to tell me? Also that doubles my need for you to answer my question — is he rich?"

Rich almost seems too small a word to describe Damon, but, "Yes."

"Old-money rich?"

"Maybe? I haven't asked him the provenance of his wealth." He does sort of give those vibes, though, sometimes, especially with his habit of scenting her wrist every single time.

"Yeah, okay, so find that out. Partly because you should know what kind of estate you'll be marrying into, but also because it does kind of change the color of the flag."

"Because old-money people are terrible?"

"Because I'm pretty sure that's literally just what they call their kids. Like in an affectionate way."

Kara frowns. "But that's still weird, right? Like I'm not crazy that it's a weird thing to hear someone say in casual conversations in the twenty-first century?"

"Oh yeah," Sue Ann drawls. "That's very weird. And it doesn't mean he's not still a weirdo traditionalist. Does he do weirdo traditionalist shit?"

"You mean like courting an Omega he can't bond or make 'kits' with?" Kara says dryly. "No, I mean, he's..." Nice is true, but it feels like not enough. "He seems genuine."

"Have you slept together yet?"

"All of us—"

"*All?*"

"They're a set," Kara says. She can feel her face burning a little. Sue Ann is a Beta from a family of Betas, and they don't really have sets the same way Alphas do. Polyamory, sure, but not in the same way.

Sue Ann laughs delightedly. "So you're being courted by, what, three—"

"Four."

"—four rich, probably hot Alphas who can knot you up all night and keep you in style. That seems like the ideal situation."

"Unless they're weirdo traditionalists."

Sue Ann sobers a little. "Right. That."

Kara huffs out a laugh. "I keep telling myself it's too good to be true, you know? And then they're nice and gorgeous and funny, and I convince myself that they're not going to drop me once it sinks in for them what it means to have an Omega that can't go into heats. And then I go back to my apartment, and reality hits me."

"So stop going back to your apartment."

"Sue Ann—"

"I'm serious," Sue Ann says. "If you think they're for real, then second-guessing yourself is just going to fuck things up. What does it hurt to give it a real, honest try?"

Because if she gives it a real, honest try and this doesn't work, it's going to kill that last little bit of hope that she's been keeping alive. If she puts everything into this and the people who have an actual reason for wanting an Omega like her still can't manage it, it's never going to happen.

"I'm just saying that 'genuine' isn't how you describe a guy you don't feel anything for. Don't listen to that voice in your head that's your mom or your shitty doctors or whoever. Let them spoil you, and if you figure out that they're weirdo traditionalists, dump their asses and come down here and get day-drunk with me while we burn them in effigy."

Kara drops her head back against the pillow behind her. "What if they break my heart?"

"Then we burn them in effigy, Kara, catch up." There's a little kid's voice in the background, and Sue Ann says, "I see that, Kitty, but the grape jelly belongs *in* the kitchen. I—thank you, Kitty. I wanted a sandwich."

"Do you need to deal with that?" Kara asks.

Sue Ann snorts. "You mean the balled-up PB-and-J that's about eighty-percent jelly that my daughter just stuck in my hand? No, Mike has her for the moment. If you ever decide to adopt a kid or, I don't know, steal one from the stork, get one that's less into mess."

"I don't think kids come with a 'less into mess' setting."

"I live in hope," Sue Ann says. "But actually, yes, I do need to go wash my hands, because they're gross and covered in jelly. Please report back on your hot Alphas and their questionable political views."

"Love you."

"Love you too. Get your life together."

Kara snorts and ends the call. She doesn't talk to Sue Ann as much as she should, but she always feels better when she does. They've known each other for something like a decade at this point, since they were roommates their first year of undergrad, and their lives have taken vastly different paths—Sue Ann married her high-school sweetheart and already has a kid, living with her husband Mike back in her hometown in Tennessee and working at a local architecture firm, while Kara has been living alone in the same Northern Virginia apartment since starting her PhD.

Sue Ann has always known what she wanted—and if she doesn't, she's much better at hiding it than Kara is. For Sue Ann, it's just about deciding what to do and figuring out how to do it, and if it doesn't work for her, then she'll figure out how to make it work or she'll cut her losses and move on. It's as simple as that, to her.

Kara has never quite figured out how to live like that. She's never learned how not to be afraid of the consequences of her actions, of picking the wrong path and getting utterly fucked by life for it.

And when she's with them, when she's spending time with the set and they're making her happy, she can mostly manage not to think about it, to live in the moment and think that this all might work.

But then she goes home, or something reminds her of just how badly this could go, how much it would hurt if it all fails, and all those fears and anxieties rush back in.

Because the thing about being an Omega—especially a female Omega—is that there is so much more of a risk of getting trapped in a situation that can become untenable, because they're damned if they do end up in a relationship with someone who turns out to be awful, and they're damned if they end up alone.

She doesn't think Damon is like that—but there's that little voice in the back of her head now, the one that heard *"kits"* and thought *danger*, that keeps reminding her that they're not that many decades past the ownership laws, and if a rich Alpha wants to control an Omega, he could figure out a way.

If Sue Ann had asked Kara what she's afraid of, the answer would have been *everything*.

Chapter Nine

When Damon texts her asking if Friday works for their date, she sends back that she has some work that she needs to get done. Then she spends Friday eating ice cream from the container and rewatching an old season of the *Great British Bake Off*.

It's not that she doesn't want to see him, exactly.

Or, well, she *doesn't*, but not in a way where she wants him to know that she doesn't want to see him.

Because there was a heartbeat of excitement, when he texted her, and the next heartbeat was him saying "*kit*," and the one after that was Ry saying "*finding an Omega you want to be with*," and she got mad all over again because she's worth more than that.

So, ice cream.

Saturday morning, Jason texts her asking if she wants to go skating, and she turns him down. That afternoon, Ry texts her for the first time with a photo of Eric and Jason cuddling on the couch. Kara sends back a thumbs up and tries not to find them cute.

Sunday, nobody sends her anything, and she tries to tell herself that she's not disappointed about it.

Kara turns down another attempt from Damon to schedule a date the following week, telling him that she has a lot of work that she needs to finish, and she spends her evenings not working and feeling guilty about it.

It's such a small thing to be reacting like this to, she knows. Damon didn't do anything but mention kits. But every time she thinks about seeing him, all she can imagine doing is demanding to know what he meant when he said that. Demanding to know if what he really wants is *her*, or is just an Omega desperate enough to say yes to anything. And demanding from Jason and Eric and Ry to know what they're doing with someone like that.

But that also seems like a good way to come across as hysterical at best and completely out of touch with reality at worst, so. Avoidance it is.

Eric calls her on Tuesday, which she misses because she is actually doing work, her phone muted and hidden all the way across her apartment because otherwise she will never manage to get through a hundred freshman papers comparing two international relations theories of their choice. There's a lot of constructivism this year for some reason.

She sees it when she does her semi-illicit phone checking, twenty essays in, but this time she can't talk, not without getting distracted from work. She still feels bad, though, when she stuffs her phone back under her pillow and goes back to work.

* * * *

"Your papers are on the desk at the front," Kara tells her International Relations Theory lecture. The microphone is out again, so she's somewhere between successful projecting and actual shouting. Her throat is not a fan. "Please take your own paper—it should have your name on it. If it isn't here and you know you submitted one, please stay after and talk to me. Good job, everyone—overall, they're looking better than the last ones. See you all next week."

There's a mass rush to the table, and she uses the time to erase her chicken scratch from the board. Other than finals, it's the time when the most people actually show up to her class, because while she grudgingly follows the university's policy on accepting all essays through their stupid anti-plagiarism system, she marks up essays by hand except for students who need an exception. If they want it back, ninety-five percent of them need to show up to get it.

And for those who don't without an excused absence, she sends them a passive-aggressive email reminding them of that requirement.

She can't make people show up to her class without being far more punitive about attendance than she wants to be, but she can make the people who decide to just not show up feel a little bad about it.

The papers are all organized by surname, so most people get them and get out pretty quickly. By the time the dust clears, there's one student left at the table. Maya...something, Kara thinks, though she's not great with the names of the students in her big lectures.

"Your paper not here?" Kara asks. "Or did you have a question?"

"The former," maybe-Maya says. "And I swear I did turn it in. I have an email confirmation and everything."

Kara heads around the table, saying, "Believe me, I have screwed up before, and the university printers have eaten more than one student's papers, so show me the confirmation and I'll go hunt through my apartment and computer to find it."

Maybe-Maya unlocks her phone and scrolls through her emails — then says, "Oh my God. Oh my *God*. I'm so sorry."

That doesn't sound good. "What happened?"

Maybe-Maya turns the phone around to show Kara a grimy screen with low light with an email confirming the submission of a file titled *IR_Theory_110_Maya_Keller.docx*.

"That looks like a confirmation email."

Maya makes a face, then taps at the top of the email. The point where it says *Submission to Global Politics 130 – TEST SUBMISSION*.

"Ah." It's not the first time someone has made that mistake, just like how Kara has absolutely stuck the wrong essay submissions and the wrong essay submission dates with the wrong classes. "Yeah, you're good. I'll adjust the submission deadline for yours to midnight tonight and let you resubmit it to me, and I'll get your grade back to you in the next few days. Actually…" Kara spins her laptop around and signs in to the system to make the change now, so she doesn't forget. "Okay, you're good. Forward me that confirmation email so I have it for my records and upload it by tonight, and you're good."

"Thank you." Maya sweeps the knuckle of her thumb under her eye in that careful way girls have of doing when they're wearing eye makeup, to not smear anything. She looks close to tears, but she's not actually crying, and Kara lets it go. "Jesus, I just—I really need to pass this."

"You can come to my office hours, too, if you want to talk through anything."

"Thanks." Maya tucks her phone back in her pocket, straightens the straps of her background, then turns toward the door. Then she asks, "Don't I know you?"

Kara looks up.

"No," Damon says from just inside the doorway. He's in a well-tailored suit, no tie, and he looks so stunningly out of place that for a second Kara thinks it's not actually him standing in her classroom. But then he says, "I just needed to talk to Professor Igan, once she's free."

"Yeah, sure." Maya glances back just long enough to say, "I'll get that to you as soon as I sit down in front of my computer," before she heads past Damon and out of the room.

"That was kind of you," he says once she's gone.

"What are you doing here?"

Damon approaches her with a few long strides, stretching his hand out toward hers when he gets close. "May I?"

Kara offers her hand on autopilot, and he bends down over it as he always does, like he can't have a conversation with her without scenting her first.

A few days ago, it seemed courtly. Now all she can think is that feels like what traditionalists do.

When he straightens out, she asks, "Is everything okay?"

"I was going to ask the same thing," he says. He lets go of her hand, though clearly with some reluctance. It feels cold when she pulls it back to cradle against her stomach. "You've been avoiding us, and when you didn't call Eric back—"

"Oh, shit." Kara rubs at her forehead as a wave of guilt runs through her. "Sorry, that was genuinely an accident."

"Unlike the rest of it?"

His tone is gentle, but she can hear the hurt there.

"I—look, can we talk about this in my office? I don't want to do this here."

Damon says, "Of course," and waits as she finishes packing up her stuff. She can see him twitching to offer to carry her bag, but he doesn't, and she appreciates it. Enough people have views about her even working there without her being seen with an Alpha carrying her stuff for her.

Her office isn't close to, well, anything, but she knows it'll be empty because they're in the two-week period between Dr. Peng leaving for their parental leave and Dr. Aster coming back from hers.

They spend the walk in silence. Kara isn't sure what he's thinking, but all she can try to do is think of the best way to have this conversation once they're behind closed doors. Or even what conversation she wants to have. There seem like a thousand wrong ways to do this and no right way.

So of course, as soon as they set foot in the office, she blurts out, "What are your feelings on Omega ownership?"

"Bad?" Damon says, sounding baffled. He closes the door behind him without taking his eyes off of her. They're both standing awkwardly near the door, too far to be companionable but close enough to be awkward. "I think the concept is awful and I'm glad the Supreme Court decided it was illegal. Is this some kind of test?"

"You, uh." Kara chews on the inside of her lip, not sure quite how to answer. This all feels so silly, now that she's here looking at the utter confusion on his face. "You referred to 'kits' and I just...I don't know. Extrapolated."

To her surprise, Damon drops his head in his hands. "Oh, fuck me."

Kara's ire rises again. "Well, *sorry* for—"

"No, no, not you," Damon says quickly. Then he says, "Sorry for interrupting. But it's not—Jason is going to give me so much shit for this. Every time I think I've managed to train myself out of talking like my parents, it comes back to bite me in the ass."

"Your parents?"

"They're—I guess you would probably call them traditionalists. More than one of them is from old Alpha set families—like, original thirteen colonies, Founding Fathers-adjacent old. And they're really, really not the type that's into Omega ownership, but they have other things that they do that are...traditional, you might say."

"Like the scenting."

"Like a scent-greeting," Damon agrees. "My mom would kick my ass if she saw me ever not greet an Omega like you like that. And everyone was a kit until they presented. I know that must sound weird to you, but that's just how it was. And then I got to college and realized that people thought I was an asshole if I referred to children like that, so I tried to stop."

Grudgingly, Kara says, "That doesn't sound too bad."

"Don't get me wrong, my family are steadfast Alphas for house, Omegas for home people. Their politics are not great at the best of times. But we're not—I promise you, we're not the kind of people who think Alphas should own their Omegas and who want you barefoot and pregnant and barred from work, or who believe in ordering their Omegas instead of asking them. *I'm* not the kind of person."

Kara takes a deep breath—then sits down in the nearest chair, which she's pretty sure is Dr. Peng's. Her heart hurts. "I want to believe you," she says. "I do. But I need you to understand the position I'm in. Do you know how rare it is, still, to have a financially independent Omega—especially a financially independent Omega woman? I have my own bank account, I have my own apartment with my own lease with only my name on it, I have my own job. And if I'm wrong about you, if you decide in a year or two years or five that what you really want is for me to be holed up in your house, in your territory, that it's not safe for me to be out in the world, that I need an escort when I go out, it would be so hard for me to ever get myself out of that situation. Who would believe an Omega like me against Alphas like you?"

There's movement in her periphery, then Damon is crouched in front of her, looking up to meet her gaze. "What can I do—what can we do—to convince you?"

"I don't know," Kara says miserably.

"Will you at least let us try?"

There's a little piece of her that wants to say no, to just walk away from all of this, but…she likes them. Whether or not she should, she does, and throwing this possibility away because she's scared of something that might never happen feels like such a waste.

It might not work. But it might.

So she nods.

Damon's face lights up. He clasps her hands in his, pressing a kiss to her knuckles. "Thank you. *Thank you.*"

"I want to figure out how to make this work," she tells him. There's something about the hope on his face that makes her chest hurt.

He kisses her knuckles again, then gets to his feet, her hands still in his. "Will you let me take you out for dinner tonight? Somewhere nice?"

"Yeah, sure. I am actually in between grading nightmare times, for once."

Something shifts in Damon's scent, goes a little sour. "So that was the truth, at least."

Kara makes a face. "Some of it, yeah. I spent the last several days grading my entire freshman class's essays and trying not to become an alcoholic. Some of them are so bad at bullshitting things. But yes, I'd like to go to dinner with you. Just you, or—"

"Just me, if you're okay with that. I would like to still have my date."

"That sounds great." Kara stands, letting Damon help lever her up to her feet. She goes on her toes to press a quick kiss to his lips. "Is this a T-shirt-and-jeans dinner or a find-something-nice-in-my-closet dinner?"

"The latter, if you don't mind. Though you'd look lovely in anything."

"You'll send me an address?"

"I'll send you a car." He gives her another kiss, then grimaces when his phone chimes. "I have a meeting in fifteen minutes that I shouldn't miss. Thank you."

"You don't need to keep thanking me." Kara nudges at his chest. His very nice chest. "Go to your meeting. I'll see you tonight."

* * * *

The car that comes is a black town car, the sort that's discreet and luxurious and comes with a well-dressed Beta man who open the door for her and offers her a hand in. Which is helpful, because she's back in her ridiculous four-inch heels, which make getting into and out of cars a non-trivial matter.

The back of the car is dark, all black leather and tinted windows. There are bottles of water in a fancy chilled container, still and sparkling, from one of those ten-dollar-a-bottle brands. And when the driver gets in, he says, "There's an intercom button on each door. Please let me know if you need anything." Then he raises a divider, leaving her in a luxurious darkness.

It's just turning to twilight outside, and the lights blur alongside the car into something ethereal, almost magical. It's quiet inside the car, too, like it's an electric car or it has some sort of sound dampening.

It almost feels like she's in another world.

They end up somewhere in Penn Quarter, or at least near it, and this time Damon is the one who opens the door and helps her out of the car. He's in an even nicer suit, with a tie that looks almost black in the light of the streetlights.

"You look stunning," he tells her. He scents her wrist as always, but he lingers, eyes closed as he breathes in her scent. "And you smell…exquisite."

"You look great, too." She reaches out to smooth down his tie, just as an excuse to touch him. "So, what is this place?"

"For fear of sounding extremely pretentious," Damon says, "it's an invitation-only restaurant." He leads her down a set of stairs to a nondescript basement, bracing her so she doesn't fall. She clutches the railing on the other side, imagining how much it would hurt to scrape herself up on the exposed brick.

There's a slender Beta woman in a sharp black sheath dress standing at the door. She takes a metal card that Damon hands her and scans it with her tablet, then hands it back. "The maître d' will show you to your table."

"Thanks."

Inside, another Beta woman in a similar black dress shows them to a table in the back corner of the room, saying, "Your waiter will be with you momentarily. Please let me know if there is anything I can do for you."

"Thank you," Damon says. He helps Kara into her seat, then sits down himself.

From the inside, the restaurant looks like the sort of place for new rich people, with stark lines and nothing too stuffy. Each table has a plate with an elaborately folded white napkin, and on top of it is a small, crisp menu.

There are no prices.

"Dare I ask—"

"Please don't," Damon says. "It is my pleasure to provide for you, and I know it will make you uncomfortable to know how much it costs."

Kara can argue—but it won't make either of them happy, and at this point it just feels kind of silly. He has literal billions of dollars. No matter how much this dinner costs, it won't make a dent in his money.

So she settles back in her seat, gets comfortable and picks up the menu.

And immediately asks, "What am I supposed to do with this?"

Damon laughs. "They do...pathways."

"These are colors."

"They do colored pathways?" He squints at his own menu. "The food is good, I promise. They're just a little conceptual at times."

"So how do you get an invitation to a place that does colored pathways for food?" Kara asks as she examines the menu. The periwinkle option looks good, based on nothing but vibes.

"Get rich," Damon says. "What the hell is mauve?"

"It's a...pinkish...off-pink. But seriously. How does that actually work?"

"What generally happens is that Shannon or my EA Jeff says, 'You have an invitation to a new restaurant,' and if it seems even vaguely interesting, we have them go eat a meal there and tell us if it's any good, and then sometimes we go."

"So restaurants just reach out to you and ask you to eat there?"

Damon shrugs, smiling wryly. "I have no earthly idea. For all I know, our EAs reach out to places like this and ask."

"Wow," Kara says with a laugh. "The lives of the rich and...well."

"I highly recommend it."

Kara is still laughing when the waiter comes.

* * * *

Kara ends up with periwinkle, which starts with a stunning beet carpaccio with walnuts and whipped feta cheese and a light vinaigrette. She gets a couple bites in, then offers, "Do you want any?"

Damon smiles, just a small little smile like he's trying not to show too much. "I'd love some," he says.

Kara pushes a little bit onto his place, feeling brave. It doesn't *necessarily* mean anything, for an Omega to give an Alpha food from her plate, but she means it to mean something, and she knows he'll take it that way.

His own food is some sort of meat spread in a jar, with toast and tiny leaves. He smears some of it on the toast, sprinkles some leaves on it and holds it out for her. She reaches out to take it, but he says, "If I may."

It takes her a second.

He waits there while she's having her realization, hand still outstretched with that piece of bread, ever patient.

So she cups a hand underneath, leans forward and takes a bite. It's an awkward way to eat, definitely, but there's something about the act of being fed from an Alpha's head that makes heat build low in her stomach. That makes her want to do this again, somewhere that isn't in public, her Alphas around her as they make a mess.

"Good?" Damon asks with a smile.

"Yeah," Kara says hoarsely.

Damon's smile grows, and he offers her the bread again for her to take another bite.

It's a rich taste, lightly herbed with what she thinks might be thyme and something else, with just the slightest addition of *green* that must be from the tiny leaves on it. She lets herself savor the taste in a way that she often doesn't, closing her eyes and feeling the crunch, the softness, the little bite of a stem.

She's going to have a good time tonight, no matter what comes tomorrow.

Damon is watching her when she opens her eyes. He looks at her like he wants her.

"So," Kara says, to distract from the heat flooding her face. "How does one become a multi-billionaire?"

"Well," Damon says, "it helps to start as a multi-millionaire."

Kara laughs.

Damon doesn't.

"The self-made man story is romantic and all," Damon adds, "but it's kind of bullshit. My family, along with being *very* old-fashioned, is also already pretty rich by almost anybody's standards. I went into college with a trust fund of a few million."

"Jeez," Kara breathes. She stuffs a piece of beet in her mouth to keep from saying something stupider.

Damon gives her a self-deprecating smile. "I was an entitled dickhead in college. I'm glad you didn't know me then. And then sophomore year I was the silent partner to Jessica Wray and Mason White when they were starting Muse-In, and when they sold it the year after we graduated, I had a couple hundred million dollars and a strong determination to make as much money as I could, as fast as I could. It was a bad couple years, especially before the set came together, when I was drinking too much and working too much and spending my weekends sleeping with every Beta and Omega woman who caught my eye."

"What happened then?"

"Ry, mostly." Damon starts tearing the stems off of the tiny leaves absentmindedly, his fingers twitching and restless in front of him.

This isn't quite the lighthearted story Kara expected when she asked the question.

"What did Ry do?"

"For starters, he called me on my bullshit." Damon's mouth quirks up in a crooked smile. "Ry and I have known each other since we were kids, and he never let me get away with the 'look at how special I am' shit. And he was—he was really sick then, for a couple years, and I had this sobering moment when I realized that I had to choose between making more money than anyone can ever use in their life or potentially never seeing my friend again. So I stopped working so much, stopped drinking so much and figured out that I was happier being at home with the people I love than going to some awful party where the entire goal is to have other people see how rich you are.

"And please don't take any of this as a 'poor little rich boy' thing—whatever mess there was of my own making."

"I won't even think of feeling sorry for you," Kara says.

"Good." Damon picks up a piece of meat blob with his fingers and sticks it in his mouth, then licks his fingers clean. It's hotter than it should be, that casual gesture. "And then, and I realize I sound ridiculous when I put it this way, at some point your money just starts…making more money."

"And that's how you have seven billion dollars."

"That," Damon says, "depends mostly on how you define 'you'."

Kara raises an eyebrow at him.

"We have set accounts and then we all have personal accounts—it has to do with taxes and money transfers and not having all of our eggs in one basket, and also about having four Alphas all in one set."

"Okay?'

146

"And so *I* have seven billion, but the set has more like twenty, all things considered."

If Kara thinks too hard about that, she's going to need to drink something stronger than the no doubt very expensive wine sitting in front of her, so she says, "Okay. So. Two truths and a lie. All things that have nothing to do with your money."

For a second, she thinks he won't go for it, but then he grins and says, "Hmm, okay. I have more than thirty first cousins. I have been to every continent but Antarctica. And I spent my childhood as a competitive fencer."

The middle one is probably true, and fencing seems like the sort of sport rich traditionalists would stick their kid in, so she says, "The first one. With the cousins."

Damon shakes his head. "I have five parents, and they all have siblings. I have...fifty-three cousins? Fifty-five? Somewhere in the fifty to sixty range."

"So the fencing one, then?"

"I did in fact spend almost ten years of my life as a fencer."

"Which sword?"

"I competed almost exclusively with saber."

Kara says, "That sounds...fencing-related."

Damon grins. "It's the fast fencing. Technically it's the fastest combat sport in the world. But I did it from when I was about eight until I left for college."

"Why'd you stop?"

He shrugs. "I was decent but I wasn't great, and you hit a point where you have to be really good for it to be worth it to stick with it." He reaches forward to tap her hand that's resting on the table, apparently just for the sake of touching her. "What about you? What are your two truths and a lie?"

The waiter delivering their entrées gives her a chance to figure out what hers should be, so by the time she's looking down at her peppered steak and glazed carrots cut in the fancy little flowers, she has three lined up. "I've left the country only once, everyone in my family has the same middle name and I once got lost in the forest for three days."

"The forest," Damon says instantly. "Actually, no, the middle name one, it would be very weird if all of your parents had the same middle name."

"And yet," Kara says, "both of them have the middle name Lee, and so do all of us kids. And I did get lost in the forest on a summer camp trip. I almost went to Canada, but we ended up staying on this side of Niagara Falls, so now I have an easy two-truths-and-a-lie lie."

"Where would you go?" he asks.

Kara holds up a finger as she finishes chewing a carrot, then swallows and says, "It's not really safe to travel to most places as a single Omega, but I'd love to see cherry blossom season in Japan, and I'd love to see the Northern Lights. I—" There's the slide of the smooth top of a shoe against the bare skin of her leg, and she laughs. "Are we playing footsie now?"

His foot slides higher, tracing up the inside of her calf, and she swallows down her laughter as it transforms into a gasp.

"I'm sorry," he says, though the smirk on his face doesn't look sorry at all. "I just couldn't go any longer without touching you."

Kara represses a shiver as his foot traces against her knee. She can smell the scent rising off of her, and off of him, heat and citrus and need.

"You were saying that you want to see the Northern Lights?"

"I—" His ankle slides down her leg, and she says, laughing, "You're not making it easy to answer you."

"Am I distracting you?"

"You know you are." In retaliation, she reaches out to take his hand in both of hers, dragging her nails lightly over the sensitive skin of his palm. A shiver runs up his entire arm, and she can smell a wave of heat from him. "I think what I like seeing is things in nature," she says. It's easier to talk now that she feels a little more in control of what's going on, now that it's not just *her* reacting to *him*. "You know, I've lived in urban or suburban or exurban places for my entire life, and there's just something about seeing somewhere... natural."

Kara drags her fingers up to his wrist—then he flips his hand over, grabbing her hands in his. "If you keep touching me like this, I'm going to say, 'to hell with dinner' and ask you home with me for the night."

"Now you know how I feel." She can still reach his wrist, so she brushes the tip of one finger back and forth against it. "You're not the only one who's allowed to tease."

He brings her hands up to his lips to kiss her knuckles. "I'm all for your teasing," he tells her hoarsely. "But maybe we should hold off in public."

Kara grins at him. "All those Alpha hormones making you lose your head?"

"Something like that." He kisses her knuckles again with a smile, then lets go. He pointedly goes back to his food, cutting off a piece like he's trying to illustrate what she's supposed to be doing.

Kara cuts off some more of her own steak, but instead of eating it, she puts it on his plate. His smile grows.

"Is wanting to see nature how you got lost at summer camp?" Damon asks. His voice sounds a little more normal now, but she can still smell his need in the air. The fact that she can make an Alpha like him want an Omega like her — it feels good.

But his question — Kara laughs. "I got lost at summer camp because I was eight and stupid and wanted to get away from a girl who wouldn't stop talking about horses. We were already camping, so I had some subset of what I needed, and I got very lucky, but it did turn me off camping for a while."

"When did you get turned back on to camping?"

"I'll let you know when it happens."

Damon laughs. "Fair enough."

* * * *

Kara's dessert, when it comes, is a chocolate mousse, layered with fruit sauce and something crunchy. She takes small bites to savor it, ready to lick it out of the glass it's in because it's so goddamn good.

Damon, on the other hand, is making longing faces at hers, while poking unenthusiastically at what looks like a pear or maybe apple tart.

"I'm not sharing," she tells him, reading the look on his face.

He pouts at her. "*Omega.*"

"I can eat a literal mixing bowl of chocolate mousse all on my own." Kara eats another spoonful, licking it clean. His gaze tracks her tongue. "Don't you like your...fruit...thing?"

"I want to taste what you taste," Damon says. He's still pouting, which he manages to turn into something cute instead of that asshole thing men do sometimes.

He cuts off a piece of the tart with his fork and puts it on her plate, giving her a proud smile like he's a cat delivering a particularly juicy dead bird.

It's more endearing than it should be.

Giving in, Kara scrapes some mousse into her spoon and hands it over to him.

His look when he puts it in his mouth is like he's having an out-of-body experience.

"I'm sure they would give you your own," she tells him, thoroughly entertained by how into it he seems to be. "I think, when you have a gazillion dollars, they will let you exchange some of that money for chocolate mousse." She picks up a piece of tart crust with her fingers and sticks it in her mouth. It leaves sticky wet cinnamon sugar on her fingers that she licks off.

"But then it wouldn't be *your* chocolate mousse," he says around the spoon. He gives it back, a little reluctantly, saying, "I'm going to have Shannon find us the best chocolate mousse in the city and then get a literal mountain of it."

"Then it wouldn't be my chocolate mousse, either."

"It would be if she gives it to you first."

"If it's mine, then I can decide not to let you have any."

Damon shrugs. "That's a risk I'm willing to take." He reaches out like he's going to touch her hand, but stops just before making contact. "Will you come home with me? Be with me tonight—be with us? There's no obligation, but everyone would like to see you."

Kara wants to, but the thought of seeing all of them after ignoring them without explanation, especially when none of them did anything wrong, makes her so anxious. "Are they mad?"

"They're mad at me for freaking you out, but mostly they just miss you. We all like you, Kara, and we want this to work."

Kara thinks about it, but more out of habit than because she has any real reluctance to go. "I have to say," she says finally, "you're nicer than what I picture when I think 'billionaire Alpha.'"

"Nice is a choice," he says. "I can hurt people. I probably did, when I was just trying to make money for the sake of making money. And the people I love now didn't like me very much. *I* didn't like me very much. So now I wake up in the morning and choose to be nice." He grins. "Eric and Jason, on the other hand, are naturally nice."

"Not Ry?"

"I love Ry to the bottom of my heart, and I think he's an amazing person, but sometimes he is an absolute asshole. So, what do you say? You want to come back with me?"

Chapter Ten

When they're nearing Damon's place, Kara realizes, "I don't have any other clothes with me."

Damon's scent goes embarrassed at that, which is *not* the reaction Kara was expecting. He says, "I hope this isn't overstepping, but we bought some clothing for you, just for this purpose. Or, well, we had Shannon buy some clothing for you. So you could stay overnight without worrying about having packed a bag."

"Oh," Kara says, surprised by his thoughtfulness. It feels a little weird, the idea of wearing clothing that someone else chose—like wearing her friend's clothes after a sleepover when she was a kid, or walking out of the store in something she just bought. But it also does make her life a lot easier, that she doesn't have to choose between heading out tonight or leaving in the morning in what would definitely feel like Walk of Shame clothing.

"You don't have to wear it," he tells her, and she realizes her response could have been taken the wrong way. "We won't be offended."

"No, no, I appreciate it." Feeling bold, Kara reaches out to put her hand on his knee — but it's a little too far away, so her hand lands on his thigh instead. Under the fabric of his pants, his muscles twitch. She leaves her hand there. "I'd like to be able to stay."

"Good." Damon swallows, and his scent shifts to the warmth of arousal, filling the enclosed space of the car. Kara's mouth waters. "Good."

They stay like that through the drive, her hand on his thigh, just sitting there. She can feel the tension building like the rising tide, desire and heat lapping at her feet, her ankles, every nerve alive with need.

It hasn't been that long since she's had sex, but she's already getting used to it, to even semi-regular sex after literal years of only getting off on her own fingers and toys. And she hasn't even done that recently, given that she's been drowning in work.

And now, in this car full of their mixed scent like syrup against her tongue, all she wants to do is climb onto his lap, get their hands between them and get off quick and dirty. After that, they can take their time.

By the time they stop in the set's ridiculous driveway and she's managed to fumble her seatbelt off, Damon is out of the car and around to open her door. He helps her out, bracing her when she totters on her absurd heels, but only until he can get her pressed against the side of the car, his thigh pressed between her legs as he kisses her and kisses her and kisses her.

"I've wanted to do this all night," he rasps against her mouth, hands hot against her skin as he hikes one of her thighs up around his leg. She ends up off-balance, leaning back against the car with only his hands keeping her on her feet. Her dress has ridden up so much she's rubbing her soaked panties against his thigh, trying to get friction that she can't quite manage the leverage for. "Do you know what you look like, what you *smell* like?"

Kara gets one hand between them, but she's not at the right angle to get to his zipper, so she just palms his cock through his pants, relishing his groan.

"It'll be a quick night if you keep at that, baby," he grits out, even as his length strains against her hand, leaking enough precum that she can feel it through the fabric.

She wants him in her mouth.

"There are four of you, aren't there?" She tilts her head to nip at his chin, then licks her way down his throat to his scent gland. It's so strong she can *taste* it in the sweat against his skin…Alpha heat. He makes a deep, vibrating sound in his chest when she sets her teeth and tongue against it.

She pushes him back, and when he goes, she sinks down to her knees right there on the driveway. The concrete bites into her skin, but it's a distant pain, because all of her attention is on getting his cock free and getting her mouth on it as soon as possible.

He tastes like precum and smells like Alpha, and he settles into that place in her head where everything is heat and sensation and the aching drooling weight of a cock in her mouth and nothing else mattering.

His hands are polite at first, and so are his hips, but she can feel every little stuttered jerk as he tries not to fuck his way down her throat. Then she rolls her eyes up to look at him, and his eyes meet hers, and it's like something snaps inside his head. His hand drops onto her hair, fingers digging in, and those last points of almost pain bring her to where she wants to be.

"Jesus," Damon breathes. "Jesus, fuck, *fuck*, that mouth on you."

Kara hums around him. His hips buck, and she has to pull back just enough not to get his growing knot in her mouth. He's close—she can feel it, that pressure and shift and sound—and she closes her hand around his knot, and he comes.

She swallows what she can, then spits the rest of it out onto the driveway, which she should probably feel worse about than she does.

Her jaw aches, but it's a good ache, the kind that she hasn't had in too long. She grins at the sight of her lipstick in a blurry ring around his cock, even though it means her face no doubt looks a mess.

Getting back to her feet is a little harder, especially in her heels, and she can feel the gritty scratchy pain in her knees that was so easy to ignore when she was blowing him.

Damon, when she rises up to look him in the eye, looks a little shellshocked. She can't help but grin and brush her cum-covered lips against his and say, "Did I break your brain?"

"In the best way." He licks his lips. "I think I want you in a bed when I return the favor."

"That would probably be the best for everyone's knees," Kara agrees. She's absolutely soaked through her panties, and her clit is throbbing like a second heart, but getting him off took enough of the edge off that she doesn't feel so frantic now, like she'd die if she didn't get her mouth on him right fucking now.

She helps tuck him back in his pants and zip him up, enjoying his shudder as her fingers brush against his half-soft knot. It didn't try to lock on anything, but knots always come down slower than everything else.

The car door is still open, she realizes when he leans over to close it, and she thinks she should feel embarrassed that they didn't get further than getting out of the car before going at it. But it was hot, there's nobody around to judge them and being a courted Omega should have some privileges.

When they get into the house, Jason, Eric and Ry are all standing in the entryway like they've been watching everything that just went down.

She asks, "Is now when I apologize?"

"Are you apologizing for protecting yourself?" Jason asks, striding toward her. The outline of his cock is tenting his pants. "Or for getting off an Alpha who's courting you?"

"Either," Kara says, even as she moves toward him, pulled inexorably toward the heat of him. "Both? I'm not sure."

He stops in front of her, lifting a hand up to smear his thumb across her lips. It comes off pink with lipstick and cum. "You have nothing you need to apologize for, though if you want make it up to us, you can let us fuck you until you don't smell of anything but pleasure and us."

"I won't say no to that."

"In a bed," Damon adds. "I promised her a bed."

"We do have one of those." Jason leans down and swoops Kara off her feet, striding toward the stairs. She holds on, swallowing down a shriek. Quieter, he says, "You don't need to say yes if this is just an apology."

"I'm so horny we didn't even get the door closed before I was getting Damon off," Kara says, and grins when he almost stumbles and she has to clutch onto his shoulders even harder. "Are you going to keep make me deal with it myself?"

"Never, sweetheart. You can come to us every time you want to get off."

"Maybe I will."

Jason gets them up the stairs and to the room with the massive set bed. Then she's bouncing down onto it, kicking off her shoes somewhere as Jason climbs on top of her.

He's big over her like this, pushing up her dress so he can follow its path with his mouth, trailing wet kisses up her thighs, her stomach. "You want it slow, sweetheart?" he asks against her stomach. "You want us to take our time with you? Or are you looking for something a little rougher? Want some teeth with it?"

"Whatever you do," Kara says, reaching down to pull him up over her, "I want you to get on with it."

"We can do that," Damon says from one side of her. He's stripped off his shirt while she's been distracted by Jason, and now he's climbing over toward her on the bed. "Let's get this dress off of you, and then we can have some fun."

"There's a zipper," she blurts out before one of them can try to get it up over her head. She sits halfway up, and there's another set of hands on her back, and Ry eases the zipper down.

Jason helps her shimmy out of the dress, leaving her in just a cute pair of lace panties and a push-up bra that has her breasts spilling up against her chest. She strips her bra off too, freeing breasts that ache to be touched. She feels good like this, wanted, and all of her thoughts and all of her fears are somewhere too far away to worry about now.

"Gorgeous," Eric breathes, from somewhere near Ry.

Damon helps settle Kara's head back onto his lap. "Our Omega asked us to get on with it," he says. "I think we should do what she asks."

"It would be my pleasure." Jason pushes the crotch of her panties aside, and his long fingers are sliding against her clit. She bucks up against his hand. He settles into a rhythm, two fingers pushing inside of her, opening her up, while his thumb plays with her clit, and it feels so good, so achingly good.

Then Eric's mouth closes over one of her nipples, and his fingers close over the other. There's so much sensation everywhere that it's overwhelming in the best way.

She doesn't realize she's shut her eyes until Damon slides a hand against her cheek and says, "Eyes open, baby. I want to see the pleasure that our set is giving you."

Kara pries her eyes open with effort, and he is right there, his gaze holding hers like a magnet. His pupils are blown wide.

Jason's mouth replaces his fingers, and everything flees her mind but sensation. It's all she can do to keep her eyes open.

Pleasure rises in her, an ocean swelling around her, and she writhes, clutching onto the sheets and chasing that pleasure until it threatens to overwhelm her. There are hands everywhere, four or six or eight, and all she can see are Damon's eyes watching her.

But it's not enough to tip her over that peak, and she pushes Jason's head back and lurches upright and says, "If I don't get one of your knots in me right the fuck now I'm going to die."

Eric's hands are the ones that reach for her, and she clambers over onto him, pushing him back so she can straddle him. His hands settle on her hips, and he grins up at her. "I like this view," he tells her.

He's a sight underneath her, long limbs and smooth skin with wiry hair running down his chest, and she takes a moment to drag her nails up his chest. Little lines of pink follow her fingers, and he shudders under her touch.

"Fuck," Eric groans. "Fuck, baby, you feel so good."

"It's about to feel ever better," Kara says, and she sinks down onto him. Both of them groan.

He's almost too thick for her, even soaked as she is with slick, but she sets her teeth in her lip and lowers herself down on him until she's resting just on top of his knot.

"Look at her," Ry breathes behind her.

Eric's hips buck under her, almost pushing his knot into her, and she moves with him, holding on to his hips.

She starts to ride him—slowly at first, then faster, until he's swearing and gasping and begging and she can barely catch her breath. He's not the longest that she's ever had, or the thickest, but that means that she can take in all of him, teasing the top of his knot with every move.

She loses herself in it, in the movement and the heat and Eric pushing up into her, meeting her rhythm, hitting all the right places, and someone drapes themselves over her back, tugging at her nipples until they're aching with pleasure.

"You're so gorgeous," Jason breathes into her ear. "Look at you, riding him. Look at you." He slides his hand between them, playing with her clit, and just like that, she comes.

It's like fireworks going off, and she sags back against Jason even as she keeps riding Eric, thighs burning. His knot is growing, and he gasps out, "Can I knot you?"

Kara nods, and Eric flips her so they're on their sides. His knot slides into her, and he comes, and it locks.

It's a shock, the sensation, and Kara breathes through it, through the feeling of intense fullness. She leans her forehead against his chest, sweaty skin against sweaty skin, and breathes.

"You good?" Eric gasps out. "You okay?"

Kara nods. It doesn't hurt, and now it's starting to feel good, hitting all those nerves that Omegas have to make this pleasurable. It won't help her get pregnant, the way evolution intended, but it's like someone being part of her, an Alpha being part of her, the way Omegas and Alphas should be.

A body slides in behind her, Damon's scent filling her nose as he slides a hand against her stomach. "You're taking his knot so well," he breathes in her ear. "Our beautiful Omega, taking her Alpha's knot so well."

Kara grabs his hand, then slides it down, down to her clit. He starts circling it, gently at first, featherlight touches to oversensitive nerves, building that pleasure back up inside her.

Eric tips her head back, leans down to press a kiss to her nose, her cheek, her lips, opening her lips until his tongue is fucking her mouth, wet and hot, and heat rises up in her again, her hips rolling against his as much as they can with that knot caught inside of her.

"There you go," Ry says. "Ride his knot, Kara."

Pleasure rises in her, washes over her in waves and waves, and she presses against her Alphas as it carries her away.

Chapter Eleven

Kara wakes to a hand between her legs. It's not moving there, not playing with her, just laying heavy, high against the inside of her thigh, brushing up against her curls. The entire room smells of slick and sex.

"I need a shower," she rasps out. She's not even sure how to get out with so many people around her, other than climbing all the way down the bottom of the bed.

The hand curls around her thigh, then lets go. Damon says, "I'll wash your back if you want."

"I do like conserving water," Kara says with a grin, rolling over so she's on top of him. She tries to keep most of her weight off of him, but he tugs her down on top of him, wrapping his arms around her back. "I'm pretty sore, though."

Damon drops a kiss on her forehead, then says, "We don't have to do anything but shower."

"Stealing our Omega away to the shower?" Ry asks from the other side of the bed. "Keeping her all to yourself?"

"Last night was *my* date," Damon reminds them. He rolls them both over, picking her up in his arms until she squirms to be put down. "I should at least get a shower with her before you all descend on her like locusts."

"I'll start on breakfast," Ry says. "Anything you want?"

"Waffles," Eric mumbles. He's face-down on the bed, head buried in a pillow.

"I was asking our Omega." Ry climbs off the other side of the bed, stretching. The muscles in his back shift and move as he does, but Kara can see that he's thin—too thin. Then he turns and smiles at her, and she forgets about how thin he is. "Anything you want me to make for you?"

"Waffles sound good," Kara admits. "If they're not too much trouble."

"As our Omega asks," Ry says with a wink.

* * * *

Kara has to head back home that afternoon, if reluctantly—she wasn't planning on spending the night, and she has household crap to deal with. But she goes back full of waffles and a promise to come back for her date with Ry.

She's barely in the door when her phone chimes with a text

From Damon: *Thank you for the date <3*
From Damon: *I know Ry's date is next but I want to see you again soon*
From Damon: *I realize I text like an old person*
From Damon: *Please forgive me*

To Damon: *that definitely doesn't make you sound less old*

To Damon: *I had fun too*

To Damon: *thank you for coming after me when I was being a coward*

Her phone rings, and as soon as she picks up, Damon says, "You weren't being a coward."

"Hello to you too."

"Yes, hi, thank you for picking up, I'm glad to hear your voice again. Protecting yourself isn't the same as being a coward."

Kara flops down on her bed, staring up at the ceiling. "I just don't want my reaction to everything to be running away. I don't want to be that person."

Damon is silent for a moment, and she waits, listening to him breathe. Finally, he asks, "Is it that you think we don't want you? Or that we'll hurt you anyway?"

"Both," Kara says, then, "neither. I don't know. I get that you want me now, but it's just because of Ry. Because you need someone who can't go into heat. But if you change your mind, I won't have any protections. I won't even have a bond to prove that I'm with you."

"Is it legal protections, then?"

"Legal protections aren't nothing," she says, maybe louder than she should. "And social protection. An Omega that's thrown away by her Alphas? Who would want to work with me? Who would want to employ me? Who would want to *be* with me?" Kara realizes, humiliatingly, that she's crying now, all of the good feelings from the night before and the morning tipping over into just *feeling*. "I'm sorry. I'm so sorry. I'm trying not to—I don't want to be like this. I spent the last few years thinking I wasn't going to be scared like this, because no Alpha was ever going to want me, and then you showed up and gave me hope. And now I keep crying."

With that embarrassing rant, she buries her face in her knees and tries to make it less obvious that she is losing her shit because she is having every feeling all at once like a fucking hormonal teenager.

"Oh, baby." Damon lets out a low Alpha croon, the kind that's meant to soothe Omegas and children, and she calms just a little. She's heard it's most effective when they're in person, but she's never had an Alpha croon to her like this before. "Oh, baby, listen to me, please. We like you for *you*—not for Ry, not because you can't go into heats, but because you're gorgeous and smart and someone we could see ourselves being with. Please don't cry. I don't know what to do when you're crying and I can't even hold you."

"I'm sorry," she gasps out.

"Fuck, don't apologize."

There's a choked-off noise from somewhere beyond the microphone, then the tenor of the background noise changes. Eric says, "Hey, baby, I'm sorry our fearless leader is so useless."

Damon makes an offended noise, and Kara laughs through her tears. "It's the rich people thing."

"Oh my God, it is." Eric lets out a low croon too, so deep Kara can almost feel it in her chest. "Did he make you cry?"

"I made myself cry." Kara shakes her head, leaning back against the headboard of her bed. "I'm sorry, I'm being ridiculous."

"Do you want someone with you?" Eric asks. He's speaking over the crooning, somehow, like they're coming from different parts of his chest. "Someone can be over there soon."

Humiliation burns through her, because she's being ridiculous. They don't need her crying to them about how she's afraid they're going to leave her. That is not how to get Alphas to be into her. "You really don't need to do that."

"I didn't ask if we needed to," Eric says. "I asked if you wanted us to. You're allowed to want things from us, even if we go out of our way for them."

She does want that—she wants to be back in their arms, with someone telling her it's going to be okay. She's so tired of being scared, and she's even more tired of being scared alone.

So she says, "Yes. Please."

"Good," Eric says, sounding like he's smiling. "Because Ry and Jason are already on their way, and otherwise they were just going to awkwardly sit outside of your apartment being protective and weirding out your neighbors. Can you keep breathing for me?"

"I'm breathing."

"Thank you," Eric says. "And it's okay if you want to cry, no matter what the idiot whose phone I'm using said. Crying is a good cathartic release."

"I feel so stupid. We had such a good day, and then I lost my shit, and now you need to come here and deal with me."

"We didn't need to do it," Eric reminds her.

"And by we, you mean Jason and Ry."

Eric laughs. "It's a set, baby—everything is *we*, unless I don't want to do it, and then it's them."

"Like cooking," Damon adds. He sounds like he's gotten over her crying, which is a relief. "Cooking is never a 'we' activity with Eric."

"That's because you're such a good cook, darling." There's a wet noise, like Eric planted a sloppy kiss on

Damon. "That was our main criteria for agreeing to join a set—had to be able to cook like a fucking dream, to make up for the fact that neither of us can boil water for shit."

Damon laughs. "Oh, is that what it was? I thought it was my stunning good looks."

"Glasses *are* sexy. But alas, we had to settle for a couple of straight men."

"The horror," Kara murmurs.

"I know," Eric says in a commiserating voice. "I give great head, and he's never taken me up on the offer. At least Ry went through his bicurious period before he decided he was also straight."

As Eric and Damon tease each other, Kara relaxes back against her headboard. She has a dehydration headache brewing now, and her nose is all stuffed up, but they're being so normal about her crying that she's feeling less stupid now.

She's not *wrong* to be scared. She just wishes she could keep her shit together.

"Thank you," she blurts out, cutting Damon off. "For all of this. Thank you."

"Of course, Omega," Damon says gently.

There's a knock on her door, and she clambers out of bed, saying, "They're here. Or my landlord wants to check my smoke detector. One or the other."

"Call us any time," Eric puts in. Then, just before he hangs up, he says, "I adore you."

Then he's gone, and there's another knock and Kara has to put that away so she doesn't start crying again.

Jason and Ry are both right outside the doorway when she opens the door, both of them sort of staring at her. She stares back, and they're all just standing there, staring at each other.

Neither of them makes any move toward her, though they're both nearly vibrating with tension.

"Are we just going to, uh." Kara swallows. "Stand here?"

"It's your apartment," Ry says. His hands are clenched into fists, but as soon as he sees her notice them, he stuffs them in his pockets. "It's where your nest is. It's your prerogative to tell us whether we can enter."

"Right." Nobody ever tries to come in here except her Beta landlord, and she can deal with that, so she forgets sometimes that she would absolutely lose her shit — again — if an Alpha came in without permission.

She steps back, saying, "Please, come in."

Almost before the words are out of her mouth, they're inside her apartment, Jason closing the door as Ry crowds her against the wall. It's claustrophobic for one half-second, then a croon starts in the base of Ry's chest and all of the tension runs out of her.

"You're okay," Ry croons. "You're okay, Omega."

Jason crowds near too, his hand sliding over her hip as his head tilts down over her. And she feels *safe* here, between them, hidden by them. Shielded by them.

Despite all of that, tears start trickling out from the corners of her eyes.

"Why are you crying?" Jason asks. He brushes a tear from her cheek.

The absolute last thing she wants to do is talk about it more, so she just shakes her head, curling forward against Ry's chest. He holds her to him, letting his croon run through her and his scent of *safe safe safe* fill her up.

* * * *

"What do you all feel about cookies?"

"Oatmeal raisin is a true betrayal of mankind," Jason says promptly. He's sprawled out on her couch with her pulled on top of him. Ry is curled up on the floor with his head tucked up against her so she can run her fingers through his hair. "Any other questions?"

Kara laughs. "Do you *like* cookies? That's the plural you, not the singular, though I guess I also want to know the answer to the singular you version of the question."

"Ry doesn't have much of a sweet tooth," Jason tells her, leaning over to nudge Ry in the shoulder. "But that just means that I can eat his cookies for him."

"Wonderful." Kara starts to sit up, then shrieks when Jason tugs her back onto his lap. "I'm trying to go make you some cookies."

"I'd rather cuddles than cookies," Jason says with a pout.

Kara pulls herself up again, and this time Jason lets her, even as he dramatically sticks out his lower lip. Ry unfolds himself, offering her a hand to help her get off the couch with something resembling the same level of grace. "I want to do something for you all," she tells them. "And as you can tell from my apartment, I'm a shit housekeeper, and you all are rich anyway. But I make a hell of a shortbread cookie."

"You don't have to—"

"Let me make you the damn cookies," Kara says, half-laughing, half genuinely irritated.

"Yeah, Jason," Ry says, wrapping his arm around Kara's waist and tugging her the short distance into her kitchen. "Let her make the damn cookies."

Jason snorts, twisting on the couch so he can look at them. "I've been banned from the kitchen out of fear that I will injure myself or others, so you will have to carry on without me."

"However will we survive?" Ry murmurs, and Kara laughs.

"I heard that!"

"I'm definitely not a baker," Ry tells her, ignoring Jason's shout. "But let me know how you'd like me to help."

"Maybe measure the flour? There's like five ingredients so it's not that complicated."

"Of course."

He stays out of her way as she gets all of the ingredients and materials out. When she looks over at him, he's smiling.

"I'm going to be creaming the butter by hand," she says as she sticks some sort-of-softened butter in a bowl with a half-cup of sugar. "So please don't judge me for my weakling arms."

"That sounds so horny," Jason comments from his spot on the couch.

Ry rolls his eyes. "Somehow I'm in a set with a child."

"Come on," Jason says. "Tell me you didn't have at least one horny thought when you heard her talk about creaming."

Kara's face is burning, but she can't manage to fight down a smile. He sounds so casual here, and there's something that feels good about that. A relationship that's all emotion and fire isn't going to make her happy, not for long. She wants to be with people who she likes as people.

Loud enough that she knows Jason will be able to hear her, she asks, "Is he always like this?"

"The number of times we have walked in on Eric and Jason going at it in...basically every room in the house is frankly horrifying." Ry grins at her. "You know what you'll have to look forward to."

"Feel free to join us at any time," Jason says. "If we're having sex out and about, it means that all comers are welcome. Pun very much intended."

That is...not unappealing, actually.

Ry groans. "If the room smells like sugar *and* like her arousal, I'm not going to be able to resist."

There's a weird pause there, a half-beat too long of silence, then Jason says, "No fucking in the kitchen. It's a set rule."

"Is the kitchen sacrosanct?" Kara asks as she squishes some sugar into butter.

"The kitchen requires a certain level of cleanliness that is not conducive to sex," Ry says dryly. "It was a rule we had to set early."

"To stop Eric and Jason?"

"Damon, actually," Ry tells her. "Back during his, uh...what does he call it?"

Jason offers, "His promiscuous phase?"

"I told him he was allowed to bring home whoever he wanted, but I was not going to live with him if he kept having sex in the kitchen. In this set, sexual activity in this kitchen is limited to heavy petting with all clothing on. Do you want help with that butter?"

"I'm good," she says, even though her arm is starting to ache. "You can measure out a cup and a half of flour for me, though, and dump it in that other bowl. Oh, and can you preheat my oven to three-fifty?"

Her oven isn't particularly fancy, not like theirs, but it defaults to three-fifty when she turns it on, so it's pretty idiot-proof to set. She had an oven in an old apartment that had a knob *and* buttons *and* no display. Three months into living there she gave up hope of ever using it successfully.

"Why shortbread?" he asks as he's measuring out flour for her. "I feel like chocolate chip cookies are the default for people who have a standard cookie that they make."

The butter is mostly creamed, so she starts adding the rest of the ingredients. "My college friend Sue Ann has an irrational hatred of chocolate, and dried fruit doesn't belong in cookies, so...shortbread. I ship her shortbread every year for her birthday now."

"Where is she?"

"Tennessee." Everything's mixed now, so she gets it out onto a piece of plastic, squishes it into a rectangle and sticks it in her fridge. "We can go back to cuddling once I get this all cleaned up."

"Nope," Jason says, popping up off the couch. "Cleaning is the one thing I can be trusted with in the kitchen. You go cuddle with Ry." He heads over to press a kiss to her lips, then pushes her gently back toward the couch.

"I see you offering up my body to our Omega," Ry says, knocking good-naturedly against Jason as he heads over to wrap his arm around her waist. "So, shall we cuddle?"

"Let's."

Chapter Twelve

For Ry's date, he has her come to the house.

The *house*. It's so much more than a house it feels ridiculous to even call it that. The mansion. The estate.

He doesn't give her any clue why, though, or whether they're planning on going somewhere else after. Maybe he knows they'll just end up back there anyway.

It doesn't look like anyone else is around when she gets there, at least based on the fact that the driveway in front of the house is empty, but it's so big that it feels like they could all be somewhere else on the property and she would never know. It's the start of summer, and she always has to remind herself that just because her schedule changes dramatically when the semester ends, it doesn't mean everyone else doesn't have their own normal work schedule.

Ry greets her at the door as her Uber driver heads off, scenting her wrist before herding her into the house and shutting the door behind them.

"The rest of them," Ry says as he leads her into a room she hasn't been in before, "are kind of idiots." He's in a loose pair of pants that look like linen with a light gray button-down shirt, and it's almost enough to keep him from looking washed out.

He's wearing a scent blocker, not strong enough to cover everything but stronger than she would expect for a date. Alphas—and Omegas, she won't pretend that they're much better—want to get their scent all over those things that they think are theirs, and scent blockers keep that from happening.

She wonders what he doesn't want her to smell.

"How exactly are they idiots?" Kara asks.

He steps away from her once they're in the room that they seem to be going to, some sort of dining-room-cum-conference-room, leaning back against the wall. "Everyone else is seeing this courting as a time to convince you to fall in love with us."

Kara's eyebrows go up. "And you don't want that?"

"I would love that," Ry says, but he's not quite smiling. His eyes are very keen. "But the goal of courting—what it always has been, what it always should be ultimately—is for us to convince you that you will be safe and taken care of with us. They forget, I think, how vulnerable you are and how vulnerable you make yourself by agreeing to join our set."

"And you don't?"

Ry shoves his hands in his pockets, glancing away for the first time. He looks tired, his lips pale. "My dad is an Omega, and the way my father treated him..." He meets her eye, and she couldn't look away if she wanted to. There's something hypnotic about the intensity of his gaze. "It's important to me that you know that this relationship will be stable and *safe* for you, if you agree to the marriage."

That sounds so much more pragmatic than Alphas usually seem to be — because they don't need to be. To Ry's point, they don't need to think about this, because Alphas will always come out on top. If this falls apart or if they decide they don't want her, they would face very few consequences. Fewer still because they wouldn't be bonded and so wouldn't need to go through the discomfort of breaking a bond or a scarred reminder to every future lover that they are broken-bonded.

But still she has to say, "You didn't want to do this in the first place."

Ry's expression twists. "I wanted to court you, desperately, from the first moment I heard about you. You may be my only chance to have a relationship with an Omega that is equal to that of my set. For most of my life, I never *dreamed* of that. But the thought of the set basing their decisions around just me... I am sorry for how I treated you when we first met. And I understand if you would prefer to keep your distance until I convince you that I mean it."

"I'm not looking for distance," Kara says, then gives in and walks over to him to press a hand to his chest and kiss him.

Ry hesitates for just a second — just long enough to convince her that she's fucked up — then he drags her against him, opening his mouth to drag her lip between his teeth. A spark of pure need runs down her spine.

His teeth run against her inner lip again, then his tongue. He turns them to press her back against the wall. She realizes her eyes are closed when his kisses turn slow, drugging. It's like he's stealing her breath, breathing her in and taking her into him until he's the only thing in the world.

One hand slides up her thigh, hitching her leg up against his, and his hips grind against hers as he pins her to the wall. He's half-hard already, she can feel it, the length of him pressing almost where she wants it, where she *needs* it.

She winds her arms around his neck and pulls him closer.

Then he lets out a low, hurt sound and pulls away, letting her thigh slide back down to the floor. He doesn't go far, just far enough that every line of his body isn't pressed against every curve of hers, but she can feel the rush of cold air between them.

He's breathing hard.

"Sorry," he breathes out. "I didn't mean—I'm sorry."

A wave of humiliation washes through her like acid, and she ducks out from under his arms to get away. She doesn't need him to remind her that he's not interested in her like that, no matter what he says.

"You don't need to force yourself," Kara says stiffly. She wants to wrap her arms around herself and hold on, but she doesn't let herself. "I'm a big girl."

"I'm not—*damn it.*" Ry shoves a hand against the wall. He's breathing hard still, but suddenly it sounds less like arousal and a lot more like something worse.

Kara opens her mouth to ask if he's okay—then closes it again when there's a knock behind her. She turns to see a woman standing in the doorway, politely pretending to not look at them.

The woman is a Beta, maybe early thirties, in a sleek shirt tucked into a pair of wide-legged pants, a leather folder under one arm. Her curly hair is scraped up into a high ponytail.

"Shannon," Ry says with relief.

"Sorry to interrupt," Shannon says. She has a light Irish accent and a surprisingly deep, pleasant voice. "I can come back."

"No, no, come in." Ry moves toward Kara but doesn't touch her. "Kara, this is Shannon, the set's personal assistant. Shannon, Kara Igan."

"It's lovely to meet you, ma'am," Shannon says, strolling forward to offer Kara a firm handshake. It's not very common for Betas to shake Omegas' hands, but she appreciates that Shannon doesn't even hesitate.

"You too." Kara offers her a smile that feels awkward on her face. She's not sure what's going on here. "Thanks for the clothes, before."

"Of course."

"I wanted to take this chance to talk you through how you can fit in this household," Ry tells Kara. He herds them both over toward the table, keeping an odd distance that she doesn't understand and doesn't know whether to be offended by.

He was fine cuddling her in her apartment—but they haven't touched sexually, she realizes, not at all that she can remember. He's the only one she's never had inside of her, the only one she's never even seen undressed.

Kara wants to ask him what the hell is wrong with her that he's unwilling to touch her, but not here with this gorgeous Beta standing there, watching them.

Nobody sits, and she realizes that they're both waiting for her like the polite Alpha and Beta that they are.

She sits.

Ry sits next to her, his thigh barely brushing hers, and Shannon sits across from her.

"Mr. Jonas asked me to walk you through the basics of how the household functions and some of the major assets that the set owns, so you can discuss how you can fit in upon your marriage."

That's very pragmatic, and it makes something unclench inside of her, because they're treating her like a potential equal member of the set.

"I'm almost afraid to ask," Kara admits. "The amount of money you have is…staggering."

"I'll start with the basics," Shannon says. She opens up the leather folder, flipping to a page with a mess of information on it. She turns it to face Kara. "Given the structure of the set, wealth is distributed in a couple ways. Obviously some amount of wealth is held in physical assets, but in terms of stocks, bonds and liquid assets, the set follows a mixed centralized-decentralized model. That means that approximately fifty percent of the wealth is held in set accounts, which are used to do things like pay staff and maintain the set's physical assets. The other half is distributed across individual accounts, which can be used for anything that member of the set wants. Obviously, real estate or other asset purchases can be done with personal accounts, but those are generally handled through the set accounts."

"You're funding medical research through yours, right?" She remembers Ry mentioning at some point that he was doing that.

He nods. "I am."

"And this is—" Kara swallows. She feels crass to even ask this. "Is the plan that I would also have one of those accounts?"

"Of course," Ry says, sounding surprised that she would even ask that. "That's the point of this conversation, so you understand that you would have this safety once we're married. We can talk about how much you'd want—I keep mine at between two-fifty and four hundred, because most of my expenditures are more on the set side than on the personal side. Eric and Jason are both in the one to two range, I think, and Damon keeps his at somewhere like seven because he's an ostentatious asshole."

Kara has to close her eyes, overwhelmed by all of this. "When you're saying one to two, you mean—"

"Billion."

"Okay." Kara breathes out, slowly, then has to do it again. This is so far from what she knows how to deal with. "And when you're talking about—about us talking about how much I'd want, you're talking about…"

"We'd start you off with at least half a billion, and we can talk logistics if you want more." Ry hesitates, then says, "I want you to have enough money that you feel like you can leave us if you need to and never need to worry about anything else for the rest of your life."

"Why?" Kara asks hoarsely.

"Because if you're going to be with us, I want you to be here because you want to be, not because of the money. And let's be clear—if you left us the moment that account was in your name, the loss of the money wouldn't matter to me at all. It would hurt, because we would be losing you, but it wouldn't hurt because we lost the money. But if we get married and then you stay because you feel trapped, that is a worst-case scenario for me. I watched my dad waste away in a relationship that he had no way to leave because nobody would hire a broken-bonded Omega and he knew it. I refuse to watch that happen to you." He touches the back of her hand. "We intend to be good husbands to you, good Alphas, but none of us are perfect.

"And just as importantly, it's what we all have. What kind of a relationship would it be if we gave you less than we gave each other? What kind of Alphas would we be?"

Five hundred million dollars is an incomprehensibly large amount of money, so large her brain just jumps over it like a skipping record when she tries to think too hard about it, so she just...moves past that for the moment to ask, "And for my role in the household?"

Kindly, both of them let it go.

Ry says, "I know it's traditionally an Omega's role to manage the household. A lot of that is already handled by our staff, but I do the majority of the household oversight for the set, given that I'm the one without a full-time job. If you'd like, I can keep doing what I do, and you don't need to take over any of it. But if you do want to, or at least might want to, I wanted to give you a chance to see what that looks like."

Kara can't imagine wanting to take over what is no doubt a big job, no matter how many times Ry has referred to himself as a house-Alpha, but the Omega part of her also can't imagine doing nothing. It's an instinct, like nesting—it *is* nesting, really, just on a bigger scale, to make the home be *just so*.

Kara says, "I'd like to be involved, I think."

So Shannon walks her through the mindboggling number of staff and *stuff* that they have, all of which a house manager—whoever that might be—manages. Then Ry's job, apparently, is to make the big decisions about all of it, of which there seem to be a lot.

The biggest decision Kara's ever made, other than getting her PhD, was to live alone. This, all of this, seems to be on a whole other level.

But there's something deeply reassuring about doing this, not about the set trusting her enough to walk her through this, but them starting to treat her like she might one day become a real member of the set.

It's so much, though, and by the time Shannon steps away to make them all coffee, Kara's head is spinning.

"I know it's a lot," Ry says apologetically. "It's probably too much to be throwing at you all at once."

"I'm definitely going to need to hear all of this again...more than once." Kara turns in her chair to look at him, taking one of his hands in hers. His hands are a little cold, and the lack of scent is still throwing her off, but she ignores both of those to say, "I appreciate this. If we do get married, I need to be a full member of the relationship, not just someone to be spoiled and, I don't know, kept in style. I'm a fully grown adult."

Ry glances down at their clasped hands, curling his fingers around hers. "Believe me, none of us think you're anything but that."

"Alpha always seem to think Omegas are basically children," she says bitterly, unfairly.

"I'd blame it on our rugged Alpha biology, but the truth is that most of us are raised to be assholes. And the fact that we can force Omegas doesn't help. But just like Omegas want to nest, Alphas want to —"

"Control their Omegas?" Kara offers.

Ry snorts out a laugh. "I was going to say, 'give their Omegas what they need.' Or, more accurately, what we think they need. Our instinct is always going to be to spoil you. So if we start acting like assholes, please just tell us."

Shannon steps back into the room carrying three mugs of coffee. She sets one in front of each of them, not spilling a drop, with grace that a barista would envy. "If you'd like," she says as she walks back to her own seat, "I am happy to connect you with the house manager to discuss anything that you have additional questions on."

"I'm good for now," Kara says.

"Do you have an accountant?"

Kara squints at her. "I...don't have enough money to have an accountant."

Shannon glances at Ry, then says, "I'll schedule time for you to meet with one of the set's accountants."

"I really don't need an accountant."

"Do you enjoy doing your own taxes?" Shannon asks dryly.

Kara laughs. "Point taken. Thank you."

Shannon smiles at her. "My job is to make the set's lives easier. If there is anything I can do..." She looks at Ry. "The food will be delivered in an hour."

"Thank you."

"Of course," Shannon says. "Is there anything else I can do for you right now?"

"Just get me the event list for the rest of the season by EOD," Ry says, "so I can bully everyone into picking at least one to go to."

Shannon inclines her head, typing something in her phone. "Will do." She glances at Kara next, and it takes Kara a second to realize that the question is for her, too.

"I'm good," she says quickly, before she ends up with an entire new wardrobe or maybe the world's fanciest hat. Then, remembering a conversation from a couple weeks ago, she asks, "How is, uh...Annabeth? Annamarie?"

Shannon blinks at her, looking startled, then says, "Annamarie is doing well, thank you. My niece is in primary school, and God love her, but every time we see her she manages to give one of us something. But my wife has finally gotten over the cold, so she no longer sounds like Elmer Fudd every time she tries to talk."

"I'm glad."

Shannon's phone lights up, and she says, "If you'll excuse me." Then she's gone, with a flourish of paperwork and a quick nod.

"She seems great," Kara says.

"She is." Ry stands, offering her a hand to pull her up to her feet. "I'm glad that you want to be part of this. We were worried that whoever we would find wouldn't want to…"

"Do things?" Kara offers.

"There's a certain type of person who only goes after rich Alphas, who wants to be—as you put it, spoiled and kept in style. And we'd have been with an Omega like that, but we wouldn't—we wouldn't love her."

Kara freezes, but Ry doesn't seem to expect her to respond, just twirls her in a circle like they're dancing, then pulls her in close so she's enveloped in the circle of his arms.

"The others should be back in half an hour or so," he says, tucking her against his chest. She goes easily, breathing in what little of his scent she can get through the scent blockers. "I was thinking we could walk through the gardens, if you'd like, in the meantime."

"I'd love that." She wants to give him a kiss, but he's been so weird about it that she refrains. They'll have to talk about it, but…not now.

* * * *

"Is she asleep?"

Kara isn't asleep — exactly — but it's so warm where she is, and opening her eyes seems like so much work, so she just stays where she is, in warm sun-drunk haziness, and lets answering be someone else's problem.

"She's sunbathing," Ry says from next to her, voice soft. "Or she was, at least."

"And you managed to get her to sunbathe topless?" Jason asks. There's laughter in his voice, but something hoarse, too.

"I figured you wouldn't mind," she says. Her voice comes out slow, a little sleepy, but she can't bring herself to be bothered. "You've already seen me naked, so I didn't think the sight of my bra would offend you."

"Offend me?" Jason asks. He sounds closer now, and Kara opens her eyes just enough to see him crouching next to her lounge chair, eyes bright. "I'm trying to convince myself not to seduce you right here."

"It's not even that nice a bra," she mumbles. She leans up, and he gives her a kiss, one that goes on and on until she has to pull away, gasping.

"If you think it's the bra I'm thinking about," Jason says with a smile, "then I'm not doing my job right." He strokes a hand against her cheeks, then says, "But I'm here to tell you know the food is here."

Kara hasn't been thinking about food, but the second he mentions it, she realizes she's hungry — really hungry, actually, because she ate a vague brunch around ten-thirty and hasn't eaten since. So she rolls herself upright, letting Jason brace her until she can get her feet under her.

He doesn't let go, and Ry crowds her on the other side, sliding a hand down her back. His scent blocker has almost worn off, probably sweated off, and she closes her eyes against the wave of scent that envelopes her from the two of them. It's almost overwhelming, the two of them so near her with her head still fuzzy from sleep, even with that tinge of bitterness in Ry's scent.

"Dinner," Ry says pointedly.

"Right," Jason says, pulling away a little. "Dinner."

Inside, there's a whole array of food laid out, and unlike the time Damon picked up Chinese food and they ate it sitting on the couch, this looks professionally laid out—roasted lamb and potatoes and some sort of purée all plated nicely, with extra laid out down the middle of the table.

"Wow," Kara says. "Did you let someone come in and lay this all out?"

"They were Betas," Damon says, a little sullenly. "And they were wearing descenter."

"And Damon will only pout about it for a month or so," Eric says, sounding amused.

Damon pulls out a seat for her, and Kara sits and lets him push her in, even if it galls her a little bit to do so. He brushes a hand against her shoulder—clothed again, because she didn't really want to eat dinner shirtless—then heads over to his own seat.

"So," Kara says once they start eating, "now I know about all of your riches and wealth."

"Is that an incentive?" Jason asks. "Or have we scared you away?"

"I mean," Kara says, "I do have questions. Like, why *do* you own so much art?"

"Tax evasion," Damon says promptly.

Kara blinks at Damon. Damon blinks back at her.

Next to her, Jason guffaws with laughter, and she sees a small smile quirk up the corner of Damon's lips.

"We like art," Jason says, "and we like to own shit. I have a security clearance—I'm not allowed to be involved in tax evasion."

"I don't think anyone is allowed to be involved in tax evasion, technically," Kara says, but she's smiling too. "And you own a *Rembrandt*."

To her surprise, Damon's face turns a dull red at that. "I bought it when I made my first billion. It was a stupid purchase. What the hell was I going to do with a Rembrandt?"

"Stick it in the National Gallery, as it turns out," Eric says dryly. "It gets us invited to all of their shindigs."

"Speaking of that," Ry says. "Shannon's going to get me the event schedule for the upcoming event season tonight, and if I have to hunt you all down to agree to go to one of them, I'm going to be pissed."

"What kind of events are we looking at?" Eric asks.

"Did you miss the part where I'm getting the list tonight? But I'm going to send it around, you're all going to look at it and we're going to pick at least one without you all being children about it," Ry says. He looks at Kara. "We'd love if you would come to one, too, if you'd like."

That feels like an odd thought—but it's appropriate, for an Omega being courted by an Alpha or Alpha set. It's what courting used to be for, in some ways, for showing off a set's Omega to society and letting everyone know what a great pick the Alphas have made.

And she'd like to be seen out with them, for people to know that they're with her, so she says, "I'd be happy to."

"And this," Eric says, "is why I won't be a child about picking an event to go to. Anything to spend more time with our Omega."

"Aww," Kara says, clasping her hands under her chin and tilting her head like she's in a beauty pageant or an old-timey movie. Eric blows her a kiss.

The food, when she gets a chance to start eating it, is amazing, the sort of thing that's like it has all the fancy technique of coming from a fancy restaurant while having all the hominess of a home-cooked meal. And it tastes fantastic, too.

"This is," she says around a mouthful of potato, "so good."

"I'll have Shannon add it to the list," Ry says.

"Where did you get it from?"

Ry explains, "We have a private chef we use sometimes. Mostly for the times when we're hosting, but we use them for dinner too, sometimes."

"Well, they are awesome. A-plus."

"Should we be jealous?" Damon asks with a laugh.

"Only if you want to be a professional chef."

"Damn."

Kara grins at him, taking another pointed bite of the food, and he smiles back.

Something shifts in his expression, goes soft, goes wondering, and even before he says anything, Kara's heart starts pounding in her chest.

"There are many points to a courting," Damon says slowly, like he's trying to figure out what words to say even as he's saying them. Kara's throat feels very tight. "It is for compatibility, for trust, for building a relationship. But one piece of it is for Alphas to prove that we are able to provide for our Omega."

Kara has a thought of where this may be going, or almost a thought, but she can't let herself think about it too hard in case she's wrong, in case she's reading too far into this.

"We have built a nest for you," he continues, and Kara sucks in a breath. Building a nest for an Omega — that is one of the most intimate things an Alpha can do, more intimate than sex, more intimate than knotting. A nest is a place that is an Omega's alone, the one thing that even in the most traditional households belongs to the Omega. Once an Omega has claimed it, it's theirs.

So to build a nest for an Omega is to say that an Alpha thinks that they know them, in those deepest ways.

"We would be honored if you would consent to share this house with us," Damon finishes, "to allow us to continue to prove to us through this courting that we can provide you with what you need. And we would be honored if you would consider the use of the nest that we have built for you, in whole or in part."

It's hard to forget, sometimes, that Damon is from such a traditional background, but it's never been more evident than just now, listening to him ask her to move in like she's a second-heat Omega in a historical novel.

"You can see the nest before you say yes," Jason says, and he sounds nervous enough that she realizes that her startled silence has been taken as rejection. "We can — I mean, you should finish eating. But after that."

"I would love to see the nest you built me," Kara says honestly, in a bit of an understatement. Her heart is pounding so hard she can feel it in her throat. "I would love —" She swallows, feeling like her throat is closing up. She never thought that they would get to this point in the courting, despite everything they've said about how much they want this.

Because there's saying it, and there's building her a nest and asking her to move in.

"Kara?"

She's crying, she realizes, hot tears running down her face. They *want* her.

They want her.

She's not been the sort of Omega that Alphas have wanted for years, and now she's sitting here and they're asking her to move in...asking her as though they expect her to say no.

And there's a part of her, that scared, instinctive part, that wants to say no. Letting go of that little bit of independence, letting go of having her own apartment and her own space and her own fallback, that scares the shit out of her.

If this goes badly—

But if she keeps living like things are going to go badly, she'll never go anywhere. She'll never do anything.

"You are allowed to say no," Ry says. "It won't end the courtship."

"I'm not saying no," Kara says, which would probably sound more convincing if she managed to say it without snotty gross crying. "Sorry." She wipes off her face, trying to make herself look at least a little bit presentable. "God. Sorry. You ask me to move in, and I become a mess." She takes a breath and lets the excitement that she's been suppressing fill her. "Can I see the nest?"

"Of course," Damon says. He sounds excited too, now, like he's managed to get past the formality and tradition. He stands, and Kara does too, following him out of the room. They're leaving the food behind half-eaten, but now that she knows that there's a nest for her, that's all she wants to see. To claim it — or to reject it, if it's not good enough.

She doesn't want to hurt their feelings, but claiming a bad nest is something that no Omega will do.

She hopes it's a good one.

"We weren't sure if you wanted a separate bedroom from your nest," Damon explains as he leads her up the stairs, "so we have both." He's walking a little too fast now, and she has to hurry to keep up. She can smell his excitement, that Alpha urgency.

Up the stairs is a hallway that leads in both directions, then branches off. The room with the set bed that they slept in that first night is to the left, and Damon leads her in that direction, but he passes that room and heads to one farther down the hallway. A more defensible part of the building, in some old traditional ways of thinking.

The door that Damon stops at is one that looks like all the rest, that beautiful dark wood with a delicate grain pattern. He doesn't open the door, though, just says, "Your nest, Omega."

"You don't want to show it to me?"

"It's your nest," Ry says from behind her. When she turns, he's leaning back against the hallway wall, watching her with a small smile on his face. "And the door swings in."

So if he opens it his hand will cross over the boundary into the room.

Kara's heart is pounding.

She turns the knob. The door swings open smoothly.

Inside is the most gorgeous nest Kara has ever seen in her life. There's a king bed pushed up against the back wall, with lush sheets and a blanket that looks so soft she wants to touch it.

But on top of it are piles and piles of pillows, arranged around the entire bed like walls on top of walls. Safe.

Kara walks in, feeling the plushness of the rug underneath her feet. To one side is a bathroom, door half-open, and in another direction is a door that probably leads to a closet, but all she can look at is the bed.

She heads over toward it, trailing her fingers over the edge. The top blanket feels like some sort of natural fiber, so soft that it's like touching a cloud. The pillows themselves are a mix of all different types, firm pillows like memory foam at the base and softer ones on top, some like regular bed pillows and others like throw pillows with all sorts of covers.

The colors are more muted, as nests usually are, but there are bright pops of color here and there.

It's the best nest Kara has ever seen, bar none — with one exception.

She plucks one of the pillows off of the nest and walks back to the door to hand it to Damon. "Not this one," she says.

He takes it.

When she turns back around, the nest already looks better without it. It was a garish yellow, almost highlighter yellow, but more than that, it unbalanced it, made it too heavy on one side, made it —

Wrong.

Damon clears his throat. "Do you like it?"

"Oh," Kara says, startled. She turns back to look at him. He's still holding the awful yellow pillow. "Yeah, of course."

"Will you claim it, then?" Jason asks from behind Damon. He looks nervous — they all do, and they smell it, too, which she had been too distracted by the nest to notice.

They really think she might say no to them.

She turns back toward the nest again, walking back over so she can open up a passage in it so she can get in. There's a good amount of space inside it, enough for her to fully lie down if she wants to, but instead she just sits in it, crossing her legs in front of her.

"Kara?" Jason asks.

Kara closes her eyes and takes a deep breath — then she lets out the pheromones that Omegas use to claim what is their own. Children...and nests.

It's hers now and everyone knows it. They're going to have to pry it out of her cold, dead fingers if they want it back.

"*Oh*," Damon breathes.

"It's mine," she tells him — tells all of them. "I claimed it, so it's mine now."

"It is yours, Omega," Damon reassures her.

Kara wants to luxuriate in it for a while — it's *so soft* — but she shouldn't actually leave four Alphas standing out in the hallway, so she grudgingly climbs out of it and heads back to her Alphas.

"It's very nice," she tells them, because they still smell a little anxious, and she would like them not to. "Thank you. Please get rid of that pillow."

"Consider it gone," Damon says, and chucks it down the hallway. Kara snorts, then starts laughing. He grins at her, looking more boyish than she's ever seen. "I'm glad you like it."

"We all are," Eric says. "We based it as best as we could off the nest in your bedroom."

"Oh," Kara says with a laugh, moving past Damon to touch Jason's chest. He leans into her. "Is that really why you came to comfort me before? To spy on my nest configuration?"

"You got us," Jason says, grabbing one of her hands to kiss her fingertips. "We didn't care about comforting our crying Omega. We just wanted to get some intel."

"Like any good military Alphas," Eric adds. He moves closer, crowding against her. "We can multitask."

"Personally, right now, I'm multitasking by thinking about food and sex at the same time," Jason says.

"Impressive."

"I do my part." He leans down and kisses her. She kisses him back and everything is good.

Chapter Thirteen

Kara keeps her apartment.

It's partly practical — she doesn't want to move all of her crap here, including the miserable process of disassembling a claimed nest — and partly pragmatic — if this all falls apart, she wants to have somewhere to go back to.

Still, she slots into their home without too much trouble. They give her an office to work out of and set up a car to drive her to and from campus to cover her summer work. There's more than enough space for the stuff she does want to bring with her, and it's big enough for her to have all the room she needs.

As used as she is to living alone, it's hard sometimes to spend that much time with other people, especially this many other people.

But in the evenings, most evenings, she finds herself in the kitchen, working or helping while Ry and sometimes Damon cook. They all eat together as a set more often than not, and afterward sometimes they watch sports or TV shows or documentaries or make out, and sometimes they all go their own ways, and life is…comfortable.

It's the nicest that life has been in a long, long time.

And she *fits* here, with this slightly weird set of Alphas that are nothing like she expected when she first read about them.

Then event season starts.

* * * *

"You want to come out here?"

"No," Kara says, still staring at herself in the mirror. She looks…like an Omega, which she always does, which is silly to think, because she's never been anything else, not since she presented as a teenager. But she's never dressed like an Omega, not by traditional standards, and this is —

This is a high neck, so high it's almost to her chin, and a back that's entirely open. Her bra is one of those bizarre sticky things that she has no idea how she's going to get off, and she's in some overly elaborate lacy pair of panties just because Jason and Eric thought it would be hot. The entire dress falls in a shimmering navy wave down to her feet, the sort of luster that looks expensive.

She doesn't know how expensive it is. They refused to tell her.

She's going to have to train them out of that. She won't be cut out of financial decisions in a relationship she's in.

"Kara?"

"Is someone willing to come in and convince me I don't look ridiculous?" She doesn't think she does, but she looks like she's playing at being rich, like she has aspirations of wealth that all these real rich people are going to see through in a heartbeat.

The door opens, and Damon stops in the doorway to her bedroom. He's in a tuxedo, with unfastened cuffs and no shoes. He looks gorgeous.

"May I enter your space?" he asks.

Kara's in her bedroom, not her nest, but she appreciates him asking anyway. She doesn't carry about muddying scents here the way she would there — and wants it to smell like them in here anyway — but him being good about asking permission is one piece of his traditionalist upbringing that she really does appreciate.

She'd thank his parents, if she weren't a little concerned they'd call her a harlot and try to excise her from the set.

"You can come in," she says, then, "thank you."

He inclines his head then slips into the room, heading over toward her. He stops a couple feet away, surveying her up and down, and a spark of heat runs through her at his gaze.

But his eyes are soft when he looks up at her to ask, "What is it that makes you think you look ridiculous?"

"I just feel like I look..." Kara grimaces, smoothing her hand down the dress. "You look like you belong at some charity event, and I look like I'm cosplaying as a rich person."

Damon steps closer, turning her with gentle hands to face the mirror and pulling her back against him so he can wrap his arms around her. "Here's the trick," he says, and she can feel the rasp of his tuxedo and the press of his buttons against her bare back. "Every rich person is just cosplaying a rich person. You don't become a different or more impressive person when you have more money. There's no magic radar to tell a person who is 'really' rich."

"So what you're saying is that I don't look ridiculous."

"You couldn't look further from ridiculous." He steps back to slide one of his hands down the open skin on her back, and she trembles a little at his touch. "You're gorgeous, and I would like nothing more than to eat you out right now and leave you smelling like *me* all night so everybody knows that we're the only Alphas who can touch you. But if what you're worried about is people looking at you and somehow knowing that you don't have at least seven figures in the bank, let me guarantee you that nobody will be thinking that."

That does help, a little.

He tilts his head to the side and says, "I could give you a couple million, if that would make you feel better."

Kara chokes, not sure if her horror or her urge to laugh is stronger. "That would *not* make me feel better."

"You do know that, assuming this courtship ends the way everyone in this set wants it to, you'll also be a billionaire."

"Oh God." Kara buries her face in her hand. There's something about the concept of being a billionaire that feels like a joke. It's not something that happens in real life. "Isn't it your money?"

He leans down to kiss her cheek, then turns her to face him. "My money is the set's money. What use do I have for it if it's not for the people I love?"

Her face heats, and she blurts out, "How did you avoid rich people brainworms?"

Damon snorts out a laugh. "Oh, I do adore you."

"Sorry."

"No, no, don't apologize." He glances down at her very nice watch, then says, "We do need to head out soon. Do you still need to…" He waves his hands in the general vicinity of his face. "Whatever women do when they're…doing things?"

"Have you never met a woman before?"

"Okay, okay." Damon holds his hands up in surrender. "I'll leave you to whatever you're doing."

She's just teasing him, so she goes up on her toes to kiss him — gently enough that she doesn't muss up her lipstick — and says, "No, I'm done, other than my shoes."

"Well then." He steps away, but just far enough to pick up the shoes she has sitting on the floor next to her bed. They're an indulgence, a pair of black pumps that are about the most comfort she's found in heels. "May I?"

Kara doesn't think she's had someone help her put shoes on since she was a kid, but it doesn't seem altogether unappealing. She nods.

"If you'll sit, Omega."

Kara sits in the chair in the corner and, shoes in hand, Damon kneels in front of her.

She wants, instantly, irrationally, to keep him there, this Alpha who is willing to kneel for her, to see what else he can do down there, mouth buried against the lace between her legs —

Damon groans, dropping his forehead against her knee, and she smells a rush of arousal from him. "If you keep thinking whatever you're thinking," he grits out, "and smelling how you're smelling, we're never going to get out of here."

"Sorry," Kara says. Then, feeling just a little wicked, she suggests, "I was thinking about what else you could do while you were on your knees for me."

That gets another punch of scent from him, and she can see that he's hard now, the long line of him tenting his tuxedo pants.

It feels good, that she can make him want her like that, even knowing that some of it is just that he's an Alpha and she's an Omega and that's how it works.

Damon musters enough self-control to pick his head up and mutter, "If we go down this road, we'll be *so* late." With a warm hand, he picks up one of her feet and slides the shoe onto it, careful to keep the back from folding under her heel. His thumb brushes her ankle, and she shivers. His next touch against her other ankle, under the guise of guiding that shoe on, is more deliberate, at least going off the small smile on his face.

Before she realizes what he's doing, he leans down and touches a kiss to her ankle bone, a barely-there brush of heat and skin.

From another room, Jason shouts, "Stop hogging the Omega!"

Damon rolls his eyes, unfolding to his feet so he can offer her a hand up. She takes it, and he leans down to touch his lips to her wrist, the way he so often does.

"You don't need to do that every time."

"But yet," he says with a smile, and leads her out of her room.

Out in the set room, Eric and Jason are cuddling, as much as anybody can cuddle in a tuxedo. Eric is leaning back against Jason's chest, with Jason's hand playing in

Eric's hair. There's something extraordinarily soft in Jason's expression. Kara's heart aches, looking at them.

Eric starts to pop up off Jason's chest, but Jason holds him back with a heavy arm over his chest. "I want to look at our Omega for just a moment," Jason says.

"Well, *someone* won't let me greet you properly," Eric says, even as Jason tugs on his hair and his eyes flutter shut. "But you look magnificent."

"Thank you," Kara says. They look gorgeous together, two hard bodies pressed against each other in well-fitted tuxedos, and she can't resist the urge to head over to them. Her heels sink in a little on the carpet, but she barely notices, because all she can see is the hot gaze of two Alphas who are watching her, who *want* her.

Eric's legs are spread where he's sprawled on the couch, and she stops between them, bracing herself with a hand on his chest so she can lean over and kiss him.

He opens his mouth to her, one hand sliding up her throat to cup the back of her neck. It's a relatively chaste kiss for them, her tongue just sliding against the inside of his lower lip before she pulls away.

Eric is slower to let go of the back of her neck, his fingers trailing sparks against her skin as he drags them away.

"You are stunning," Eric murmurs. "I could look at you for hours."

"You don't look too bad yourself."

"Yes, yes, you're both very pretty," Jason says, with a grin that makes it clear he's joking. "But where's my kiss?"

He's a little far away with Eric between them, but Kara lets Eric take her weight as she leans over him to press a kiss to Jason's cheek. Then she pulls away, ignoring his offended noise.

"Omega," he whines.

"You told me Alphas don't mind a little bit of Omega teasing," she says, then turns away before he can convince her to change her mind. It won't take much, but she doesn't want to let him know that.

She wants him waiting for her, anticipating her.

Against the wall, watching them with a small smile on his face, is Ry. He's also in a tux, and she thinks that when they all stand next to each other, they'll look like they belong together. Like a set.

Ry is gorgeous too, with that Alpha presence that they all have, but he looks even paler than usual, with bruises under his eyes like he hasn't slept. Which she knows he has — or at least she thinks she has — but looking at him now, she's doubting herself.

Like he can tell what she's thinking, he gives her a small smile and says, "Don't worry, I'm not quite as bad as I look."

"You look like you could use some sleep," Kara tells him. She stops in front of him, touching a hand to his chest. He's warm, his heart beating solidly under his shirt, but there's something off about his scent, bitter against her tongue.

She wonders if the rest of them can smell it, too.

"Are you okay?" she asks.

Ry takes her hand to press her knuckles to his lips. "I am as I have been."

That's not a *yes* but it is a pretty clear *let's not talk about it*, and she knows all about those. She's spent her life full of them.

So she just leans up to kiss him, ignoring the bitter smell that threatens to choke her.

* * * *

The event is held at a large open hall with a soaring glass-and-metal ceiling. Kara's not sure what it's usually used for, but at the moment it's filled with art — paintings line the walls while sculptures on pedestals cover the hall floor.

They're not late, not much, but the room is half-full already, men and women across all dynamics in tuxes and gowns. Kara's pretty sure she can play spot the male Omega just by seeing whose tuxes aren't black. This seems like the sort of place where Omegas still don't wear black, not without getting some real side-eye.

She has a fleeting moment of relief that the AC is cranked high enough to push through the muggy DC August heat.

"All of the art is made by people we've helped," an Omega man says, stepping up next to her. He's in an open-neck gray suit, no tie, and she can see that he's unbonded. "The proceeds from sales here all go to supporting the Rainbow Initiative, but we also recommend supporting the artists beyond what you see here."

"Do you work at the Initiative?" she asks, even though she's pretty sure the answer is yes.

He nods, offering a hand to shake. He wouldn't do that if he were an Alpha, or if she were — and even Betas get weird about it sometimes — but Omegas are normal about touching each other. "Austin Kelton. I help run day-to-day operations at the Initiative."

"Kara Igan. I'm with—" Four Alphas, all of whom seem to have disappeared into the crowd. "People, who are somewhere."

"Well, Kara Igan of the people who are somewhere, do you have any questions for me about the Initiative?"

"Do you have an elevator pitch?"

"Only for giving in elevators," he says, but with a grin. "The Rainbow Initiative is a DC metro area non-profit that provides safe housing, job training, counseling and other human services to queer individuals of all dynamics. We have two main parts — services we provide to queer youth, which consists mostly of day services — afterschool programs, college prep, counseling — and services we provide to queer adults, which include housing. We also provide some dynamic-specific services, like job training and interview help for Omegas."

"Why not provide housing for kids?"

"The rules are different when it comes to providing shelter to kids and we don't have the resources right now — money, staff or locations. We do connect them with emergency shelters and other services when possible."

"Are you — " It's a stupid question, and she feels like she shouldn't really ask it, but it's how she judges most organizations, so she asks, "How are they about their Omega staff? I know human services is an 'Omega' job" — she puts air quotes around the word — "but we both know that doesn't always mean much."

A smile widens across Austin's face, and she picks up the scent of something like pride — not pride in himself, but the sort of pride that parents have in their children when they do the right thing. It should have felt condescending, but instead all she gets is a little thrill, like getting an unexpected A on a test.

"Nowhere's perfect," he concedes, "but this is better than most. We do our best. We aim to have at least one-third Omega staff and at least one-third Omega board members, both of which we've met for the last three years."

One-third Omega staff members isn't the most impressive—it's human services, and like she mentioned to him, that's one of the standard Omega jobs, like nursing and childcare, the places where they can be most nurturing. But one-third Omega board members is better than almost anywhere she's seen.

The university's leadership Board of Trustees has one Omega of the twelve, and they're only there because they give an excruciating amount of money.

"I'm impressed," she says. She glances around, but she still can't spot any of the set—either they were waylaid by someone, or the fact that she's at least a head shorter than half the crowd isn't helping them find her any more than it's helping her find them. "I should probably go—"

"Sorry, sweetheart," Jason says, appearing from the other side of her to touch a hand to the small of her back. "We got—holy shit. Austin?"

Austin's face lights up, and even under the mélange of scents in the room, Kara picks up something that smells like joy. "Jason. How the hell have you been?"

"I should be asking you that, man." Jason leans over to clap Austin on the shoulder, and Kara does her absolute best not to react. She's not going to get jealous of Jason touching another Omega, one that he's clearly friends with. "I didn't realize you had gotten out."

"Yeah, it's been almost nine months at this point. I thought I'd try my hand at something completely different instead, so here I am." Austin scans the crowd. "Just you here?"

"You asking if your favorite is here?" Jason asks in a teasing tone.

Austin laughs, a good strong laugh that's underlaid with that note that Omegas get when they're with Alphas that they like, a half-purr. Kara freezes.

This isn't just an Omega that Jason is friends with — someone he knows from the military, she's guessing, even though military Omegas are rarer than rare. They were together, were something — or Austin wants them to be.

And neither of them is flirting, not really, not in a way that would be disrespectful to her — but there's something there, something she can't hope to begin to compete with, not against this man who can surely bond, and get pregnant, and be what every Alpha wants.

Ry wouldn't be able to bond with him, the problem that started all of this — but he was the one most against this whole arrangement to begin with, so he will no doubt see the advantages of this when Jason brings it to him.

Because she has no doubt, looking at them, that he will — probably not today, but eventually, when he realizes that being with someone he can bond with, who he has this connection to, trumps a relationship with her, with her broken glands.

This is going to hurt, she thinks blankly. She *likes* them, despite knowing that she shouldn't get too attached, and now she's going to have to figure out how to extricate herself from this while doing the least amount of damage.

"Kara?"

Maybe it would be better to get herself out now, walk away and save face, but she doesn't want to. She doesn't want to walk away from them.

What an absolute mess.

"Kara?"

"Sorry," Kara says, smiling at Austin, who's looking at her with concern. "It's just a little overwhelming in here. You'd think more people would wear scent-blockers before coming to something like this." Kara has a low dose on, not so much that it covers who — and what — she is, but enough to quiet it. She was always taught it was just good etiquette, but apparently not.

Austin gives her a commiserating look. "It is a lot in here, isn't it? There's a room in the back if you need a little bit of breathing space — I can't guarantee it'll be empty, because we use it as a general sensory space, but it should be a little less overwhelming, I hope."

"I'm good, but thank you." Kara glances up at Jason, but he's still watching Austin like he's a revelation, or a miracle. She swallows. "I'm going to go figure out where everyone else ended up, if you want to stay and chat."

The look that Austin gives her is kind in a way that hurts, deep in her chest, like he knows all the things she's not saying, but all he says is, "It was nice to meet you, Kara."

"You too," Kara says, and she means it, mostly. She likes him, too, at least from the brief exchange they've had. He'll be good with them.

Jason's hand slips off the small of her back as she heads into the crowd, and she tries not to let it feel portentous.

By the time she finds Damon — pushing her way through a crowd that seems to grow thicker with every person that she gets past — she's pretty sure she's being ridiculous. Jason isn't throwing her away just because he wants to catch up with an Omega he knows, and the fact that the Omega wants him doesn't mean anything about what Jason feels.

They agreed to this courting, and she's not so insecure or possessive as to freak out because he talked to someone else.

Damon turns to her just as she reaches him, and she can see the wild look in his eyes just before he says, "Kara! Come meet Dr. Silas." He sounds like a man desperate to escape, which Kara understands as soon as she sees the woman in front of him lean forward to smooth down Damon's tie. She's a Beta, from what Kara can tell, and she's standing *very* close.

"Mia, please," the woman says. She pats Damon's stomach, and Damon jerks away from her, toward Kara. "Oh, dear, is this the Omega you were talking about?"

"That's right," Damon says, taking Kara's hand in his like that will save her from Mia's attentions. "Kara Igan, meet Dr. Mia Silas."

"She's lovely," Mia says, with barely a glance at Kara. "I am willing to share, you know. Omegas make such…fun bedmates."

It takes Kara a second—then she realizes what Mia is suggesting. Some traditionalists—the awful, old-school traditionalists—had primarily Alpha-Beta relationships, where Omegas were kept as little more than pets, to care for the house and bear the children and be *fun bedmates.*

"I'm afraid that we're not looking to add to our set," Damon says stiffly. "If you'll excuse me."

"Oh, there's no need to pretend," Mia says. She leans closer, and Kara sees Damon's jaw work. He seems more bothered than she is, frankly—what the woman is insinuating is horrifying, but the ownership laws were rescinded almost eighty-five years ago in Virginia, and Kara has the ability to say no.

If she couldn't laugh at people like this, she never would have gotten through university.

Ry steps up on the other side of her, his hand brushing against hers, to say, "You seem to have gotten a little lost. You know that this Initiative does Omega rights support, right? I'm sure you can find an ASPCA instead if you're looking for a pet."

"Oh, I support Omega rights," Mia says enthusiastically. "There's nothing wrong with Omegas working as long as they come home at the end of the day."

"A ringing endorsement of Omega rights," Ry drawls. Then he says, "Shall we go?" to Kara.

"Let's," Kara says, because she doesn't want to spend any more of her life talking to someone who wants to keep her barefoot and knotted.

They escape the crowd near a marble sculpture of an Alpha sinking his teeth into another Alpha's throat, right over where a bonding mark would go. Ry asks, "What do you think about this for our front entrance?"

Damon snorts out a laugh. "That's one way to dissuade visitors."

"I think it would encourage visitors," Ry says, wrapping an arm around Kara's waist. "We could have the best erotic sculpture garden in Virginia. And, on the plus side, it would probably keep your parents away."

"Ah, your real goal." Damon sighs, looking out over the crowd. "I want to buy at least a couple things before we leave."

"Not the sexy sculpture?"

"If you really want the sexy sculpture," Damon says, "you figure out where to put it." He glances at Kara, then around the room. "Maybe we should each get one."

"Speaking as the official curator of shit in our house, we are absolutely going to run out of space in the house for art," Ry says. He pulls Kara close. "You are welcome to be joint curator of shit in our house."

"I'm flattered," Kara says, and means it. It's traditionally an Omega's role, minding the household, but Ry's been doing it at the set's house for a lot longer than she's been there. She's not planning to usurp his place. "But with as big as your house is, do you really not have space for another four pieces of art?"

"Five," Ry and Damon say together, and *oh*.

She never imagined they meant her.

And that, somehow, makes this all a little too much — not Jason reuniting with his old Omega friend or the batshit traditionalist Beta, but the idea that they want her to be adding things to the house outside of her own room and her own nest.

Because homes — Alpha's homes, set's homes, Omega's homes — they're more than just *homes*. Because they're territorial, the lot of them, more than Betas can ever really understand. It's instinctive, it's *intrinsic* and she will bite another Omega who tries to enter her nest without permission.

Alpha's territories tend to be larger, houses rather than nests, but it's the same. They don't let go easily, and they don't let people in and they hold on with clenched fists to those things they want to keep.

They invited her into their territory, but this feels like more.

Lips touch her throat, on the other side from her gland, and Ry says, "You smell pensive."

"Just thinking," Kara says, then smiles when she realizes how stupid that sounds. "Do you know where Eric ended up?"

Ry noses against her throat, the warm heat of his breath against her skin. It's a little forward for somewhere like this, out in public, but far less than it would be between two Betas.

Right now, with Mia's *"fun bedmates"* comment not too far from her mind, she's not sure how she feels about that.

But she doesn't push him away. She doesn't want to push him away.

"If you really want to mess with people like *Dr.* Mia Silas," she says into the lull, "you can introduce me as Dr. Kara Igan."

She means it as a joke, but Damon stiffens. Looking abashed, he asks, "Do you want me to introduce you that way? I didn't think—I didn't realize how that would sound."

Kara laughs. "You absolutely do not need to introduce me like that. I only go by doctor in academic settings, not personal ones."

"So if we meet someone from your university..."

"Then you can call me Dr. Igan to your heart's content. Or professor."

"You don't want to show it off more?" Ry asks.

Kara tilts her head back and forth in a so-so movement. "It's complicated. There are, as of right now, fewer than two dozen Omega women in tenured or tenure-track positions in the country. There are a few more Omega men, but it's still fewer than fifty. Even the number of Omegas with doctorates is only maybe ten thousand or so, last I saw. In academia I make damn sure they know that I'm one of them, but in social situations, it tends to cause more problems than it solves."

"Is it really that few?"

"The numbers get masked by the fact that the majority of Omegas in academia end up in non-tenure-track positions, so if you're not involved in academia it seems like there are more of us. But it really is that few. Most universities wouldn't even accept Omegas into doctoral programs until about twenty years ago, much less hire them as professors." She shakes her head. "Anyway. Eric. Did we lose him to the hordes?"

"I think he was admiring Omega softcore porn 'art' somewhere on the other side of the room."

"Unlike the sculpture we're standing next to," Kara says dryly, amused by the judgmental tone in Damon's voice.

"You know what," Damon says, "just for that, we're buying it, and you all are going to look at it every day."

"Starting our erotic sculpture garden?" Ry asks.

"Yes," Damon says determinedly. "Keep our Omega company while I find someone to sell it to me?"

"Keep her company yourself," Ry says with a laugh. "Art's in my wheelhouse." With a kiss to Kara's cheek, he heads off through the crowd.

"You do realize that now you're going to actually own this sculpture, right?" Kara says, turning to look back at the sculpture. It is beautiful, done in the style of the old masters, threading the line between erotic and loving. She can almost see the shift of the muscles under marble skin, the tension and play as though they could come to life at any moment.

Damon laughs. "I do like it, even if I don't want to put it in our front entryway. And Jason and Eric will like it, I think. There's not a lot of Alpha-Alpha art, especially between two men. And I like supporting local artists."

"You could commission them to make the rest of the erotic sculpture garden. Become a patron of the arts."

"Oh, God, please don't say that within earshot of Ry," Damon groans.

"Don't say what within earshot of Ry?" Eric asks, emerging from the crowd. "Also I bought two paintings that he's going to tell me we don't have space for."

"We're buying the sexy sculpture," Kara tells him. "And I'm not supposed to suggest that Damon commissions a whole set of sexy sculptures."

"I think that sounds like a good way to keep your parents from ever showing up," Eric says.

Kara laughs. "That's what Ry said."

"Perfect. We're all in agreement."

"My parents are not that bad in small doses," Damon protests, though not very loudly.

There's a shift in the crowd near them, and Ry reappears near them with Jason and Austin next to him, saying, "One erotic statue is ours. And I found Jason."

"And now the set's all together," Jason says, leaning over from next to Ry to give Eric a kiss. "And look who I found."

Eric looks up — then blinks, his jaw dropping. "Holy shit, Austin, is that you? I thought you were still — well, not in Afghanistan, but in whatever hellhole they're sending the OMC these days."

Of course Austin used to be OMC. The Omega Medical Corps is the only place Omegas are allowed to serve in combat, and they're known as the best of the best of Omegas.

Eric leans forward to wrap Austin in a hug, and Kara keeps the smile firmly on her face. She's not going to overreact to it. She's not.

"It's really good to see you," Austin says. "And I appreciate your support of the Rainbow Initiative. All of you."

"All this money has to be good for something, right?" Damon says. His smile is a little different now, more *glossy magazine* than *normal human being.*

But Jason just laughs, nudging Austin's shoulder with his own. "Have to pay it back, don't we?"

"Well, on behalf of a lot of queer kids — and adults — it's appreciated."

Austin surveys them, and Kara doesn't know what he's seeing. Four rich, gorgeous Alphas with a very regular Omega with no bonding marks. And Damon's been seen with every Omega and Beta in the DMV.

She's not exactly arm candy.

"I realize I never really introduced myself," he says. "I'm Austin Kelton, formerly of the Omega Medical Corps, now Deputy Operations Manager at the Rainbow Initiative."

"Best damn medic in the entire armed forces," Jason says. "Or he was."

"*Hey,*" Eric says, but he's laughing.

"I saved your ass, didn't I?"

"That you did," Eric concedes. "You're really out? I thought you'd be a lifer."

Something tightens behind Austin's eyes, but he just says lightly, "Not a hell of a lot to do for the OMC now that we're out of Afghanistan."

"I guess not." Eric looks at the rest of them like he's just remembered that they're there, then says, "I realized I didn't introduce the set—this is Ry Jonas, Damon Silva and Kara Igan."

"We've met," Austin says with a nod to Kara. "And it's lovely to meet the rest of you. If you'll all excuse me, I should go socialize some more."

"Give us a call," Jason says. "Actually—" He pulls a business card from his inner pocket, scrawling something on it before handing it over. "Here's my number and Eric's. We should meet up some time."

Austin takes it with a smile, then gives a jaunty half-salute and disappears back into the crowd.

Kara feels—

Something.

She's not sure what, just that it's sitting uncomfortably on her hard palate. Eric and Jason look *so happy* to see the Omega, like it made their whole day—their month.

And he was nice to her, and professional. He didn't flirt much, or act inappropriately. He wasn't cruel to her.

He seems like the sort of Omega they would all want. The sort of person who knows about all of this charity stuff, who's clever and successful and, most importantly, can no doubt bond.

He was Omega Medical Corps, and she's a mid-tier academic.

While Eric is saying something to Jason, Kara turns to Ry and asks, "He was their…"

"They were together," Ry says quietly. "As much as they could be, at least. OMC aren't allowed to bond while they're in the Corps. In the end, Jason and Eric left and he stayed, or so they tell it."

Of course. The thing keeping them apart was that they couldn't legally be together—and that's gone now.

That numb feeling grows, twists.

She makes herself smile. This isn't the time to get upset about this. There's a charity to support.

With a nudge to Damon's shoulder and a curling of her fingers around his, Kara makes herself go back to being a normal human being supporting this event. She smiles, she laughs, she teases Jason about the art he's considering buying. She drinks a glass of champagne, then two, decides that getting drunk tonight is not a good idea and switches to surprisingly decent lemonade.

And the whole time, all she can think is, *here's another Omega that they want.* There's another Omega that they want, and they thought they couldn't have him, but now they can. And he's better suited for them than she is.

Damon will be kind about it, at least. They'll *all* be kind about it, because they are kind. Which is why she likes them so much to begin with. That they're kind, and they like each other, and they like her. So they'll let her down gently.

But courting ends one of two ways—in bonding—or in their case marriage—or in a breakup. And if Eric and Jason already have an Omega, then by default the set has an Omega—and it's not her.

At least she still has her apartment, so moving out won't be too awful. And she'll miss them, obviously, but—

Well, maybe it's for the best. She can't imagine Alphas being happy with someone they can't bond with, ultimately.

They're almost to the car at the end of the night when Kara says, "I want to go back to my apartment tonight."

Eric was saying something, she realizes when he breaks off abruptly. Everyone is staring at her. That numb feeling is burning through her stomach. "Is everything okay?" Damon asks carefully.

Kara nods. *This is for the best.* "Please."

"Do you want any of us to stay with you tonight?" Jason asks.

"No, I'm okay." She makes herself smile. "Please."

Nobody looks quite sure what to do, but they all get in the car. Kara curls up against the window, and Damon tells the driver, "Kara's apartment, please, first."

The drive to her apartment isn't too long, in the grand scheme of things, but her stomach is twisted into knots and nobody is saying anything and it feels like it takes forever.

This is for the best.

This is for the best.

The car stops finally in front of her apartment, and she lets herself out. She smiles at all of them. "I'll talk to you tomorrow, yeah?"

"Of course," Damon says. "And please — come back?"

"Yeah," Kara says, and closes the door.

She has her fob and key in her purse out of habit, and she gets herself in the building, up the stairs and into her apartment.

Then she weeps.

Chapter Fourteen

About half an hour after getting back into her apartment, when Kara is lying on her bed in just her impractical underwear, she has the humiliating realization that she's being ridiculous.

Here she is, in *fuck me* lingerie, sulking in her sad little nest in her sad little apartment because Eric and Jason had a couple conversations with an Omega they used to date. Here she is, preemptively breaking up with them because she's afraid that they might break up with her later.

Here she is, running away again.

And she can keep lying here, alone and miserable, or she can get off her ass and go back to her Alphas. If they want to break up with her, they're going to have to have the courage to do it themselves.

She's not putting that dress back on, though, so she throws on a T-shirt and jeans and calls an Uber to their place. To her place, now, too.

She never did pick out a piece of art for the house.

The Uber driver slows when they get near the gate and he says, a little uncertainly, "I don't think you'll be able to get in here."

"I have the code," she tells him. He lets her out to type it in, and she can see the surprise on his face when it opens.

"You work here?" he asks.

Explaining seems like more trouble than it's worth, so she just says, "Something like that."

"They pay well?"

"Well enough."

"Fair enough," he says as he pulls toward the entrance. "But I don't know if there's any employer that pays well enough to have their employee showing up at this time of day."

Apparently not explaining was the thing that was more trouble than it was worth, but she's already gone down this road, and there's no good way to turn back now. "I'm good," she reassures him. "I promise."

"Fair enough," he says again. He stops in the driveway, saying, "Good luck, I guess."

"Thanks."

It's only as Kara's walking up to the door that she realizes that they might already be asleep. Not that it matters, given that she has a key, but—

If she just goes straight to her nest tonight and pops up in the morning, they might not ask. They might let her get away with it, and they might never have this conversation.

And she needs to have this conversation.

She hesitates for one moment, then unlocks the door and heads inside.

Everything is lit up, and there are voices coming from the living room. She closes the door behind her and locks it, then takes her shoes off and sets them aside.

There's a stillness in the air out here in the main entrance that she's reluctant to break…not like waiting, but like a clear night in an open field. She pads across the stone floor, stopping in the entrance to the living room so she can see her Alphas in their natural state.

None of them are looking in her direction. Ry's on the couch with Eric and Jason, near enough to them that Jason's arm, thrown over Eric's shoulders, is brushing against him as well. They all look soft, from the backs of them, with the loose posture of the sleepy or tipsy.

Eric says something, but it's too quiet for her to hear.

Damon, on the other hand, is sitting stiffly in one of the armchairs, a crystal glass of something that looks like whiskey dangling from one hand. He doesn't look happy.

Kara's heart aches, looking at him. She didn't mean to make him sad.

She must make a noise, because Damon's eyes dart over to her. There's a second when he doesn't register that she's there, then he startles. "Kara."

Everyone turns to look at her, Ry twisting so much he nearly climbs into Eric's lap in the process.

Self-consciousness hits her, and she blurts out, "I'm sorry."

"Kara, what—"

"I like you," she says. "I like you a lot, all of you. You're smart and funny and nice, and you've gone out of your way to make me feel like I belong with you. So I'm not going to let my insecurities convince me that you're going to leave me."

"Why would we—"

"Austin," Ry says quietly. "I assume that's what it was, at least."

"Oh, sweetheart," Jason breathes. "Yes, Eric and I had a thing with him, but it was years ago. We're not looking to get back into that relationship."

"I know," Kara says, and she mostly means it. "Or at least I assumed, once I got past the blind panic of you talking to another Omega you so clearly liked. I'm not running away again." She bites her lip. "I'm sorry for ruining the night."

"You didn't ruin the night," Damon tells her. He gets to his feet, setting the whiskey down, then strides over to her. She goes to him, meeting him in the middle and throwing her arms around his neck so she can pull him close. His hands settle around her waist. "Thank you for coming back."

"Thank you for putting up with my neuroses." Kara kisses him once, twice, then leans into it, sliding her fingers into the short hairs at the base of his skull. She tugs on them, just a little, and he gasps into her mouth. She can taste whiskey.

"Kara—"

"I'm still wearing my ridiculous underwear," she tells him, and his hands tighten around her waist. "I don't think we should let it go to waste."

She steps back from him, his hands letting her go reluctantly, so she can strip off her T-shirt and drop it down on the floor. Then she shimmies off her jeans, revealing dark purple lace panties. They're not quite a thong, but they're cut high on the hips, hugging her in all the right places and nearly sheer all over.

"Jesus," Damon breathes. He reaches out to slide a hand down her stomach, his thumb just barely flirting with the top of the lace. The look on his face is reverent.

"Beautiful." Jason steps up behind her, settling his own hands on her hips. The hard length of him presses up against her back. "You want to show our Omega how beautiful she is?"

Damon's gaze flicks up to Jason, then he smiles and sinks down to his knees in front of her. He hooks his fingers around the sides of her panties and slides them down, then he presses his mouth between her legs.

There's no slow rise of desire there, no wave or tide, just *pleasure* like the sun and gravity and the hot wet drag of a tongue that has her knees going out under her. Jason holds her up, one hand around her stomach while the other slides up to cup the base of her throat.

"You're ours," he murmurs in her ear, tilting her head back so it's pressed back against his chest. She can barely keep her eyes open, barely listen to him, overwhelmed by the pleasure building and building between her legs. "Our Omega, our gorgeous Omega, who came back to us. Feel how he worships you. Feel how I want you. Look at how Eric and Ry can't resist touching themselves, just watching you."

Kara gets her eyes open just enough to look over at them, to make eye contact with an openly masturbating Eric—then Damon's tongue slides just right over her clit, and she buries her hands in his hair and comes.

She just has her legs under her when Damon rises to his feet and kisses her, and she can taste herself on his lips.

Behind her, Jason makes an impatient noise, then spins her around so she's facing him. He pulls her up on her toes and leans down to kiss her. His mouth is hot on hers, and he just *takes* and she lets him, dragging her hands up under his shirt. She tweaks a nipple, and he bites her lip.

Jason slides his thigh between her legs, pressing on a clit that's verging on oversensitive but throbbing with need, and she gasps into his mouth.

"I want to fuck you," he says into her mouth. "I want to knot you all night and then wake up and knot you again."

"You'd better take me to bed, then," she tells him.

And he does.

* * * *

Kara wakes to a body draped over hers, one hand pressed to the bottom of her sternum, just between her breasts. She's sore, but not so much that she doesn't press back against whoever is behind her, half asleep and ready to go for another round.

Behind her, Ry groans. He drags his thumb against the underside of her breast, and she shivers.

"Kara," he murmurs in her ear. "You smell so good."

She drags his hand up so she can press a kiss to his palm, a little sloppy and uncoordinated, then sets her teeth against the meat of his thumb. He gasps.

"I don't have anywhere to be this morning," she says, in a tone that aims for seductive but only reaches horny.

Ry hesitates, and she takes advantage of the silence to slide his thumb in her mouth, laving it with her tongue then scraping up the pad of it with her teeth. He's breathing hard behind her, his hips rutting up against hers. She can feel how hard he is against the line of her back.

Then he rolls them so he's on top of her, hands and knees bracketing her so he can lean down and kiss her lips, her throat, the top of her collarbone. She arches up into him, reaching down to slide her hand down his length. His hips jerk down.

"You're so beautiful." Ry presses a hand between her legs, and she's already so wet that he can slide his fingers in easily, just the littlest bit of friction to give her almost what she needs. "You're so beautiful that it's hard to breathe around you sometimes."

"You're not so bad yourself," she says with a grin, then tugs him up to kiss him firmly. "Fuck me?"

Something goes across his face, too quick for her to track, then he lines himself up and slides into her. He's big, bigger than she expected, and she clings onto his wrist until she can breathe through the stretch.

He stays there for just a moment, eyes fixed on hers, then he starts to fuck her in earnest. It's a slow slide, dragging, his other hand playing with her clit so pleasure washes over her in waves with every thrust.

It's wordless, breathless, the two of them breathing into each other — then the angle of his hips shift, and he hits just the right place, and she gasps, "Oh, fuck, *fuck*, do that again."

His hips snap forward, faster now, and she clings onto his back as pleasure rolls over and over her.

He collapses on top of her when he finishes, then rolls off to the side, breathing hard. Kara's breathing hard too, shivering as the last of the aftershocks run through her, but she reaches down and grabs his hand, lifting it up to press the back of it to her lips. His fingers are cold.

When she looks over at him, he's already asleep.

With a smile, she follows after him.

It's later when Kara wakes, but not that much later — she doesn't have that stiff ache that comes from sleeping too long. Ry is still sleeping next to her, his cheeks flushed.

He looks tired, somehow, even in his sleep.

So she doesn't wake him, just brushes a kiss over his lips and eases off the bed. Fortunately, there's nobody around to see the amount of shimmying and fumbling required to get out from the middle of a bed this big.

Downstairs, Damon and Jason are both nowhere to be seen — at work, probably, or doing whatever else it is that they do — but she finds Eric sitting in the kitchen, eating toast with one hand as he scrolls through his phone.

Kara walks over to him, leaning in to kiss the back of his neck, and he turns to give her a smile. "Hungover?" he asks, pressing a kiss to her collarbone. "Damon spent the morning squinting at me."

Kara laughs. "I didn't drink that much. I did have a *very* good morning with Ry, though."

Eric goes very still. He hides it quickly, but not fast enough for her not to notice when she's pressed up against him like she is. "Is he up yet, then?" he asks, in a voice that doesn't hit as casual as he's clearly aiming for.

Which is weird. Kara can't think of a single reason why they would have an issue with her sleeping with Ry, when they've been okay with her sleeping with anyone else in the relationship individually.

Or could it be because of last night? Did something happen, beyond her briefly losing her shit? None of them said it last night, but she wasn't tracking anything at the event beyond her own fear of Eric and Jason leaving her.

She asks, "Why?"

"Kara," he says quietly.

"He was still sleeping when I left," Kara says. "If the rules about me sleeping with one of you individually have changed, I'd appreciate you just letting me know instead of getting weird at me about it. I'm a big girl."

"It's not that," Eric says, but he's pulling away, getting up to head out of the kitchen.

Kara watches him go, then sits in his seat and puts her head in her hand. That was not how she imagined her morning going.

* * * *

After a sad ten-thirty meal of dry toast, Kara calls her mom out of a misguided sense of…something.

Her mom greets her with, "I met a nice man that I think you should meet."

That misguided sense of something evaporates into just feeling misguided. Kara drops her head back against the armchair pillow so she can stare up at the ceiling and pray for the ability to travel back in time two minutes and not call her mom.

"I'm already in a relationship," she reminds her mom. "Also, hi, how's it going, what's your day been like?"

"I just worry that you're going to have your heart broken," her mom says. "Casey found a nice girl to marry. I just want you to have the same happiness."

Casey is five years older than Kara, and they've never been close — it's just enough of an age gap that it's always been a little weird. They were never in the same school together, never in the same time of their lives.

Casey is also a Beta, lives in Seattle and had a string of lovely Beta girlfriends before he married Mina and settled down to design bridges somewhere far, far away from their family.

"I'm not Casey," Kara says, "and I'm not you."

"This isn't about me."

"It is about you. I don't—I don't want to talk about this." Kara drags her hands over her face. "I just wanted to catch up, but clearly that was not a good idea."

"Don't be like that," her mom says, sounding offended. "You know that Alphas don't stay with Betas—"

"*I'm not a Beta*," Kara snaps, sharper than she's ever talked to her mom before. "I'm just not. The fact that I don't have heats doesn't change my dynamic, and it doesn't make me less lovable or desirable. Stop calling me a Beta. Stop implying that I am one. I'm not."

Her mom goes silent at that, and Kara can hear her own breathing in the silence. She's never said that before, not like that, and she's not sure if she feels good or not having said it. Mostly her stomach hurts.

Finally, slowly, her mom says, "I know you're not a Beta."

"Then why do you always sound like you think I am?"

Her mom doesn't seem to have an answer to that.

Kara closes her eyes. She can smell her own sadness, filling up the space.

Today is not going how she wanted it to.

"I just want you to be happy," her mom says. "And I think they're going to break your heart."

"You've made that very clear." Kara gets up to start pacing, because she can't keep sitting here with a twisting stomach and so much anger. "I don't care that you think that they're going to break my heart. I I—I like them very much, and they like me, and they are courting me. Stop treating me like I'm you."

Her mom doesn't have an answer to that either, which is just as well, because Kara's not sure she wants to know what her mom's answer would be. She's spent the last few years with everyone around her treating her like she's somewhere between defective and not an Omega at all. Being with Damon and Eric and Jason and Ry has been one of the first times that she's actually felt like an Omega in a positive way in years. She's done with letting other people tear that down.

She likes them. They like her. She's done running away.

"How's your baking class going?" Kara asks, instead of continuing to push. She doesn't want to have this conversation anymore. She just wants to talk to her mom the way she used to, before everything happened.

"Not bad," her mom says finally, a concession. "We made these custard things during the last class, and mine only a little bit turned into scrambled eggs."

"And that counts as 'not bad'?"

Her mom laughs. "Bad would be Maria Carter's — you remember Maria, right? You were in that one class with her son."

Kara does not remember Maria Carter or her son — whoever her son might be.

"Anyway, Maria, her custard *exploded*. Actually exploded. She took it out of the oven and it just splattered everywhere."

"Oh no."

"It was extremely gratifying," her mom says vindictively. "Maria is a smug, smug woman who spends every class talking about how she *almost* went to culinary school. Except she pronounces it like *cyoolinary*."

Kara laughs, and everything is a little more okay again.

Chapter Fifteen

Ry doesn't come down until almost dinnertime. He's pale and wan when he does, and he doesn't cook, just sits down at one of the seats at the island and watches Damon finish up what he's stir-frying. He's back upstairs almost as soon as they're done eating, having spent the entire meal picking at his food.

He doesn't smell like anything.

Kara keeps quiet, because she can read a room and the *don't ask* vibes are out in force, but everyone except her seems to know what's going on, and it's starting to piss her off.

This is the sort of shit that they do to Omegas all the time, all over the world. It used to be that they wouldn't tell Omegas about tragedies or deaths, sometimes for days, out of fear that it would "unbalance" them — that it might risk their pregnancy, or their fertility or their ability to take a knot just right.

Alphas always say that they want to protect Omegas, that it's in their best interest, but that slips so easily into keeping secrets, into lying, into turning a shield into a cage.

Kara refuses to live in a cage like that.

She goes to bed frustrated that night, and alone.

Ry isn't down until after lunch the next day, and he's still wearing so much scent blocker it's like he barely exists at all. There is nothing that screams *I'm hiding something* more than doing that in their own home.

So finally, fed up, Kara demands, "What is going on?"

Everyone looks at her, in an odd tableau like they're all trying too hard not to look like they're frozen. Jason, thumb still pressed on his phone screen, asks carefully, "What are you talking about?"

"You've all been weird since I had sex with Ry, and Eric said that it wasn't because the rules have changed about me having sex with one of you individually, but clearly it was *something*. So. What's going on?"

"Nothing's going on," Eric says.

"Stop *lying* to me." Kara looks at Ry. "Do you just not want to have sex with me? Is that it? You can tell me. I won't be offended."

Ry swallows. He doesn't smell like anything, and it's pissing her off to no end. "It's not that."

"Really? It's the only time we've had sex, just the two of us, and don't think I haven't noticed that you barely touch me, barely even kiss me. If you're just not into it, or into me, *that's okay*, but you need to tell me, because right now I'm floundering."

"I want to have sex with you," Ry says, but not like he means it.

Kara bites down around a whole series of swear words that she wants to say. "Really?" she demands. "Really, I'm supposed to believe that? You didn't want me in the first place, and you've been avoiding me for like twenty-eight hours at this point, which, professional tip, is not that subtle when we live in the same house."

"It's not that."

"So is it that you're sick that you're hiding? Don't want your Omega to think about things like that, because it might make me hysterical? Do you just plan to drench yourself in scent blocker for the rest of your life, or is that just for when I'm around, because, what, you think it'll turn me off to know that—"

He snaps, "*Stop*," and she—

Does.

She feels odd like this, like she's floating a little bit outside of her body, or maybe a little bit inside of it, shrunk half an inch all around so whatever makes her *her* has come unmoored from her body.

She wants to stop, is the thing. She wants to do anything he asks, for as long as he asks it. Maybe if she does that, he'll pet her hair and tell her she was a good Omega for him.

"Baby?" one of the Alphas near her says.

"Yes?" she asks. Her voice sounds dreamy, drowsy, and it comes to her through so many layers it feels as though she's underwater.

"Fuck," an Alpha says.

Someone lowers her into a chair, pressing a hand over her eyes until she closes them, and she goes easily. She's being a good Omega for them.

"That's right, sweetheart," an Alpha says. "You're being a really good Omega for us right now. But the one thing that would make this even better is if you can come back to us. Can you do that?"

"I'm right here," she tells him. The hand against her face feels good.

The Alpha asks, "Do you remember what we were talking about before?"

"That Ry's sick and you're all lying to me about it," she tells him peaceably.

"That's right," the Alpha tells her approvingly. She smiles. "And I know Ry ordered you to stop talking about it, but he changed his mind. Isn't that right?"

"That's right," the Alpha who ordered her says. "I changed my mind, Kara. You can disregard my order. I changed my mind."

For a second, nothing changes, all of that heavy floating still dragging her away from everything, then she blinks under the hand covering her eyes and she comes back.

It's like being hit with a hangover all at once, and she turns and gags, almost throwing up. The hand moves to the back of her neck, holding her hair back, and Eric murmurs, "You're okay, you're okay. Just let it out, if you need to."

"If you ever do that again," Kara gasps out, "I'll leave you. You get"—she dry-heaves, her stomach clenching so hard her ribs hurt—"exactly one fuck-up."

"I'm so sorry," Ry says. He sounds farther away, and very hoarse. She doesn't look at him. "I'm so sorry."

"Please don't talk to me right now," she says, because if she hears his voice again right now she's going to lose it. "Just give me—give me a little bit of time."

He doesn't say anything, but his scent fades, then a door shuts.

Kara sags, clenching her eyes shut around the tears threatening to seep out. She hurts, her head pounding, but more than that, she feels so betrayed it's hard to comprehend.

She's never been ordered by an Alpha before, but she's heard what it feels like — that desire to do what an Alpha says, submission made willing. It's like having every piece of her stripped, pulled away, until she's just the ur-Omega, nothing but instinct.

She's heard some Omegas have their Alphas do that to them intentionally. She understands that.

She would rather die.

"Do you mind if I check your heart rate and blood pressure?" Eric asks quietly. "Your breathing is really fast, and I want to make sure you're okay."

Blindly, she sticks out her arm to him, and he clips something on her finger. His other hand is still on the back of her neck, and it's helping, but not much.

But if she lets herself think about how much she feels like she's going to throw up, she actually will, so she distracts herself by asking, "Do you just carry a pulse-oximeter with you, or do you have them stashed around the house?"

"Both," he says. He takes the clip off, then puts a cuff around her arm. She feels it start to inflate. "Your heart rate is pretty high, baby. Would you be willing to take something to try to get it down?"

"Absolutely the fuck not." Her stomach is starting to settle, just a little, and she drags herself upright. "You're not giving me anything. None of you are giving me anything."

"Kara—"

The cuff beeps, and all of a sudden she can't stand it, can't stand having it on her or having him touch her. She tears it off, pushing away to get to her feet and away from him.

Eric, still standing where he was, gives her a concerned look. "Your heart rate and your blood pressure are both really high, and I'm worried about how fast you're breathing. Please let me take care of you, baby."

"I need —" She gasps in a breath, looking around the room. Damon is gone, but Jason is still there, standing by the door, watching them. He looks very pale. "I need to not be here. I need to not be around any of you right now."

"Do you want to go back to your apartment?" Jason asks. "I can drive you if you do, or we can call a car for you if you'd rather not be in a car with me."

"What?" Kara blinks at him, feeling too awful to parse what he's saying. "No, I just — I'm going to go sit in my nest for a while. I need you all to just…leave me alone."

"Of course, sweetheart," Jason says. He starts to move, then stops, looking at her like she's a wild animal that he's trying not to startle. "Just let us know if you need anything, and we can —"

Kara can't deal anymore, can't be here with him looking at her like that, so she gets out of there.

She smells like Alphas, and she doesn't want that anywhere near her nest, so she strips naked and shoves all of her clothes out of the bedroom into the hallway. She turns on the shower as hot as it will go, then she gets in and sits on the floor and cries.

They weren't supposed to do this. They were supposed to be better than this.

And if she didn't like them so much, it wouldn't hurt this damn much — but she does. She likes them so fucking much, and all she wanted to do was figure out how to help Ry, and he just —

He took away *her*.

Standing up, she scrubs descenter all over her entire body, to get every last bit of Alpha off of her. She doesn't want to smell them at all right now.

Her nest smells like her when she curls up naked in it, pulling a pillow against her stomach to hold on to. She's surrounded by pillows here, layers and layers with just enough of an opening for her to get in and out, and she closes up that opening once she's settled so nobody else can get in.

Here, at least, Kara feels safe.

Curled up in her nest, she just keeps going back to that thought she had in the shower—that this hurts like a son of a bitch because she *likes* them. She doesn't want to walk away from them. It would be so much easier if she did, if she could just fuck off and leave, burn them in effigy with Sue Ann and never think about them again.

But Jason is funny and Eric is bright and Damon is so much kinder than she ever expected, and Ry put so much work into making her feel safe here. And they treat her like she's precious, but not like she's useless. They haven't tried to put her in a gilded cage, or make her quit her job or take away her financial independence. They want to give her *more* financial independence.

Ry said that he wanted to make it so she could leave them if she wanted to.

That's when she really started to fall in love with them, she thinks.

She grabs her phone and calls Sue Ann, setting the phone down next to her head so she can stay curled up in her nest while they talk.

It rings once, twice, and her chest hurts at the thought that Sue Ann won't pick up. She needs to talk to *someone*, and there's no one left. She's thrown out bits of her life for years, made it smaller, excised all those pieces that hurt too much because of what she couldn't have.

And her mom — there are a lot of things she can talk to her mom about, but not this, not when her mom's views on Alphas are still shaped by that one bad breakup back in college. Her mom wants what's best for her, but — she can't have this conversation with her.

Then Sue Ann says, "Hey! What's up — *Kitty, take that out of your mouth right now.*"

Kara chokes out a laugh. "Dare I ask?"

"My daughter managed to put an entire — small — stuffed animal in her mouth. Why do you sound like you've been crying?"

"Because I have been." She curls even tighter around her pillow. "Please tell me I'm being stupid."

"You're being stupid," Sue Ann says obligingly. "How are you being stupid?"

"If I tell you something, do you promise not to freak out?"

"No."

Kara laughs again. She's already feeling better, just hearing Sue Ann's voice. "I love them, I think."

"Isn't that the goal here?"

"Yeah."

Sue Ann must hear something in Kara's voice, because she asks, sharply, "What happened?"

"One of them ordered me."

"*Son of a* — no, Kitty, I wasn't going to say a bad word. Can you go into the other room so Mommy can talk to her friend alone?"

"I think Mommy was going to say a bad word there."

"Yeah, well, the fuckers deserve it. What did they make you do?"

"Nothing." Kara squeezes the pillow. "Nothing. They — one of them wanted to stop talking about something, and he told me to stop, and I — I don't know how to explain what it feels like, but I knew. And they got me out of it, and they tried to make sure I was okay, and they — *fuck*. Sorry. Sorry."

"You have nothing to apologize for," Sue Ann tells her. "And you don't need to defend them. Isn't that shit illegal?"

"Not if you're courting. Or bonded. Or married."

"How is that allowed?"

Kara laughs. The sound hurts to hear, even for her. "We're barely people, in the eyes of the law. Who the fuck is going to make it illegal for our Alphas to tell us what to do?"

"They should," Sue Ann snaps. "Your Alphas have all the money in the world, right? Tell them to do that. Or leave their asses. Maybe both." She lets out a slow breath. "Do you want me to come up there? Or do you want to come down here? I can play keep-away between you and the Alphas for a while."

"You have Kitty."

"I have a husband, too — he can deal with our kid alone for a few days. Do you want me there?"

Kara does, but... "Not yet. I want to — I love them, Sue Ann. I thought I didn't, or I didn't think about it, and then this happened, and I just...."

"I get it."

"Do you? Because I don't."

"Well, no, I think you should make them grovel at your feet and beg you to take them back, but I get being in love, Kara. Just let me know if you change your mind about me coming up there, and I'll be on the next plane I can get."

"I love you," Kara says, and means it.

"I love you too. Now don't let them off too easy, okay?"

"Yes, ma'am."

Kara listens to the call end, then she closes her eyes and cries.

* * * *

She must fall asleep at some point, because she wakes up to a sore neck and a text on her phone.

From Eric: *Let me know if you want food and we can drop it off outside your room or make ourselves scarce so you can get it yourself. Or if you need anything else.*

As she's staring at the text, trying to figure out what to do with it, another one comes through.

From Eric: *I'm so sorry*

Awkwardly, one arm still half-trapped under her body and mostly asleep, she types a message back.

To Eric: *Are you the designated spokesman for the set?*

From Eric: *We didn't want to overwhelm you.*

That's a yes, then.

Kara doesn't want food, doesn't want to do anything but lie here in her nest and cry, but she knows if she lets herself stew in her hurt feelings, she'll just talk herself into making the absolute worst of this.

Because that's so, *so* tempting. Because Ry violated her, because he hurt her in a way that only Alphas can hurt Omegas. Because he was supposed to be better than that.

But he stopped, immediately. And she doesn't know if the rest of the set stopped him or he stopped himself, but—

They could have hurt her, so easily. They could have made her do anything, and she would have, willingly. Happily.

And they didn't.

That's what she has to hold on to. They didn't.

To Eric: *I'll be back down soon. You don't need to clear out.*

There's a long pause, and she watches her phone. Waits.

From Eric: *Are you okay with Ry being there?*

No.

But she has to be. She has to trust that he won't do that again, or she won't be able to do this.

To Eric: *Yes*

She waits, but he doesn't respond.

So finally, Kara reopens the passage in her nest and climbs out, naked, phone in hand, truth coming out of her well to shame mankind. She dresses, taking her time, putting on her own clothes — plain panties, a nude bra, leggings, an oversized university T-shirt.

Her clothes are gone from the hallway. One of the Alphas must have grabbed them, but she doesn't care one way or another.

Downstairs, she heads to the living room first. Eric and Jason are sprawled out on the couch there, tangled against each other, but neither of them looks relaxed. Damon is in one of the armchairs, his head bowed, his glasses dangling from one hand.

All of them look up when she walks in.

"Where's Ry?" she asks.

"In the kitchen," Damon says hoarsely. "Do you want — do you want me to — "

"Please," Kara says.

He stands and walks out, jamming his glasses back on his face. He doesn't come near her as he leaves.

Eric and Jason are both watching her, but neither of them moves. Neither of them has moved at all, since they looked at her. She's not entirely sure they're breathing.

"I'm just going to…" she says, then walks over to sit in another armchair. She curls up in it, pulling her feet up toward her chest. Their eyes track her, but they don't say anything.

They wait.

It feels like an age before Damon comes back, but nobody says anything in that time, and nobody moves.

She feels almost serene now, her tears having washed away the worst of her feelings. She loves them. She loves them. She loves them.

She doesn't move.

Damon sits back down in his chair, but Ry just stands there, in the doorway, watching her. He looks very pale. "I'm so sorry," he says.

"Please sit," she tells him.

He sits at the far end of the couch Eric and Jason are on, about as far from her as he can get without sitting on the floor.

"I'm so sorry," he says again. "I didn't mean to do that — but that's no excuse. All I can say is that I'm sorry, and I'll never do it again."

"If you do it again, if any of you do that to me again, I'm leaving. Do you understand me?"

"Of course," Damon rasps out.

"I want that to be illegal," she says. She's been thinking about it, and Sue Ann is right, no matter that she probably wasn't being serious. They have more money than almost anyone else in the world. It has to be good for something. "I want non-consensual Alpha orders to be illegal. The repeal of ownership laws doesn't mean a damn thing if you can still do that."

Ry flinches.

"But most of what I want right now is to finish the conversation we were having before. Something is wrong, and all of you are lying to me about it, and that needs to stop. Right now. So we can talk about what's wrong, or we can talk about the best way to end this courtship. Which would you prefer?"

For a long moment, they're all silent, then Ry says, "Along with BRD, I have an extremely rare condition that, among other things, makes it so my body produces inconsistent but broadly negative reactions to the Alpha-specific hormones produced during sexual activity. It doesn't change my desire, or my libido — it doesn't make me not want you."

"But it hurts you to have sex."

Ry grimaces. "Not exactly. The results are more similar to the post-exertional malaise that people with chronic fatigue syndrome get. I'm fine during, generally, but I will sometimes crash afterward, often badly. Sometimes I can't get out of bed the next day, or even longer than that. My blood pressure will bottom out, or my heart rate will spike, or I'll — there's a litany of symptoms, which are wide-ranging and inconsistent and all make me fucking *useless*."

"You're not useless," Damon puts in.

"I haven't been able to hold down a job, ever," Ry says. "I call myself a house-Alpha, but the reality is that I'm tired all the goddamn time. Half the time I can't drive. Sometimes I spend all day lying down, even when I haven't had sex. It's all the time. And it's not going to get better."

That explains what she's smelled on him, and what he's tried so hard to hide. Omegas tend to be able to smell illness better than anyone else, as a way to take care of their people.

"Why didn't you tell me?" she asks.

Ry gives her a hollow smile. "It's not the sort of a thing an Alpha should be, is it? It's hardly going to incentivize you to stay with us, tying you to someone like me."

"And you thought…what, exactly? That I just wouldn't notice? Or that you'd spring it on me once we were married?"

He looks away at that, rubbing at his eyebrow. "I thought that, if the rest of them could convince you to stay, it might be okay."

Kara rubs at her eyes. The serenity is starting to wear away now, and she just feels tired. "Is there any way that you can have sex? If you want to, I mean?"

"There are experimental drugs," Eric says. "We've been funding research — well, Ry has, mostly — for years. And there are techniques that can help."

"Then we try those techniques, right?" She looks at Ry. "Or we try — we try whatever, if it'll make your life easier. Unless the techniques are, I don't know, you whacking me with a folding chair or whatever. I don't think I'm willing to go that far."

He smiles at that, which is what she was hoping for. "Nothing like that," he says.

"Great." Kara smiles back at him. "We can try that, then."

"Just like that?" Jason asks.

"I mean, not right now," she clarifies. "I am still really fucking mad at Ry, and I don't have sex with people I'm really fucking mad at, but I will forgive you. And you're not useless," she tells him. "Don't call yourself that."

"But you're staying?" Jason presses. "You're not ending the courtship?"

"I'm not." Kara hesitates, then says, "I love you."

Everyone goes very still — then Damon is on his feet, striding over to kneel next to her chair. He doesn't quite touch her. "Thank you," he breathes.

Kara tugs him up, and he goes easily, bending to kiss her. It starts soft, almost chaste, but then she pulls him down further, chasing the taste of him, opening up her mouth and sucking his lower lip into her mouth.

He's the one who pulls away, breathing hard. His lips are red and swollen, and he looks so, *so* good.

She loves them.

"I do want to marry you," she tells him — tells them. "But I want to do that because you've treated me like a real human being and someone who can be a full member of the set. *That* is what I want to marry."

"I'm sorry," Ry says again.

"I'm still mad at you," she says. "Apologizing won't fix that. Treating me like an adult will."

With that, she nudges Damon out of the way enough that she can stand, then leans up to give him another kiss, quick enough that it does stay chaste this time. Then she walks over to where Jason and Eric are sitting. They're both in that same tense sprawl, like they're trying to pretend that they're more relaxed than they are.

She leans down and kisses each of them. Neither of them relaxes fully into it, but by the time she straightens out, both look a little less like they're about to jump out of their own skins.

Jason gives her a little grin. "We love you too, sweetheart."

Kara smiles back, then walks past them, over to where Ry is sitting. He looks pale and drawn, and she can smell the illness on him. It makes her want to fix it, want to fix *him*, even in ways that she knows she won't actually be able to.

She loves him.

She's so fucking mad at him.

Kara leans down to brush a kiss against Ry's cheek, and he startles so hard they almost knock heads.

"Why?" he asks.

"Because I have to trust that you'll be better," she tells him. "Because you could have hurt me—really hurt me—and you didn't. Because I love you."

"We'll make it illegal," he tells her.

She nods. "Good."

Chapter Sixteen

The conversation doesn't fix everything, of course.

But time goes on, their courtship continues and they settle into something that feels like a life that they could live together.

And Kara thinks.

* * * *

The email comes while Kara is sprawled out on the couch with Damon bracketing her. He reaches out to hand over her phone with what looks like muscle memory more than anything else.

Nearby, Ry snorts with laughter. "You have an email kink now?" he asks.

Above her, Damon's face turns a dull red. "It might be important," he mutters.

"How do you manage not to check your phone every fifteen seconds?" Kara asks, even as she leans up to give him a kiss. Her phone is still pressed between them where she's holding on to it, but he doesn't seem to mind. "Aren't all of your emails important?"

"You'd be amazed at the number of useless emails I get," he tells her. "But also that's why I keep my phone in a different room when I'm doing this." He leans down to kiss her, then says, "Please check your email so I can stop worrying about it."

Laughing, Kara indulges him — then sits up so fast she almost headbutts Damon in the face.

"Kara —"

Dear Professor Igan, the email reads. *My name is Alex Tseung. I am reaching out in regards to a potential doctoral supervision. I am currently completing my M.Sc. in International Relations at the London School of Economics and Political Science. I intend to research the impacts of Omegas on the disarmament, demobilization and reintegration (DDR) process. A full proposal is attached here.*

Even if we don't end up working together, I wanted to tell you — you're the first Omega I'd ever heard of in this field and the first one that I know of that's a full professor, and you gave me hope to get my Master's and even consider my Ph.D. So I just wanted to say thank you. Our generation will have more Omegas in fields like this, and it's thanks to people like you.

Very respectfully,
Alex Tseung

"Oh my God." Kara is crying — she realizes when Damon brushes a finger across her cheek. "Oh my God."

"What is it?" Damon asks, sounding worried. "Is something wrong?"

"No, I—" She can't manage to explain it to him, so she just pushes the phone at him, then shoves her own hands against her face. She's not sure whether to cry or to laugh, because neither seems quite right here—but neither does anything else.

What she's doing isn't like that. She's not some sort of Omega icon, and she's never tried to be.

There are so many Omegas who are doing so much more work than she is, who are moving things forward for Omega rights, who do activism or are at least willing to speak out in public. But Kara has spent her career doing her best to not do that, because she knows that talking about being an Omega will always make her life harder.

So for someone to not only want to work under her but to say that she gave them hope—

That means more than she ever expected it would.

"This looks like a nice email," Damon says, sounding a little baffled.

"I know," Kara says, still weepy.

"Can I see?" Ry asks.

Damon hands Kara's phone over to him, and Kara takes that opportunity to try to get her shit together. This is such an overreaction to the email that she can't help feeling a little silly now that she's gotten past her first impulse.

"Are you going to take them on?" Ry asks. He hands the phone back to Damon, who gives it back to Kara. She cradles it against her chest. She wants to read the email again, to confirm that she read it right, but she thinks that if she does, she'll just start crying again.

"I'm not sure," Kara says. "It's not solely my decision, but even if it were, I have to base it on the merit of their research. I can't just work with an Omega because I want them to succeed on the basis of them being an Omega. And it might make their life harder, having an Omega supervisor. People will think that they're getting through on the merit of us being the same dynamic."

"But they'll still have to defend their dissertation in the end, right?" Ry asks. "And you won't be the one to decide that."

That's true.

"I'll read their proposal," Kara says, then puts her phone out of the way. It's still within Damon's reach, in case he decides that he wants to make her check her email again, because he has stupidly long arms, but there's not a lot she can do about that shy of chucking it across the room and hoping the screen doesn't shatter into a million pieces. "But right now I'd really like to get back to making out."

"I second that vote," Ry says from his position on the ottoman, close enough to watch as much as he wants—and touch, if he decides he's up for it.

He usually doesn't, but it's a compromise that's been working for them.

Damon laughs. "I won't say no to that." Then he tips her back over so she's sprawled out on the couch again, staring up at him. His eyes are very dark behind his glasses, his pupils so big they seem to disappear into his irises. But before he kisses her again, he says, "I'm really proud of you."

Heat sparks through her, even as she tries to hide her face to conceal that she's no doubt *very* red, and Ry says, "Oh, I think she likes hearing that."

"Do you?" Damon asks. He leans down to brush his lips against hers, barely more than a feather's touch.

"Do you like hearing about how you're our good Omega?"

Kara makes an actual face at that, because *no*, and Ry and Damon both laugh out loud.

"If you call me your good Omega, I'm going to pinch you," she warns him.

"Not that, then," he says, and kisses her again, a little deeper this time. "But you like hearing that we're proud of you, our Omega? That we're impressed by you? That you're the smartest Omega we know —"

Kara laughs at that—then gasps into Damon's mouth as he kisses her again, tongue sliding into her mouth, stealing her breath until all she can do is *feel*.

"You don't need to lay it on so thick," she says through pants when he pulls back again. She's gratified by the fact that he's breathing hard, too.

"He's not," Ry says near them. His voice sounds thick, and she wishes she could see him. "That's really how we see you. Smart and impressive and beautiful, and you've agreed to let *us* court you."

"I'm not —" *special*, she starts to say.

But Ry cuts her off to say, "You are."

"You are," Damon repeats, then leans down to kiss her again. "Our beautiful, brilliant, kind Omega."

She knows that they're right, in an objective sense, at least about her accomplishments—but this time, she lets herself believe that they see her that way.

* * * *

"I think my calendar is fucking with me."

Ry looks over from the risotto he's been stirring for forever to give Eric a sardonic look. "Do tell."

"I have an empty block for all of Saturday evening," he says, clomping over to wrap his arms around Kara's shoulders. She leans back against him. "And it will neither delete itself nor reveal its secrets to me."

"Oh, that's me," Kara says.

"You're fucking with my calendar?"

"I put that time on your calendar. Or, well, I had Shannon do it, because I don't have access to your calendars."

"We should get that fixed," Ry says. He takes out his phone and starts swiping one-handed through it, then stops. "It's on my calendar, too."

"It's on all of your calendars," Kara informs him.

"And what is *it* exactly?" Ry asks.

"If I wanted you to know, do you think it would be an empty block on your calendars?"

"Then how are we supposed to know where to go?"

"We all live in the same house, don't we?"

"True," Eric says with a laugh. He kisses the side of her face. "I love you being all mysterious like this. It's sexy."

"I'm glad you think so," she says, "because I'm still not going to tell you what it's for."

"I think I can seduce it out of you," Eric tells her with a grin.

"I think you're welcome to try."

"No sex in the kitchen," Ry reminds him, but he's laughing.

Eric sighs, overdramatic and loud, then sneaks a quick kiss before pulling away. "My days spent toiling away, saving lives, and I'm not even allowed to seduce my own Omega in my own house."

"Just not in the kitchen."

"Well," Eric says to Kara, "would you like to leave the kitchen so I'm allowed to seduce you?"

"I'm grading papers," she protests, but weakly. Mostly she's just been watching Ry cook and admiring his backside in his well-fitting jeans.

"This is for your giant intro-level class?" Eric asks.

"My seminar on the ethics of insurgencies. It's pretty small, only fourteen students, but the papers are longer than I give for my big lecture classes."

"What are the papers about?"

It doesn't seem like the sort of thing anyone else would be interested in beyond her coworkers — but she remembers the first time they talked, when he mentioned that he read her work. "They all pick an insurgency and have to write about their engagement with civilians, police and military — how they're the same, how they differ, et cetera. I try to encourage them to branch out, but every year we get a lot of al Qaeda, Taliban, Daesh — ISIS."

"I know what Daesh is," he says, amused.

"Right." He was in the military. He probably knows better than she does. "Anyway, it's about helping them understand the idea that insurgencies don't work in one way across the board, and that their goals and ideology will change how they interact with different groups. It's not necessarily groundbreaking, but it requires some good solid research."

"How accurate are the ones about the Taliban?"

Kara waves her hand back and forth in a so-so gesture. "The biggest issue is getting them to focus on a specific time period — there's a real temptation with the Taliban to start with ninety-four or ninety-six or sometimes seventy-eight and just run right through to today, which gives a range that's frankly too wide to be meaningful."

Eric smiles at her. "You seem to like talking about this."

"I do." Kara makes a face. "Sorry if you don't want to talk about the Taliban, though, or any of it, really."

He shrugs. "I don't mind. A lot of it was shit, but— well, if I hadn't been there, I wouldn't have met Jason. And I wouldn't have saved his life, which I can now hold over him every time we have a disagreement. I wouldn't go back for anything, though."

"And you got out."

"We got out. I even managed to avoid any bullet holes along the way." He wiggles his foot against hers. "Broke all my toes at one point, though."

"Ouch."

"He's just trying to get sympathy," Ry says from the stove.

"Girls swoon over war wounds."

Dryly, Ry says, "Your weird, fucked-up toes are not going to get her to tell you about the calendar block."

Eric laughs, bringing Kara's hand up to his mouth to kiss it. "It's worth a try."

"You'll find out on Saturday," Kara says.

* * * *

Saturday dawns with the sort of pale brightness that means that winter is well on its way, but it's almost warm by the early evening when everyone gathers in the living room. They all look impatient.

Kara says, "I'm sure you're all wondering why I've gathered you here today."

"Finally," Eric groans.

Kara grins at him. "Well, you'll have to wait just a little longer."

Jason snorts out a laugh. "She got us there. Just tell me—is this some sort of sex thing? Because I can definitely get behind it if it is."

"I have faith that you can make anything a sex thing if you put your heart into it," Kara tells him. Her phone goes off. She checks it then says, "Our car is here."

"I could have driven," Jason says, sounding good-naturedly offended.

Ry rolls his eyes, strolling over to loop his arm with Kara's and head with her toward the door. "Hard to keep a secret if you're driving."

The car is one of the fancier black ones, with two rows that face each other so the five of them can look at each other. It was one of her requests for Shannon, when she was setting this whole thing up.

It's only once they're in the car that Kara starts to get nervous. She's confident about what she's doing—but there's always a chance that this will go horribly wrong.

Her pocket feels very, very heavy.

She ends up between Ry and Damon, with Eric and Jason facing backward. Jason stretches out one of his legs to twine around her ankle.

"If you're taking us all somewhere to murder us..." he says in a joking reference to their first ride here, and she laughs.

It's not a quick drive, getting into DC at this time of day, but it's faster than heading out of the city, even on a weekend. It's nearly dark this time of year, but the city lights are bright enough to make up for it.

They stop at the National Mall, and Kara grabs Damon's hand to lead them toward the Reflecting Pool.

It's almost empty, given the time of day and the chill in the air, but Kara can see a light near the water.

"I have a sneaking suspicion you've been conspiring with Shannon," Damon says. He sounds amused about it, at least.

"She's amazing," Kara says. "And I wanted to make this special for all of you. You've all taken me on dates, but I've never gotten a chance to take you all on one. So...here we are."

Here is near the edge of the Reflecting Pool where Shannon is waiting with a picnic blanket with a lit-up space heater out next to an extravagant picnic basket.

"Thank you," Kara says, and Shannon nods and heads off.

They all fit on the blanket—barely, with Kara squished between Damon and Eric with the space heater and basket in the middle.

"Basically what we have is a bunch of fancy sandwiches," Kara says, talking a little too fast. "And alcohol, though I'm not sure if we're technically legally allowed to drink it out here."

"It's lovely," Eric says, starting to unpack the basket with Ry. They're all from the same fancy restaurant or private chef—Shannon figured it out—and they're wrapped in butcher's paper with neat labels written in Sharpie. There's homemade potato chips, too, and desserts of some kind. They all dig in, laughing when Jason almost drops his entire sandwich onto his lap trying to stuff it full of potato chips.

"I need to figure out how to make this," Ry says around a bite of his sandwich. "I've never actually made brisket before, at least not successfully."

"I do remember the extremely unsuccessful attempt," Eric says, grinning when Ry waves an irritated arm at him. They're across the space heater from each other, too far for Ry to hit him without getting up. "It ended up somehow both burned and undercooked, which I didn't think was possible."

"I cooked it at too high a temperature," Ry says grumpily. "And you have zero grounds to stand on when it comes to cooking, so don't even try to pretend you could make it better."

"Oh, I don't think I could make it better," Eric says easily. "But I wasn't the one who said I could make it in the first place."

"You're not allowed to judge my cooking until you can make it yourself."

"Try and stop me," Eric says with a grin.

Ry throws a potato chip at him. Eric catches it and eats it.

Between them, Jason rolls his eyes. "Is this really the set you want to be stuck with?" he asks, joking.

And Kara thinks, *yes*.

It's a beautiful night, despite the chill, a nearly full moon reflecting off the water and helping illuminate the world around them. It feels like the DC from the movies, when the only things that exist are the monuments and the White House, all glassy shots and the three helicopters of Marine One flying overhead.

It feels like the kind of world that Kara could live in forever, surrounded by these four Alphas.

So she takes out the box from her pocket, cupping it in one hand. It's wider than a normal one, smooth and a little bit rounded. She swallows.

"I know this isn't traditional," Kara says, and everyone looks at her. "But you all have spent the past months showing me how much you want me, and I wanted to return the favor."

"Kara," Jason breathes.

"Please let me finish this," she says in a rush, "before I lose my nerve."

Nobody says anything. Ry's eyes are very bright in the reflected light.

"I know this isn't traditional," she says again, "but I love you, all of you, and I want to spend the rest of my life with you. Even if we can never bond, even if I can never bear your children. Because you've shown me that we can be a set without that. So." She turns her hand over, opening it to show the set ring box she's been carrying around all day. "Will all of you marry me?"

Damon is the first on her, cupping her cheek and kissing her once, twice, so many times it's like he can't stop himself. "Yes," he tells her between kisses. "Today, tomorrow, any time you'd like. Yes."

"Quit hogging our Omega," Eric says, tugging her away from Damon so he can give her a long, *long* kiss. They're both gasping when he pulls away, their breaths mixing as they're so close their lips are almost brushing. "I love you," he says. "This is the best surprise you could have given us."

"*I* want to see the rings," Jason says, leaning across Eric to look at the box.

Kara pulls his out, offering it to him. He takes it with reverent fingers, slipping it on. Shannon said it would be the right size, but Kara's still relieved to see it go on easily.

"The inside of each of them is engraved with all of our initials," she explains, and grins when he immediately pulls it off to squint at the inside. "And the outside of each is inlaid with a diamond and two rubies." She hands Eric his, then Damon. Finally she's left facing Ry, who is still watching her with those bright, bright eyes.

He's the only one who hasn't said anything.

So she pulls away from Eric and Jason to step over the space heater, stopping just in front of him. He stands, reaching out toward her hands. She offers him the box with the last ring, but he takes her other hand instead, lifting her wrist to his nose to breathe in her scent, the way Alphas do when they greet Omegas.

The way she forbade him to do, the first time they met.

"I love you," she tells him. "Whether I was your first choice or not."

"You will always be my choice," he says, voice low. "You will *always* be my choice." He takes the ring, then closes the box in her hand. "Where is your ring?"

Suddenly feeling shy, Kara says, "I thought I'd go traditional on that part and let you pick what you want me to wear."

"It would be our honor," Damon tells her. He stands so he's beside her, Eric and Jason on her other sides, and everything around her is her Alphas, her set.

Here, she's home.

Sanctuary: Winter Howl
Aurelia T. Evans

Excerpt

Renee took the last sip from her Samuel Adams and set the finished bottle down next to the first one. She smiled and nodded at Marie, who had come over to take the empty bottles and leave the receipt. There were no words between them. Usually Marie would chat to her customers, but she'd learned when she'd moved to Antoine five years ago that Renee Chambers would not look at her, half of the time wouldn't talk and the other half of the time would stumble through some painful attempt at conversation. Renee had got better as she'd come to know Marie, but it was still more comfortable for both of them when Renee didn't try to talk and Marie didn't try to make her.

Renee left the cash tip on the table, clenched the leash and slid out of the booth. Her legs stiffened when she saw Josh Beall and Marcus Levinson a few booths down. She had not seen them come in, and although she had heard their laughter, she hadn't recognised it as theirs. She would have to walk by them to leave. The warm body against her leg reassured her, nudged her in the right direction. She took one step, then two. Her knees loosened and let her walk. She instinctively — and fruitlessly — tried to hide in her long, light blue coat.

"…saw her at the supply store getting her checklist squared away," she heard Josh say.

"What's it been, two months since she last came down here?" Marcus asked.

"Three months. Won't come back down till spring. You can practically set your seasons by her." He belched, then coughed, pounding his chest a bit.

"What does she do up there all alone, anyway?" Marcus asked.

"Roswell says she gets a lot of mail," Josh said. "He says she has help, but I don't believe it. She wouldn't let anyone up there. I bet she does it all herself. Completely crazy."

Renee closed her eyes and breathed in. She was not so egotistical as to believe that everyone in Antoine talked about her, but it was just her luck that she had to walk by these two rubes when they were. Neither was too far into his mug for slurred speech, but they were far enough that they couldn't gauge their volume.

"Maybe she does porn," Marcus suggested. "You know, video stuff."

Josh snorted. "Frigid bitch like her? Don't think so." He leant forward conspiratorially. "Hey, what if we went up—?"

"Hey, Renee," Marcus said, even more loudly then they had already been speaking. Josh turned around, his scruffy but reasonably attractive face lighting up with a sly grin when he saw her huddled against the booth table behind them.

"Speak of the scared little devil," he said, raising his glass. "Want a drink? You look a little tense."

Renee's eyes darted from Josh to Marcus to Marie to the door. At another nudge to her leg, and she stepped towards the door.

"Yeah, come on, sweetie," Marcus said, misinterpreting her direction. "We'll make it worth your while."

How? Renee thought. *By drooling on me and trying to feel me up with all those smooth moves you've cultivated over the last ten years?* She didn't say anything, of course, just kept inching along until she finally started past the table.

She lurched forward when Marcus delivered a hearty smack to her ass. It didn't hurt, but Renee could feel her face start to burn and her chest tighten. At least she could move her legs faster now that she was past them.

"Hey, now, none of that in here," Marie called from behind the bar. "Have a good day, Renee. Don't be such a stranger."

"You always run away," Josh shouted after her.

"I wonder why," Renee muttered, her tongue looser now that she was out of the bar and no one was looking at her. "Come on, Britt, one more stop before we go home."

"Hey, Mommy, can I pet the dog?"

Renee winced at the high frequency of the voice and hoped that the mother would know the appropriate way to answer her child. No such luck.

"Hello, miss. Can my daughter pet your dog?"

Antoine was not exactly a highly populated town, but it had a fair tourist trade, particularly downtown Main Street, which was described in most tourist guidebooks as colourful, cheerful, folksy, and unique. Renee did not know about unique or folksy, but many tourists liked to come by for the ambience. And like most townies, the Antoine population had both respect for tourist dollars and frustration with the tourists themselves.

Especially when tourists did not know a service dog when they saw one.

"I'm sorry, ma'am," Renee said, emphatically not looking at the woman. That sometimes helped, and the warm feeling of Britt against her leg reassured her. "She's working."

"Oh, I'm sorry… Hey, wait, you're not blind." The overly polite apology turned into a similarly grating voice of parental annoyance. "If you didn't want Lisa to pet her, you could've just said. There's no need to lie."

"I'm not lying," Renee said. In fact, she was a terrible liar, but that was not the issue at hand. "They do more than help blind people. Please… I need to…"

"Well, that's just rude, having a dog around when you're not really blind and then not letting a little girl pet it," the mother said indignantly.

"I'm sorry. She's working." The words came out short and clipped and curt, but Renee was not really that angry. Her throat was just tightening, and she could feel her shoulders curling in.

"Bitch," the woman muttered under her breath as she grabbed her daughter's free hand — the girl's other hand had been playing with Britt's tail. The little girl was lucky that Britt was an extremely well-behaved dog. The woman led her daughter across the street.

"Good girl," Renee whispered, rubbing Britt's ear gently. "Ready to go?"

She barely had to tug the leash in the direction of the grocery store. Britt had a deep bond with Renee, had been with her most of her life and been her service dog for about five years. She could feel where Renee wanted to go.

Renee admired Britt's beauty beneath the deep green service vest. So many people confused her for a Siberian husky, and Renee understood the mistake. They were both northern sled dogs, but malamutes were bigger, with thicker fur. Britt was a little larger than average, and the darkest parts of her fur — set off by the usual white accents — were almost black. Malamutes were not traditionally service dogs. But Renee had loved Britt since the first time she'd met her, and the feeling had been mutual. There was friendship and respect between them, a connection that she had never managed to make with any of the people at school. It was really no wonder she spent all her time around dogs — she understood them and got along with them so much better than she did with most people.

With Britt in front of her, Renee felt secure in her steps. The sides of her coat hood blocked out her periphery, like blinders on a horse, and she felt a little more confident where she put her feet. Besides, with a large dog like Britt with her — a dog that was occasionally confused for a wolf — she felt more protected. Like a celebrity with a bodyguard, thankfully without the paparazzi.

They made it to the grocery store in about a ten-minute walk. That was what she liked about Main Street. Almost everything was within walking distance, so all she had to do was drive into Antoine, walk around a bit, then drive back home when she was finished, rather than drive from one place to another, and another, and another. Renee was able to stretch her legs after the long drive into town, and certainly Britt needed the exercise as well.

Renee did not need to go to the grocery store often, and she did not necessarily need to go now, which just went to show how much better she had become in public places. But she wanted to get a few treats to tide herself over before all her orders were shipped in. That was actually how she did most of her shopping — online through bulk providers. She had the space, the money and the resources, and most of the things shipped in *needed* to be shipped in bulk. Besides, it was such a long drive between Antoine and where she lived.

There had been a time right after her father had died when she could not even walk into a grocery store without panicking, a time when she could not walk off her property without feeling everything coming in to crush her, as if the entire world had a force field of inhospitality. That was what each successive building had felt like once she stepped out into the world — like a heavy, unpleasant curtain surrounded each of them, and it would take all her effort to pass through. And sometimes she couldn't.

With Britt, though, she was able to walk into places much more easily about ninety per cent of the time.

A grocery store should have been easier, in theory. All those people should have made her feel less conspicuous — she should be able to do better in crowds where she was anonymous and no one really cared. She should do worse with one-to-one interactions. But quite irrationally, it was the other way around. While she was quite bad at one-to-one interactions outside her sanctuary, she was even worse in places that tended to attract more people. Marie's bar, The Benefit, was small and close, and although it tended to get more crowded by around four in the afternoon, Renee avoided it at that time. The grocery store, however, was another matter altogether. It was more than just a public place —

it was a *frequented* public place, and that meant that the unwelcome energy surrounding it seemed to pulse against her.

Swallowing, Renee squinted at the people she could see inside. None of them were looking, none of them were judging. They were all going about their business. She was not the centre of the universe, she reminded herself sternly. The muscle of her heart felt as though it was forcing itself against the thin walls of her lungs, rattling her ribs.

Britt whined slightly as Renee retrieved a shopping cart. She could do this with Britt at her side. Then she could leave. If she could just get through this, she could go back home. That was good motivation to do what she needed to do. Her heart was still racing and her breathing was still a little shallow, but Britt stayed next to her, with her fur brushing Renee's jeans.

When she had finally finished, she pushed her cart to the self-checkout. Once she wheeled the cart out into the parking lot — relieved to be outside and breathing open air again — she saw a few dry flakes of snow fall on her coat sleeves. She guessed there was not going to be anything more than a flurry, but it would only be a sample of what was to come in future months.

Renee took the bags out of the cart and opened her duffel to pack them in. The bag was heavy on her shoulder when she started walking again, but aside from altering her gait, it did not bother her much.

The cold air felt great on her face, since she was beginning to sweat a little. She went around Main Street this time, behind the shops, among the employee parking and the dumpsters.

She rushed through the alleyway and finally reached the intersection between downtown Main Street and the beginning of Antoine proper. Her blue

2000 F150 was waiting at the end of the downtown parking lot. She was going to break into a jog to reach her truck that much faster, but two things held her back. One, Britt did not let her hurry. And two, Josh stepped out from behind the hood, where he had been leaning against the driver's side door.

"Hello, peaches," Josh said. "Plan to leave town for the rest of the winter and use the snow as an excuse?"

Renee hesitated at the edge of the last building, as if she had run into a glass window — but then she pushed through and circled around the truck, away from Josh. There was a chest in the covered bed of her truck that she usually put her groceries in. Her keys clinked as she pulled them out of her coat pocket and unlocked the back of the truck.

"Sit," she murmured to Britt. She needed both her hands to climb into the bed.

"Just going to ignore me?" Josh asked. "That'd be nothing new."

Renee opened the bed and lifted her duffel up into it, then crawled up to open the chest at the other end of the bed.

A low growl that made even the truck vibrate alerted Renee to the fact that something was wrong. She glanced back as Josh pushed himself up into the bed and started to crawl in after her. Renee had to hand it to him. He was crawling after a woman with a wolf-like dog growling at him, and although his face showed a trace of concern, he did not seem scared enough. He was either very persistent or just very stupid. Britt's brows twitched as she looked from Josh to Renee, waiting for Renee to decide what to do with the situation and whether she could handle it herself. But what Josh had not anticipated was that the truck was part of Renee's space, just like her land. And Josh had just entered her space.

"Don't you ever get lonely up there those dark winter nights?" Josh asked. "Don't you ever wish—?"

"I didn't go out with you in high school. What makes you think I'm considering it now?" Renee said.

Josh blinked.

"Time," he said, overcoming his surprise. "You're all alone, and it's been what? Seven years? Things change. *I've* changed."

"I'm not alone," Renee said.

"Oh, that's right," Josh said. "Your dogs. As though that's a substitute for good human companionship, especially in front of the fire with no lights on and sweet music playing… Unless they are a substitute, and I severely misjudged you."

Renee's face twisted in automatic disgust.

"Well, that's a relief."

"You haven't changed," Renee spat, unloading her groceries into the chest, then shoving his arm. "You haven't changed at all."

"And neither have you," Josh said. He grabbed her arm, and although it didn't hurt Renee, Britt's growl kicked up a notch. "Up there, nothing ever changes, and nothing ever happens. It's all safe and easy and alone, and don't you wish something would happen? Something new, exciting, different?"

Renee slid out of the bed and tugged Josh out. She felt a little shaky, but she knew Josh was mostly talk, no action, so she did not feel as threatened as she might have with Marcus or someone like that.

"Every day," Renee said. "You have no idea. But it's also not you I'm looking for. God, it's so not you."

Josh's jaw twitched as he clenched his teeth. She tried to pass by him, but he grabbed her arm again. His face was too close, and his gaze drifted down to her lips.

"You sure about that? You really sure about that? 'Cause it is awfully out of the way where you live, and if…"

It was Renee's turn to blink. Maybe she had underestimated him, with that glint in his brown eyes, the set of his jaw.

But she narrowed her eyes and murmured, her voice almost inaudible outside the truck, "You try and come on my land, and I promise it will go badly. And it won't be any fault of mine. I'm sorry."

She tugged herself away, and he let her go without much of a fuss. Renee looked around to see whether anyone had been watching their little altercation, because if they had, she would have been mortified. But where she was parked, the last building on Main blocked most of the view.

"So I guess this is the royal brush-off again," Josh said, leaning back against the truck as she fumbled with her keys. "Frigid bitch."

She unlocked the door and whistled to Britt, who came over and jumped into the driver's seat, then into the shotgun seat, settling down and keeping a sharp eye on Josh. Renee pulled herself up — it was a big truck for a small girl. Before she shut the door, she said, "Don't I know it."

Renee thought she heard Josh snort before she revved the engine and left him and Main Street behind. She breathed a sigh of relief and felt a muscle in her body unwind for every second she headed out of Antoine.

About the Author

E. Rose Lynn has read most romance genres under the sun and tried her hand at a fair few of them. She writes queer and polyamorous romance with a touch of fantasy.

E. Rose Lynn loves to hear from readers. You can find her contact information, website details and author profile page at https://www.firstforromance.com/

PUBLISHING

Sign up for our newsletter and find out about all our romance book releases, eBook sales and promotions, sneak peeks and FREE romance books!